WHY HAS THE PRACTICE OF ARRANGED MARRIAGES CONTINUED IN VULCAN SOCIETY?

HOW DID SCOTTY TRANSPORT ALL THOSE HORDES OF TRIBBLES TO THE KLINGON SHIP AT EXACTLY THE SAME TIME?

ALTHOUGH KIRK WAS AN ADMIRAL AT THE START OF THE STAR TREK MOVIE, WHY WAS HE CALLED CAPTAIN AND SEEN WEARING CAPTAIN'S BRAIDS THROUGHOUT THE FILM?

HOW DID THE KELVANS MAKE THE *ENTERPRISE* INTO A SUPER SHIP?

These are just a few of the puzzles examined in this exciting new collection of articles about the universe of Star Trek. You'll delve into the lives of characters like Scotty and Spock, unravel some of the paradoxes posed in various episodes, fight evil menaces with Kirk and his crew, and experience all the wonder and fascination that has made Star Trek so important to people the world around.

THE BEST OF TREK® #5

About the Editors

Although largely unknown to readers not involved in Star Trek fandom before the publication of *The Best of Trek* (*#1*), WALTER IRWIN and G. B. LOVE have been actively editing and publishing magazines for many years. Before they teamed up to create TREK® in 1975, Irwin worked in newspapers, advertising, and free-lance writing, while Love published *The Rocket's Blast—Comiccollector* from 1960 to 1974, as well as hundreds of other magazines, books, and collectables. Both together and separately, they are currently planning several new books and magazines, as well as continuing to publish TREK.

THE BEST OF TREK #5

FROM THE MAGAZINE FOR STAR TREK FANS

EDITED BY WALTER IRWIN AND G. B. LOVE

A SIGNET BOOK

NEW AMERICAN LIBRARY

TIMES MIRROR

SIGNET, SIGNET CLASSICS, MENTOR, PLUME, MERIDIAN AND NAL
BOOKS are published by The New American Library, Inc.,
1633 Broadway, New York, New York 10019

First Printing, August, 1982

  1 2 3 4 5 6 7 8 9

PRINTED IN THE UNITED STATES OF AMERICA

CONTENTS

INTRODUCTION

Thank you for purchasing this fifth edition of articles and features from our magazine, *Trek*. We are sure that you will enoy this collection just as much as you did the previous four.

As always, the articles included in this volume reflect the continuing growth of Star Trek fandom, as well as the increasing interest in science and space exploration. The recent successes of the space-shuttle missions have once again inspired millions with the awe and mystery of space exploration—and have brought about a renewed enthusiasm for Star Trek. As this is written, the new *Star Trek II* movie has just gone into production and will serve as an even greater spur to our hobby.

We have a fine assortment of articles in this volume; each, we feel, reflecting an important and interesting aspect of Star Trek. We think you'll find them extremely readable, informative and educational, and downright fun!

If you enjoy the articles in this collection and would like to see more, we invite you to turn to the ad at the back of this book for more information on how you can order and subscribe to *Trek*. (And, please, if you have borrowed a copy of this volume from a library, copy the information in the ad, and leave the ad intact for others to use. Thanks!)

And if you have been stirred to write an article or two

yourself, please send it along to us. We would be most happy to see it, as we are always on the lookout for fresh and exciting new contributions. (As was the case in our last volume, almost all of the contributors featured in this collection sent us material after buying and reading one of our earlier collections.) We are especially interested in seeing material from artists, as we are continuing to expand our efforts in the art area.

We want to hear from you in any event. Our lines of communication are always open. We welcome (and heed!) your suggestions, comments, and ideas; you readers are the bosses. Although we cannot give you the addresses of Star Trek actors or forward mail to them, or help anyone get a professional Star Trek novel published, we *do* want your comments on *Trek* and Star Trek in general. It is only through your letters that we know if our efforts, and those of our contributors, have been successful.

Again, many thanks, and we hope you will enjoy *The Best of Trek #5!*

WALTER IRWIN
G.B. LOVE

THE MUSIC OF STAR TREK:
A VERY SPECIAL EFFECT

by Eleanor LaBerge

If you've ever sat up until the wee hours of the night to see one of the very early, classic "talkies," you may have been vaguely disquieted by the lack of "background music"—a musical score. Today, however, scoring is omnipresent in both films and television, and we tend to take it for granted. The music featured in a production is an integral and important part of its dramatic impact. Good music enhances a show; bad music detracts from it.

In the following article, Eleanor LaBerge examines the music of Star Trek, and the ways in which it affected both the series episodes and Star Trek: The Motion Picture. *We think Eleanor's article will send you running to your tape recorders to replay several episodes. . . .*

We fans have read thousands of words about Star Trek's cast, the problems of scientific accuracy, the construction of sets and model miniatures, and the multiple difficulties arising from production. We also love to read and reread articles that give insights into the characters created by Gene Roddenberry. But seldom is there more than a brief reference to the *music* of Star Trek, which provided exceptional enrichment to seventy-eight television episodes as well as to *Star Trek: The Motion Picture.*

Here is a twofold challenge, Star Trek fans. First, who is Alexander Courage? No, not the small person in "Plato's Stepchildren." Anyone out there recall the name as that of the composer of the Star Trek series music? Correct. Now try Gerald Fried and Fred Steiner. As you may have guessed, they are both composers of the background themes for the series.

Now ask your memory banks about Jerry Goldsmith. That's easier, of course. The name is more familiar, since his score for *Star Trek: The Motion Picture* was nominated for an Academy Award. This was a remarkable *kudos,* as many in the "business" were inclined to dismiss (if not ignore) the large-screen Star Trek as an upstart fugitive from the video tube.

The mechanics of bringing a series from idea to production was the subject of a 414-page book, *The Making of Star Trek,* by Roddenberry and Whitfield. Not until page 375 was the music given more than a one-line passing reference. Interestingly, not a word about the motion-picture score was to be found in *Trek* 15, the issue devoted to *Star Trek: The Motion Picture.* I do not point to this omission in a spirit of criticism, but only to submit that this particular aspect of Star Trek seems to have been neglected.

Neither in the motion picture nor in the series was the score just so much noise in the background. From composition to synchronization of music with the action there are many steps. There must also be an innate sense of dramatic appropriateness. Achieving the proper balance of these factors demands the skill of many technicians and the judgment of an experienced director. When these technical maneuvers are accomplished with beauty of melodic line and harmony in action, we have something special: a special effect deserving of our conscious appreciation.

The musical themes repeated throughout the Star Trek episodes would be a significant part of the fans' treasured devotion to the series. There were sequences that meant Vulcan; musical phrases that signaled McCoy's quick reparté or Spock's lifted eyebrow; there were tender melodies that provided accompaniment for Kirk's *affaires d'amour;* there were clever segments resembling a Doppler effect that revealed evil under the guise of an innocent appearance; many passages heightened a feeling of mystery;

and, of course, there were those which complemented the *Enterprise* and its crew when they were underway and ready for action.

While the viewer of Star Trek television did not have to listen to the constant musical background so popular in the vintage motion picture, timely and appropriate orchestrations were selected week after week. There was much more than stock abstract canned musical phrases.

Remember "The Trouble with Tribbles"? There was a special humorous theme for the furry beasties. In one bridge scene this was extended to a Far Eastern mode which seemed to indicate that the crew was as tranquil as a Tibetan monk in meditation. In the same episode the fist fight between Scotty and the *Enterprise* crew and the insulting Klingons was accompanied by a frolicking Scottish dance. This plus the rising strains that meant *Enterprise* combined in a neatly balanced classic melody of Star Trek adventure.

In "The World Is Hollow and I Have Touched the Sky," one of the many mystery themes appeared when an elderly man of *Yonada* told Kirk, Spock, and McCoy of his journey to the forbidden limits of his world. The same sequence of notes was repeated for "The Wink of an Eye" as well as other episodes.

Another familiar melody meant Vulcan. It fit well. There was a staccato melodic line played by a bass viol accompanied by a high-pitched, alien sound. It heightened our awareness that a Vulcan had roots in traditions not easily understood by humans. We heard the same theme in "Amok Time," as Spock reluctantly confided his biological problem to Kirk. In "Mirror, Mirror," it was repeated as the alternate universe's Spock entered a mind meld with McCoy. We heard it again as Amanda begged her son to relinquish command so that Sarek's life might be spared in "Journey to Babel."

Another Vulcan theme was heard in "Amok Time" during the combat for T'Pring. There was a warlike rhythm that gave the impression of unleashed savagery. It was a theme often repeated for a variety of combat scenes, but most fans upon hearing it would recall Spock's dramatic compulsion to satisfy the demands of *pon farr*. "I burn," Spock told T'Pau, and the music described his torment nonverbally. Once again accented by the musical background we faced that sense of mystery in Spock's divided being.

In "Shore Leave," we heard a theme that was both tender and wistful as Kirk faced his tangible dream of Ruth. This melody was used frequently in the episode to amplify Kirk's nostalgic memory of romantic interludes. Of all the romantic themes there was a special one for Edith Keeler in "City on the Edge of Forever." It was a haunting ballad in keeping with the style of her historical time. In the same episode, we heard the notes typical of many humorous scenes in the series when Kirk tried to explain Spock's ears to a New York City police officer. It also occurred when McCoy saw his Alice in Wonderland rabbit, and when the mistakenly beamed guard arrived aboard the *Enterprise* in "Tomorrow Is Yesterday."

The Star Trek fans, whether consciously or unconsciously, were accustomed to these and other themes. They were at home with them. In the series these shorter compositions could be used and repeated in a variety of situations, becoming a familiar part of Star Trek memories. Bracketed by the unforgettable Star Trek theme melody, plots were further enhanced by the modest musical background. There was little need for spectacular musical fanfare. The *Star Trek: The Motion Picture* score was, as one would expect, conceived on a grander scale. It was not meant for the cozy comfort of a series seen on the family-room television set but for the wide screen and the sophistication of modern sound systems.

One of the potential obstacles in winning fandom's support and devotion to the film would be related to taking the series out of the habits of viewing and listening intimacy. Many Star Trek enthusiasts sat in the theater waiting to see *Star Trek: The Motion Picture* with as much apprehension as eagerness. The lights darkened and without visual distraction we heard the first strains of Jerry Goldsmith's score: Ilia's Theme.

In Ilia's melodic line there was mystery and the rising beauty of tenderness filled with pathos. It was unmistakably romantic, but a listener could close his eyes and seem to float on a tall ship whose sails were filled by the winds. The navigator's song evoked the image of travel through vast empty space. The interweaving of percussion and strings rose and fell, interacting as if in dialogue. It seemed to be a musical conversation with the voices of violins, piano, and horns which ultimately blended into a suggestion of the *Enterprise* theme to follow. It was as mysterious as the Deltan herself: sensual as if pheromones were projected from sound to reality in the undulating melody.

After the theme became more familiar, speculation regarding the "dialogue" here could run rampant. Is it Ilia/Decker? Is it Ilia/Vejur/Kirk/*Enterprise*? The sequence of notes and their interaction are there. Meaning is the individual listener's emotional response. Ilia's theme lingers as a melody impossible to forget.

After Ilia's introductory theme we heard the brief opening, stirring in its martial rhythm. It surrounded us in stereophonic sound and we were back in that world where there are no impossible dreams. Jerry Goldsmith's opening is not just another march: It was and is a celebration—strong and direct but with subtleties of orchestration that delighted the ear and set feet tapping. French horns and violins alternated with the trumpet section, and the full symphonic arrangement gave body and support. Only a small percentage of the fans were concerned about the "special" effect of the musical sound track, but by the time the introductory footage was completed on the wide screen, it was clear that Goldsmith's contribution to the world of Star Trek would be satisfying.

The Klingon Imperial Cruiser *Amar* appeared in deep space and the melodic line was a clarion call blended with hollow clackers. The musical mood created in this sequence was appropriate and graphic: chase, attack, counterattack. In tonal language the segment clearly complemented the clipped dialogue as hunter and hunted clashed. The challenge ended with a single electronic sound fading into discord as the viewer saw empty space where the arrogant Klingons had been. The score told us, as if we had not known, that the Klingons were compulsively warlike.

The scene on Vulcan gave us our first view of Spock. It was introduced by electronic sounds which we later learn were to be associated with V'Ger. It accompanied the privileged initiated of *Kolinahr* as they began to confer the honor of perfect logic upon Spock. As he failed to meet the demands of the discipline, the music took on a more melodic, poignant aspect which spoke to us of great dignity and yet sadness. It was a melody all its own with a particularly compelling, if brief, beauty.

It is interesting to note that when Spock subsequently appeared in the entry lock after docking with the *Enterprise* in his warp-drive shuttlecraft, the Vulcan theme was repeated but with a distinctive difference: three descending piano chords greeted Spock as he boarded the ship. The music selected for Spock as he appeared on the bridge for the first time was that of "Enterprise," the love song. The same theme was used for Spock later in the film when Kirk received the Vulcan's limp body back from the inner chambers of V'Ger.

One of the first musical variations the motion-picture viewer might have noted in the film was that the martial strains of the opening changed in tempo and orchestral arrangement to become the lovely *Enterprise* theme. This musical technique can be used so effectively the hearer may not realize that the notes are identical. Remember Meredith Wilson's *The Music Man?* Some audiences took a while to pick up on the fact that "Seventy-six Trombones" was also the waltz-time love song. Similarly, Jerry Goldsmith selected the powerful opening theme with its precise rhythm and adapted it to the lyrical melody of "Enterprise." As Montgomery Scott ferried Admiral Kirk from the space station in the travel pod the music told us what we already felt: that this was a matter of love.

Some of the comments regarding the motion picture have cited this particular scene as unnecessarily long and dull. Considering the beauty of the musical background, it would be difficult to imagine even a brief portion of the composition cut. There is another way of evaluating the scene, as Walter Irwin points out in his comments on the motion picture in *Trek* 15. We needed and deserved that "long, lingering look," as he termed it. Kirk had waited for a mere two and a half years for this view, while the fans had wailed for more than a decade!

Goldsmith's *Enterprise* theme tenderly reflected the loneliness of past separation and led us to the joy of reunion as Kirk saw the *Enterprise* shining and majestic in dry-dock orbit. The music rose to a crescendo with the horns, bells as clear as stars on a winter night, violins, and the single trumpet in its own counterpoint. Is this trumpet

Kirk speaking to his lady *Enterprise?* Or is it what *he* hears: a Lorelei call from her? Or is it the longing in every human heart for union with that one great love wherein we become whole, that one great desire that gives life purpose? Listen well. It may be all of these things.

In the docking of the pod the musical thrust is reminiscent of such classical compositions as Tchaikovsky's *Romeo and Juliet.* It was a powerful musical symbol explicit in its description of Kirk's desire to possess the ship once again. The climax of this scene was particularly satisfying to the viewer as the long awaited adventure was once again beginning.

In "Taking Her Out," we heard a hint of the powerful engines in the low piano rhythm followed by variations on the *Enterprise* theme. When the intermix was set and the ship sped forward through the solar system, Goldsmith incorporated the well-loved, lyrical television theme. It lasted but a few moments, but fans should be grateful that the composer honored the series in this musical compliment.

Jerry Goldsmith was undoubtedly briefed on the new Star Trek theme. (One is tempted to wonder if his scenario was delayed until all was definite, forcing his composing to be done at warp speed to accommodate the many factors that did not "gel" until the last moments.) Once the composer received the outlines and the time sequences, he would have the problem of translating the meaning of one art form into another. Any critical evaluation of creative work might inspire one to question whether too much is being read into the subject under consideration. It is a valid question, and the answer depends not only upon the imagination of the one writing the analysis, but upon the depth of the author whose work is being analyzed.

In literature it would not be difficult to write a thesis-length commentary on the specific and symbolic uses of one great author's imagery—light and darkness, for example. A reader might be tempted to think that such an analysis was contrived. However, repeated imagery on the part of a literary genuis is, if not intentional, a subconscious use of one aspect of his art. Symbolism and interpretation in musical composition is essentially the same.

Musical criticism is not critical in the sense of finding fault; it is interpretation in the spirit of delving into the deeper meaning of a work. Admittedly, it is a speculative matter, especially when one comments on symbolic significance. The music of *Star Trek: The Motion Picture* is a major and important aspect of the film. How it relates to the meaning we perceive through characterization and story line is a valid question for speculation. If through the music we can come to a more profound understanding of Star Trek's philosophy, then the analysis is well worth the time.

One of the most difficult tasks in the composition of appropriate music for *Star Trek: The Motion Picture* must have been the long V'Ger sequences. How, one may ask, would a composer show us in his tonal language the awesome scope, the mystery and power of an entity 82 A.U. in diameter? We heard power in the deep bass and brass section, especially in the blaring tuba. One might expect the electronic elements of arrangement, but this composer gave us that extra bit we have learned to expect from Star Trek. Through the music he seemed to say that V'Ger was locked into "pre-melody." He showed us that the entity had life, technique, but no soul. He used sounds which represented a heartbeat amplified and pulsating—a being very much alive. He used tonal progressions not only of chords but in the do-mi-sol-do exercise-like repetitions shifting from major to minor scale with electronic variations. All the musical theory learnable would not enable a composer to create *music*; neither could V'Ger make that critical leap from logic and accumulation of knowledge (technique) to intuition (melody) without that extra something that surprises us at the end of the motion picture. For all its store of information, V'Ger had knowledge without purpose and was sterile. "It is cold," Spock told us, ". . . no beauty."

In the musical description of "Spock Walk," the Vulcan passed through the eyelike passage to observe V'Ger's incredible data storage banks. We again felt the deep power and mystery but also more than this. Up to this point V'Ger's theme had been controlled. Now sounds of confusion illustrated V'Ger's frustration. After Spock's traumatic mind meld with the device on Ilia's form, string section and brass broke into a wild orchestration that seemed to spin out of control. This was the instant when Spock's lifelong idea was shattered; it was the moment when we were in V'Ger's mind experiencing its bewilderment and disillusionment. Tht music seemed to place us in a maze with no way out, and the feeling could have been discribed as blind panic. We were one with Spock and one with V'Ger as each of them asked: "Is this all I am?"

After this scene of visual and musical abstraction, the director gave us the stark silence of sickbay. As Spock spoke to Kirk in that touching moment, the silence itself was a profound theme of oneness. There was the union not only of deep and abiding friendship, but that of Spock the Vulcan and Spock the human. Significantly, this aspect of the film needed no accompaniment.

The heart of V'Ger turned out to be Voyager VI, which, having achieved consciousness, yearned for what the motion picture tells us were "other dimensions." Decker signaled the final code sequence to the entity through the ground test computer and moments afterward V'Ger "touched the creator." Decker had overcome the fear that union with an alien might rob him of his individuality. He was no longer the man who left Delta 4 without saying goodbye to Ilia. This was now a man who was ready to step into a new dimension by his own free choice, ready to experience whatever transformation might result. V'Ger's theme in this last scene was also transformed. Even as the *Enterprise* crew approached the heart of V'Ger the music revealed longing interwoven with the electronic sounds by the use of Ilia's theme. As V'Ger and Decker were united and Ilia entered the aura of light, the musical background that had begun with a single electronic sound grew into rising cadences of brass, flutes, strings, and french horns. The effect was one of wonderment—our own and V'Ger's. Caressing sounds illustrated the delicate approach of V'Ger and its now melodic measures described the consummation of its quest. The transfiguration mounted musically until a new life was a reality. The melody ultimately blended gently into the *Enterprise* theme and its particular beauty which was, by now, familiar.

The space-fiction films of the past several years have given filmgoers remarkable soundtracks. It was a pleasure to listen to John Williams' score for *Close Encounters of the Third Kind*, and for *Star Wars*. These works gave young people who might never have listened to symphonic music a taste of something beyond country and hard rock. Jerry Goldsmith's *Star Trek: The Motion Picture* score is equal to these in melody, symbolism, and musicality. It captures the spirit of what the series became in the perception of the fans.

If Star Trek fandom idealized Roddenberry's creation, it was idealization based upon a reality of optimism and positive philosophy. The television themes and the score of *Star Trek: The Motion Picture* seem to have been written by two composers who were sensitive to the unique bond between the world of Star Trek and its deeper meaning. Both contributors to the special phenomenon it has become have undoubtedly been congratulated for their achievements. It is fitting, however, that here in the magazine for Star Trek fans, Alexander Courage, Gerald Fried, Fred Steiner, and Jerry Goldsmith be offered our particular gratitude. Belated thanks, guys!

A REPLY TO "BRIDGING THE GAP"

by Sherry Crowson

We've been getting more mail commenting on Joyce Tullock's articles than anything since the "Spock Will Die" rumors of several years ago. The mail has been both pro and con, but always thoughtful and stimulating—the kind of mail we like to see.

Sherry Crowson went one step further. She wrote her own article. It incorporates commentary on Joyce's original article, but takes an extra step forward. It is more than just a reply. It is a perfect example of how one reader can use the work of another to springboard thoughts and insights that are completely new and exciting. And that's what a magazine like Trek is all about. Sharing, growing, learning. Enjoy Sherry's commentary—it is a fine one.

Joyce Tullock's article "Bridging the Gap: The Promethean Star Trek" in *The Best of Trek #3* deserves careful consideration. I was so intrigued by the article that I sat down to read it a second time with pencil and paper at hand so I could take notes. When I finished, I realized I wasn't going to be happy until I wrote a reply. So, since I usually choose happiness, here it is:

I'm an avid reader of anything in print, but I like science fiction best. It is demanding. It challenges me to consider alien life-styles, alien philosophies. It challenges

13

me to *understand* even if I cannot agree. It demands that I suspend personal prejudice, customary outlooks, and cherished viewpoints in an attempt to see that other motivations and other cultures are worthy of my best attempts at understanding. If I examine what is alien to me, maybe I can understand more fully what it is I consider human.

Man longs for Paradise—and may not recognize it when he finds it. Our conception of Paradise comes from the dim time when it was hard, brutal work just to survive, and there was little energy left for anything else. Paradise for our beleaguered ancestors would have been a place where it was possible to live without struggling; a land of milk and honey where there would be time to enjoy pleasurable things, where there would be peace and ease and safety.

Today, in many parts of the world, we have those things already—physical necessities, even luxuries, leisure time, security, and on the whole, peace. There are exceptions, of course; there are peoples and countries to whom our ancestors' vision of Paradise still looks pretty good and is about as unattainable. But in the parts of the world that have achieved "Paradise" on earth, there is a restlessness and a searching for something—something we may only be dimly aware of wanting.

This is something James T. Kirk has already achieved —a personal sort of Paradise. Ah, I hear muttering already. . . . But consider, as Joyce does, "This Side of Paradise." Kirk rejects the spore influence; he does not need or *want* their outmoded, antiquated concept of Paradise. He wants the *Enterprise* and everything she stands for. He is satisfied with his life, right down to the core of his being. If that's not Paradise, what is?

And what is it that constitutes Kirk's personal Paradise? People to love, responsibility, intellectual challenge, the emotional satisfaction of doing a difficult job that demands everything he can give and doing it well. If everyone could have that, if each person could have whatever kind of life most appealed to him or her, then there'd be Paradise on the whole Earth. Maybe. And maybe we'd decide it was time to come up with a new concept of Paradise.

McCoy might look for love and marriage, as he does in "For the World Is Hollow and I Have Touched the Sky," because he has already experienced (for however short a time) that kind of sharing, that particular joy. So he might be tempted by some vision of Paradise that offers him this kind of love, with all its responsibilities and pleasures. McCoy has not given up on romantic love. McCoy is still searching.

Spock might be tempted by a Paradise that makes it possible for him to express and delight in the emotions that he, as a Vulcan/human hybrid, can't help feeling—as in "This Side of Paradise," for example. Or he might be equally tempted by a Paradise of logic and nonemotion, as represented by the *Kolinahr* disciplines or V'Ger. Spock has not yet come to a final peace with his hybrid nature and expectations. Spock is still searching.

But Kirk is no longer searching. He has found Paradise, and for him it is the *Enterprise*. Kirk has come to accept that he will never know all the answers. With the courage that represents the best of what is human, Kirk faces the uncertainty of *knowing* he will never be sure.

In "Who Mourns for Adonais?" Apollo asks, "What else does mankind demand of its gods?" and Kirk's reply is, "We find the one sufficient." It seems he is affirming that the "one" is Man's vision of the Unknowable Truth. Man has outgrown gods he can understand. Man has accepted that there are some questions that are truly unanswerable: *Is there life after death? Is our concept of God a true one? What is a soul? Where are you, God?* The fact that there can be no final answer doesn't diminish the importance of asking the questions. It does, however, free us from the emotional frustration of constantly seeking to prove the unprovable.

Does Kirk believe in God? I think he does—out of choice, for the comfort the vision of a Prime Mover offers and because it's hard to see the wonders in our universe and imagine that there is nothing beyond the physical, tangible reality. God admits no proof, only the choice of belief or disbelief.

God is not a question we can answer. It is humanity that we need to concern ourselves with; it's what we believe constitutes humanity that is best explored in Joyce's article.

My view of "For the World Is Hollow and I Have Touched the Sky" differs from Joyce's view. I took Joyce at her word: She said, "Take what you like from it," and I did.

I agree that McCoy, facing a terminal illness, *was* seeking comfort and safety—not blindly, but *consciously*. He saw the Oracle for what it was, not an all-powerful god, but an essential stability control for a ship that would not reach its goal for generations. Without this rigid structure of restrictions and taboos, the Fabrini knew it was all too possible that divisive splinter groups would form and war among themselves. This would lead to degeneration and possibly to the destruction of the carefully selected remnant of the race. The Fabrini ship builders and saviors chose to temporarily sacrifice "dangerous" individuality in order to save the last and best hope of their race.

Facing death—the sweeping disorientation of it—McCoy realized he could *now* form an intimate relationship with Natira because Starfleet would not allow him to continue on the *Enterprise*. He would be replaced. Feeling bereft of his security, he sought a replacement for it—much to the dismay of his friends Kirk and Spock.

What changed McCoy's mind in the end was not the realization that he had made a mistake, but rather the fact that circumstances had changed for Natira, his wife. McCoy's very special brand of humanity helped him release Natira.

McCoy, with his own unique gift for empathic insight, released Natira from her emotional commitment to him, a commitment that might interfere with her ability to lead her people.

Natira was, essentially, in the same position as Captain Kirk. Freed of control by the Oracle, the ship *Yonada* needed a captain who could make the appropriate decisions, who could command. The ship might still be physically run by the Oracle, but the people of *Yonada*, coping with the shattering revelation that their Oracle was not God . . . well, they needed a living, breathing *individual* who understood their problems inside and out.

Yonada needed Natira more than McCoy did, and consistent with his history of self-sacrifice and empathy, McCoy gave her back to her people. Her job would be as demanding, as vital, as complex as any captain's, requiring the same qualities and the same attention. McCoy understood this and thought Natira equal to the task . . . *if* she was undistracted by personal commitments.

If you have been looking for a strong, capable female character in Star Trek, Natira certainly qualifies. Her whole concept of the universe, her fundamental beliefs, even her self-image were all shattered, and still she had the strength and will to overcome her shock, readjust her thinking, and continue to lead her people. No wonder McCoy was impressed with her! He recognized and respected her greater responsibility—and McCoy earned our admiration for the depth of his understanding and his unselfish caring.

Now to "The Empath," which happens to be a particular favorite of mine. Star Trek was always good at sympathetic villains: you were supposed to be able to see both sides of the question. The writers often went out of their way, as in the case of the horta, to make us conscious of the fact that every participant in a story had his or her own viewpoint.

So imagine, if you will, what it was like to be a Vian, to be Lal and Thann. They were responsible for choosing from among several races the one that would be saved from destruction by a nova. We assume it had to be an intellectual, logical decision, considering what we know about the Vians themselves, but it was still a terrible, devastating responsibility. The races that could not be saved would perish, with all their unique accomplishments and beauties, with all their might-have-beens.

The Vians had to make sure that the race they saved was worthy of that kind of risk, that expensive salvation. The saved race would have to be something very special and rare. The Vians felt that if Gem's race could develop some additional characteristics it would be worthy of salvation.

Knowing they could not reach the necessary virtues, they selected (after an unsuccessful first attempt) our triumvirate, Kirk, Spock, and McCoy, to teach Gem, as her race's best representative, what the Vians regarded as essential: self-sacrifice, selfless love.

They devised their experiment to reveal to Gem those qualities they thought most admirable and essential—and it began with pain. Pain is amoral; it serves a useful function in the body, warning of illness and danger, protecting injured parts against abuse. It helps preserve the body.

The Vians used pain to preserve a race and protect Gem's people. Kirk, in his torment, struggled to live, to protect his friends. He faced his death with courage and nobility, and when it seemed he could do nothing but die, he cried out for it to have some meaning—death for a cause, not a fruitless waste.

All three friends could understand and even accept death: the breaks of the game, a known hazard, and inevitability to be avoided for as long as possible. In this situation, McCoy was the most perceptive, and (forgive me, Spock) the most logical. He understood, better than the others, that it is possible to fear something worse than death.

Kirk was offered the choice of death for McCoy or permanant insanity for Spock. Spock's offer to go with the Vians has an excruciating poignancy because his intellect and rationality are his essence. His body would continue to exist, but Spock would be worse than dead—a tragic shell that served no useful purpose, a constant, cruel reminder to friends and family which they would be helpless to affect or aid. McCoy was right again. A clean, final death would be preferable for Spock, or for anyone. McCoy and Kirk could both teach Gem that death with meaning might, under some circumstances, be better than living. And that is part of our humanity.

McCoy also know that together, Kirk and Spock had a better chance of getting the Vian control mechanism to work. For him, there would be the possibility of rescue. A realistic assessment of his own limited skills told him there would be no such possibility for Spock.

In a clearly logical decision, McCoy chose to go with the Vians. He also knew that Kirk, sick and exhautsed, burdened by the choice, would oppose him. So he took swift, sympathetic action to knock out the opposition, literally. Faced with Spock's almost smug usurpation of the decision while Kirk was incapacitated, McCoy decided that what was good for the captain was equally good for the stubborn first officer. And he was right.

However, there was a flaw in the Vians' carefully worked-out plan—a common one, true, but one that can easily invalidate any experiment: the narrow, singleminded pursuit of a previously visualized goal. The Vians decided, in advance, that Gem's self-sacrificing death would be the only valid conclusion to their experiment. They were working with blinders on, nearly helpless to recognize any but their preconceived goal.

Rather than the villains they appear to be, the Vians were intelligent, thoughtful beings with an awesome responsibility—a responsibility they were poorly suited to shoulder and one they couldn't abrogate or avoid. They did the best they could.

They found beings who *could* demonstrate the qualities Gem's race needed, qualities they themselves were incapable of giving to Gem. They devised the experiment, they brought everyone together and supervised the affair. Even though their own survival was never in question, they were *desperate* to prove that their choice of Gem's race was a valid one.

We don't know what the alternative might have been, but if Gem could absorb some essential human qualities like love and loyalty, like the will to survive and the comfort of a meaningful death and the spirit of sacrifice, then her race would be worthy of its costly salvation. Her death, while healing McCoy, was to be their final proof.

Kirk wasn't telling the Vians anything new when he said they didn't understand what they had brought Gem there to learn. Of course they didn't! That's why they needed the humans in the first place. The Vians admired the humanity of the *Enterprise* officers and chose them as Gem's teachers. They were faced with a heartbreaking, impossible task of their own choosing—who would compel them to save *any* race? I think they chose wisely. Gem's race will be a rare and beautiful tribute to their compassion. The Vians were not human, but if we want to be proud of our own humanity, we should grant them understanding and respect.

And on what qualities does our humanity rest? On curiosity, for one thing. Like Rudyard Kipling's Elephant Child, we have "satiable curiosity"; the will to know, to discover, to reach beyond the obvious to the next step. And like the Elephant Child, our discoveries may be painful, pushing us into new shapes, but the new shapes may be as interesting and as useful as the Elephant Child's new trunk.

V'Ger's Program was not to learn the unlearnable, rather it was "learn all that is learnable." And that is man's goal. Does it matter that no one man can hope to learn all that is learnable? No. Does is discourage the inquisitive to know that they will never know even a fraction of what we've already learned? No. The curious person wants to find out for himself; to learn by doing, thinking, reading, exploring, and thereby making what he learns a part of himself.

It should not prove to be man's undoing if he decides there are some questions that have no answers. In *Star Trek: The Motion Picture,* V'Ger sends a message to the Creator. Decker says to Kirk, "It wants an answer, Jim." Kirk's reply is typical of the man. "I don't even know the question!" And that's not so bad.

Our questions demonstrate our humanity. How can we give each person what he needs physically, emotionally, spiritually? How can we learn respect and understanding? How can we appreciate our differences? We have trouble with these questions now. Let's learn *all* that is learnable and see if we can find the answers.

Suppose we learn all that is learnable; we would still be free to speculate on the unlearnable. And who knows? As we grow, our definition of unlearnable or unknowable may change the same way our concept of Paradise is changing.

There are no forbidden answers. Who would forbid them to us? Creation is meant to be explored, studied, and examined. How else can man grow? How else can he appreciate the wonder of the Unknowable Truth? Whatever God we may choose to worship, we know that he has already given us gifts of such immeasurable wealth: love, curiosity, courage, beauty . . . ad infinitum. He has given us the universe to enjoy them in. He has given us the universe to challenge and strengthen us. He expects us to use it. Let's not keep Him waiting. Enjoy and grow strong and wise.

THE MYTH AND THE JOURNEY OF DR. LEONARD MCCOY

by Joyce Tullock

There's not much need for an introduction to this article—the title says it all. When Joyce queried us about submitting it, she said, "I just wanted to see if anything more could be said about the good doctor." The answer is a very definite yes.

Rumor has it that the race of man had quite humble beginnings.

Man was—so they say—a shadowy, uncertain creature who stood up one morning, reason and imagination in hand, and began an awkward, roundabout journey to selfhood. About that journey we have very few facts and many theories. But we do have the myth. It is the best part of the story; the part which is most worthwhile to us as intellectual creatures. Through the myth, we relive the journey, building on it with personal interpretations and observations. Most of all, the myth makes the facts and theories more charming—and ironically, more believable.

It's the same with a man. Whether he is real or the product of some writer's imagination, the myth is what is seen from outside. Such a man is Star Trek's Dr. Leonard "Bones" McCoy. He began humbly enough—ink on paper. The real myth began on that day when the actor picked up his first script, read it to himself, and scribbled notes in the margin. As unimpressive as it sounds, it was the beginning of life.

McCoy's story is one built upon legend, implication, and imagination, for the series provided very little direct information about his character. But every man, be he real or imagined, is 50 percent facts, figures, dates, and events . . . and 50 percent myth. Just as we are, in part, the product of the evolution of our own imaginations. The adult, looking back, realizes he did not develop through a straight-line sequence of events: The intellect, pretty much ignoring time and space, grows in an almost haphazard way, until imagination and reality converge in just that right combination and balance to form that state of mind which we refer to as *maturity*.

It's a journey, that's all. Every form of fiction, from Shakespeare to Twain to Heinlein, deals with the basic "journey story." It is a simple, all-encompassing theme which provides a constant, spiraling turn of new perspectives on that old subject, mankind.

McCoy experiences this "journey of life" both within single episodes and throughout the series' filmed entirety. And there comes a time when the viewer suddenly realizes that it is not so much what he sees on film that makes the character of Dr. McCoy, it is what the actor and writers *imply* creatively. That's when the viewer becomes participant in the development of the character . . . and the myth begins to grow.

As the Star Trek phenomenon moves well into its second decade, and the age of oh-my-gosh superheroes gives way to something new, the myth and the character of Dr. Leonard "Bones" McCoy is demanding more and more attention. In fact, Bones is causing a kind of gentle murmur among those viewers who are just now beginning to suspect that he was given too little attention in the series. But there is a fine marvel to it, too, as it becomes evident that this character, who was so often slighted in favor of the more marketable Kirk and Spock, is perhaps as strong and as complex a personality as filmed science fiction has ever seen. McCoy has become his own phenomenon.

At the root of Bones' myth is a simple formula: He is designed (much like Heinlein's Lazarus Long) to appeal to the most basic and unpretentious parts of human nature. In fact, he bears an uncanny resemblance to Heinlein's "Laz"; he is from the nation's South (Lazarus was a Missouri boy), he is a doctor (as was Laz, among other things), and both are a little bit shy and old-fashioned for a space-age world. Both carry some of the inbred guilt feelings connected with the religious and ethical standards of their fathers; they're stubborn, quick-witted, sometimes selfish; they've lost love and expect to love again. McCoy and Lazarus are embarrassed idealists, sentimentalists, and stubborn fighters who nevertheless know when to leave by the back door. And like Laz, McCoy sometimes wants to give up, but those who love him will not permit it. Both are reluctant heroes, reluctant leaders, who often must be "called" to service by those who need and respect their abilities.

But McCoy is more protagonist than hero, and as the events of the series unfold, we see him develop his own roughhewn humanist philosophy. He becomes many things: doctor, teacher, scientist, philosopher. He is the gentleman rogue, the fool on the hill, the Merlin to Jim Kirk's Arthur.

Little wonder that it is easy to become fascinated with the dubious evolution of this character who is claimed (by co-creator DeForest Kelley) to have "come in by the back door".

Somehow, even *that* is fitting.

But McCoy's late entrance into the series is camouflaged (rather awkwardly, perhaps) by the sequence in which the episodes were aired. In "Man Trap" we get the beginnings of the myth about McCoy, the character whose role will rise and fall in an uneven, rhythm throughtout Star Trek's existence. McCoy's is an admittedly frustrating career to any viewer who develops a keen interest in the character; if you are a dyed-in-the-wool McCoy fan, chances are that you're still waiting for the good doctor's Big Moment.

But at least there is the myth. And McCoy's myth is in many ways the story of man. Fans find a great deal of entertainment in trying to "fill in the blanks" of his mysterious life before joining the crew of the *Enterprise*. Is he running? What about his divorce? Did he know Jim Kirk before serving aboard the *Enterprise?* And the guilt—you can see it in his face, can't you? And why, for Orion's sake, is the open-minded "humanitarian of Star Trek" so hard on everyone's beloved Mr. Spock?

Of course, the fun is in the speculation.

The McCoy myth evolves, not so much as a series of facts and events, but as a kind of circular "whole" of experience. As with real human beings, his life journey has little to do with time. It is a matter of inner experience.

He begins almost as a weakling in "Man Trap," fretting over his long-lost love Nancy Crater. He lets his sentiment take charge to the extent that (for a while) he completely loses sight of his professionalism. His behavior jeopardizes his captain's life and allows the episode's hideous salt monster free reign of the ship. And for the only time during his tour aboard the *Enterprise*, he willingly takes medical advice from his captain. (Kirk advises him to take those "little red pills" to get some sleep.) Goodness! If this is Mr. Spock's initial exposure to Dr. McCoy, then there is little wonder about the Vulcan's leeriness toward the "emotional" human.

Rest assured, never again will McCoy let his emotions get that much out of control. He has his ups and downs, of course, but from here on he "breaks down" only when under the influence of some great physical or drug-induced stress. Eash stress-situation experience serves to contribute to his character and to extend his frame of reference. With each problem, he grows. And as his frame of reference broadens, so does ours. We learn about him—not about his past, but about *him*. We see his sensitivity develop into a philosophy of feeling. We become familiar with his attitudes toward medicine, technology, prejudice, love, and his purpose in life. We watch him grow and develop a positive, if extremely individualistic, life-style. In "Man Trap" he is an emotional baby, licking wounds from the past. Is he thinking of Nancy or himself? She is married. She is not his responsibility and yet he is afraid of losing her again. One suspects that the pain of his mysterious divorce somehow plays a part. It all contributes greatly to the myth.

But McCoy quickly learns that his ties to the past, be they those of guilt or love, have the power to destroy the present. When he destroys the salt monster (and its illusion of Nancy Crater) he cuts himself free of the terrible bonds of a mysterious history. He grows up a little.

McCoy doesn't turn away from his emotions, though—
he just learns to use them more efficiently. And when his
self-control does break down from time to time, the
concerns revealed to be foremost in his mind are primarily
humanitarian ones.

In "City on the Edge of Forever," he is the victim of an
overdose of cordrazine, a drug which causes him to rage
in paranoia. As the drug begins to wear off, his fear turns
to despair . . . and he reveals his feelings of horror and
contempt for the barbaric medical methods of our own
twentieth century ("Doctors cutting and sewing people like
garments . . ."). With his usually well-fortified defenses
torn away, McCoy's abhorrence of human suffering becomes more apparent. He displays the unhappiness which
he has heretofore successfully kept well hidden in his day-
to-day life as a physican. This scene touches unmercifully
upon the very raw nerve of the man's deepest feelings. It
inspires a greater respect for McCoy's mask of cynicism.
Suddenly, we understand.

We are allowed few such insightful glimpses into
McCoy. "City" is a good example of this, for while the
doctor actually appears for only a few minutes of the
story, he nevertheless makes us acutely aware of his power
and complexity as a character. In one or two scenes we
come to know the very root of his character. And something more is added to the myth in this episode, for one
can imagine that McCoy carries a very painful—if illogical—guilt for the tragic events of the story and Kirk's subsequent sorrow. It's a thing which the doctor must
somehow assimilate into his own character; a thing which
he must deal with in his own private way. It too is part of
the myth.

And so myth and man develop together. On the one
side is an individual mysteriously burdened with guilt,
tired from the suffering which surrounds him daily. One
the other side (as in "This Side of Paradise") is a more
carefree McCoy, the lighthearted "boy from Georgia." In
this episode (and in "Wolf in the Fold") McCoy's worries
are allowed to drop away along with his inhibitions. He is
seen as he might have been if he had chosen to be anything but a doctor. He is unusually relaxed, gentle, trust-
ing—a friendly "good ol' boy" with nothing on his mind
but mint juleps and having a good time.

In "Wolf in the Fold," when McCoy has been tranquilized, we see his inherent (and sometimes dangerous) capacity for trust and goodwill as he approaches the mad, knife-wielding Hengst (i.e., Jack the Ripper) with open hands and a wide, gentle grin. We get a glimpse behind the mask, and wonder if we are seeing a trace of the younger, more innocent McCoy. His tranquilized state doesn't fully explain the open, caring, outgoing manner—there has to be something more. This could be the McCoy who married with full intentions of living a life of comfort, love, and unfettered happiness. It could be a quick glimpse of the young med student who idealistically believed that he could cure the sick and ease the misery of others.

We see shadings of a young man (perhaps twenty or thereabouts) who merely wants to *help*. There is something a little unsophisticated, even naive, about this McCoy; his "down home" charm, the assurance that he hasn't an enemy in the world (even at knifepoint!), and a manner which speaks of an essentially carefree, sheltered childhood. Loving parents must have set Good Examples—and someone, sometime, has definitely encouraged him to dream.

And what happens to all dreamers one day? The cynic Leonard McCoy will tell you. With sharp tongue and searching eyes, he'll cut a bit too keenly to the core of truth. He'll use his wit to belittle his own "foolish" dreams, easing failure's pain with the balm of wry humor . . . or maybe it is better said that he *hides* the pain that way. McCoy protects those he loves most by reminding them caustically of the harsh reality which threatens their dearest notions. He is frightened for them. He is clearly a man who has too often seen his own dreams crumble. He's felt like a fool for it, as if he had done something stupid or wrong. It's a great complexity, an esential part of the myth; he will allow others to dream, even encourage it in his own backhand way, but he persists in camouflaging his own idealism in a well chosen vocabulary of terse, cynical humor. This is what makes the McCoy character the honest and humanly realistic puzzle that he is. He is often openly sentimental about those he cares for, but ask him about his hopes for mankind and he might well scowl and say, "I'm a doctor, not a philosopher!" But watch him

. . . he'll turn his head away as he speaks, so as not to show the embarrassed hope in his eyes. This is the man who is hesitant to reveal his own optimism about the human race because experience has shown him that "evil usually wins out, unless good is very, very careful."

This is the careful, suspicious McCoy. It's the McCoy who watches his troubled captain closely in "Obession" and has honest doubts about Mr. Spock's reasons for rejoining the *Enterprise* in *Star Trek: The Motion Picture*. And if the fans have a real gripe with McCoy, chances are that it is about his way of speaking so harshly to those he loves. He is, indeed, unmerciful with the truth. He's been criticized for his rough treatment of Spock in such episodes as "Galileo Seven," "Bread and Circuses," "Immunity Syndrome," and "The Tholian Web." DeForest Kelley has revealed in interviews that powerful McCoy lines were cut from the script of *STTMP* because someone felt that the doctor was "being too hard on Kirk."

And so the frustration continues; McCoy's single most valuable contribution to the story quality of Star Trek is his unrelenting realism. He sometimes comes down hard on the human race, punches us in the gut, making us face the toughness of life and self. A powerful loneliness is part of his drama, his secret, his myth. His "surface harshness" is the key to his impact . . . and he suffers for it in the scripts just as any such person does in real life. When it comes to marketing Star Trek, it is McCoy, not Spock, who is ofttimes the "outcast." His realism is kept tethered; evidently the general attitude is that there is something vaguely unacceptable about it. The doctor is censored— not to protect Kirk or Spock, but to protect that part of the audience which dislikes seeing them as imperfect human personalities.

But Star Trek isn't purely escapism for everyone. Otherwise the concept of IDIC and appreciation of the whole would not hold such interest. In Star Trek, McCoy, with his mystery and complete humanness, can be seen as representative of the entire human race. We respect him for his fallibility, recognize his confusion, and gradually discover his boundless warmth. We are impressed with the fact that he views himself and others with something which is not so much "bleeding heart" kindness as it is logical, human wisdom. McCoy recognizes the flaws in his fellow man, but he also appreciates the beauty.

In fact, of the Big Three, McCoy is the one who is most clearly awed by the human creature. Like a loving parent, he forgives mankind its failings. In "The Enemy Within," Kirk is divided into two parts, one good, one evil. Faced with the stark reality of his darker side, the captain finds himself loathing the powerful, egotistical half of his nature. He wants to reject that portion of his "self." But human ugliness is no shock to McCoy; he is not repelled by Kirk's evil side, but is only concerned that it be kept in perspective. One suspects that the doctor has already come face to face with the darker side of his own nature, and has learned to respect it. He advises his captain: "We all have our darker side. We need it, it's half of what we are. It's not really ugly, it's human." (A glimpse of the McCoy philosophy, echoes of IDIC, and a prophetic foreshadowing of the line "Why is everything we don't understand always called a 'thing'?") So McCoy the cynic is really McCoy the open-minded realist. We forgive him his sharp tongue just as we forgive the porcupine its quills, remembering the tender belly beneath.

Besides, it's hard to be a cynic all the time. Catch him at the right moment, and Bones will prove himself to quite the sentimentalist. He is deeply "honored" by Spock's request that he be present at the Vulcan's wedding ceremony in "Amok Time." He's the proud "father figure" in "Friday's Child" as he unashamedly plays his role with Eleen's newborn son. And during his earlier experiences in "Shore Leave," McCoy woos Yeoman Tonia Barrows with the statement "A princess should not be afraid—not with a brave knight to protect her." . .

So the myth becomes more involved. In "Shore Leave," McCoy and crew visit an amusement planet where their innermost fantasies may suddenly materialize. Through the no-holds-barred approach of this episode, we are given a peek at McCoy the ladies' man, the old-fashioned romantic, and we see hints of those stories of the knights of old. Those stories are imbedded firmly in McCoy's memory, seeming to be an important part of his conscious and subconscious mind—so important that in "Shore Leave" they overpower him for a time and turn into a nightmare. He is inadvertently (and quite temporarily) killed by the jousting knight he dreams up as his imaginary foe. We get the feeling that it'll be a while before Bones picks up another copy of *Le Morte d'Arthur*. (And the next time we see him, he's dreamed up two showgirls—one for each arm. Well? He said he was a "brave knight"—not a "true" one.)

The McCoy in "Shore Leave" (unquestionably the happiest and more carefree McCoy we have ever seen) is a McCoy we rarely see aboard the *Enterprise*. This episode takes him away from the tremendous duties of ship's surgeon and lets him relax just enough to provide a good look at the man beneath the title. The myth of McCoy the Carouser is proudly born.

A lusty myth it is, too. McCoy again enjoys shore leave in "Wolf in the Fold" and is no doubt pretty darn disappointed when the episode's events prevent him from taking Kirk to that little place "where the women are so . . ." The good, kindly doctor, it seems, has a wandering eye. Even when in danger he sometimes has problems keeping his mind on the straight and narrow—if a beautiful girl is at hand. In "Omega Glory," we catch him leering (well, it was a *charming* leer) at the pretty young woman who brings him his meal. If it hadn't been for McCoy's burly "Com" guard, the good doctor might well have tried to carry things a little further than a smile. You can count on bullies to spoil it every time!

Unlike Kirk, most of McCoy's more intimate friendships with the opposite sex are kept private . . . with one exception, of course, and even that exception is not really an exception.

In "For the World Is Hollow and I Have Touched the Sky," McCoy marries the lovely Fabrini priestess Natira. That's about all we know, and so speculation runs rampant. (McCoy was dying in this episode too. Call it the "Bonanza Syndrome" in reverse—every time McCoy gets involved with a woman, *he* dies—or at least comes awfully darn close. No wonder he's a loner!) And so, the questions: Did he marry Natira for shelter? To make up for a lonely past? Did he really love her or was he just rationalizing? Whatever happened to poor Natira after she set him free? And . . . good grief! Everything happened so fast. Did they have a "wedding night"?

Wouldn't we like to know.

Might as well forget it, though. As far as Leonard
McCoy is concerned, it's none of our damn business; no
more than are the details of his first marriage or of his relationship with Nancy Crater. The "myth" strikes again! But
McCoy, with all of his closed-mouthed mystery, may actually have revealed a bit more of himself than he'd like to
in "For the World . . ." when he admits to Natira that he
cannot hide himself in the security of marriage. He is a
doctor, first and foremost; everything else, even his personal life, is secondary. Chances are (opinion goes) that
while McCoy's second "divorce" lacks the bitterness which
is imagined to be part of the first, it is very likely a
shadowy replay. Somehow, McCoy's brilliance and devotion to his work is suspected to have interfered with his
marriage. The details, of course, are left to the gossip-
mongers.

But McCoy's marriage to Natira isn't even the most important role "For the World . . ." has to play in the story
of his evolution as a character. In the novelization of *Star
Trek: The Motion Picture* we hear of the Fabrini again.
The McCoy who stands before us in the movie's transporter scene is somewhat of a revelation. He is changed. He
stands straight, alone, like some long-forgotten eccentric
king—noble, proud, and just enough the clown to hide his
own sorrow. He is angry. He is wary. He is every bit the
doctor, eyeing his beloved Captain Kirk with the warm
sternness of a psychologist and trusted friend. In this one
scene, his only *real* scene in the picture, he is a powerful,
elegant mystery.

Thank goodness the novel tells us a bit more about the
doctor than does the movie. Mr. Roddenberry graciously
reveals the fact that McCoy has lived a life of seclusion
since his return to planet Earth. It seems that he resigned
from Starfleet after a rather vocal tussle with the service's
top man, Admiral Nogura; something to do with McCoy's
having his own ideas about what is "best" for Jim Kirk.

The movie's Dr. McCoy is tougher than the one we've
known. Just as fittingly, he also appears to have mellowed;
a peculiar paradox for anyone but Bones. The bearded civilian is cross, impatient, suspicious; the clean-shaven chief
surgeon is an objective, if rather sharp-tongued, adviser.
McCoy leaves his own concerns back on Earth for a time
and takes full charge of the duties at hand.

But what of his life on Earth? Of course, it's none of our business again, yet we can't help but wonder. Scuttle-butt has it that he has spent his time researching Fabrini medicine. Not surprising, really. He's been working hard, and pretty much on his own, at finding ways of applying Fabrini techniques and knowledge to Earth medicine. He's the renegade still, and it isn't hard to imagine that he's had a great deal of trouble introducing "alien" cures and prac-tices to Earth's medical establishment. He's made inroads aplenty in Starfleet medicine, though. The novelization mentions that the *Enterprise*'s sickbay utilizes his precious Fabrini technology. (And one can't help but wonder: Could this have partly come about through the quiet pressuring and constant recommendations of a certain devoted admiral?) Whatever, the novel makes it clear that a grumbling, complaining "old country doctor" takes a warm inner pleasure in seeing his own research put to good use. But McCoy's success in Fabrini research in-volves quite a bit more than simple human pride.

The McCoy "myth" derives largely from another myth—that of the duty-bound, guilt-ridden "work ethic" of middle-class Protestantism. Closely related to this are the old Southern traditions of loyalty, honor, and duty. Here we may have a valuable clue to the McCoy puzzle. Although McCoy must have grown up in what we would today call a "liberal society," he was likely also nur-tured—through family attitudes and local traditions—with a simpler, more conservative, but nonetheless desirable philosophy of a bygone time. Not only is he Old South, he is Old Earth. Intellectually, he is no less a hybrid than Mr. Spock. He is the child of two ofttimes polarized philoso-phies—liberalism and conservatism. If McCoy is a man who seems to run hot and cold, who is generous at one moment and unkind the next, then perhaps this explains it in part.

He is, after all, not so different from the man of today; he is trying continually to reconcile the unreconcilable. Like all of us, he is trying to "keep balance" in a world of confusion. And with an enviable degree of grace, he does just that. He honors the traditions of his southern Ameri-can heritage and carries them proudly into the ever-chang-ing, space-age world of the twenty-third century. His ethnic background is as important to him as Uhura's

Swahili heritage is to her, as Spock's Vulcan upbringing is
to him. By means of McCoy's warm genius for understate-
ment, the noble traditions of his fathers take their rightful
place aboard the *Enterprise* . . . in accordance with the
philosophy of IDIC. If McCoy's ethnic background is responsible for his approach to life, then it is only natural
that he feels a great sense of indebtedness and loyalty to
the Fabrini people. It isn't simply that Fabrini medicine
saved his life, it's also that his physician's mind is in awe
of a technology which grew, flowered and died long before
mankind was truly a "thinking" creature.

McCoy's experiences in 'For the World Is Hollow"
change him, all right. He meets himself for a moment,
shakes hands with his gravest fears, and returns to the *Enterprise* still believing that he has only one short year to
live. He plans to use his allotted time well—to find answers for those who suffer as he does. No doubt it even
crosses his mind that researchers may at least be able to
discover a few clues about his disease through the inevitable examination of his corpse. So McCoy puts aside the
life "he longs for" in order to seek answers. (Symbolically,
he does this again in *Star Trek: The Motion Picture* when
he leaves his beloved Earth for another tour with the *Enterprise*.) In "For the World Is Hollow," McCoy discovers
once and for all that his happiness directly involves his
work. He faces something in himself. With that typical
Star Trek religious irony, McCoy finds life only by facing
the grave.

He is a step closer to the grand catharsis.

As McCoy submits to the life-saving Fabrini medicine
aboard the *Enterprise,* Kirk promises to find a way for
him to meet and thank the Fabrini people again for their
help. The captain knows his friend well. He understands
McCoy's sense of indebtedness. He certainly understands
McCoy's "affection" for Natira. But as for the doctor's
eventual reunion with the lovely lady, we can only
guess. . . .

After the five-year mission, McCoy quickly takes on the
job of "paying back his debt" to Fabrini medicine. He is
enthusiastic about sharing its many long-lost secrets with
the world. He considers his task to be an honor and a
duty. But he has to pay a penance beforehand, spending
his last two years aboard the *Enterprise* learning the Fab-

rini language firsthand . . . under the strict tutelage of the all-too-knowledgeable Mr. Spock. Knowing McCoy, it wouldn't do to simply have a computer translation of the medical knowledge. No sir, that wouldn't be complete enough. McCoy is, after all, an intelligent man, a brilliant surgeon, and if he appears to be doing things the hard way, it is only because he is thoroughly interested in the task at hand. He takes his work very seriously indeed. He is almost a fanatic. This is one point in which the acceptable standards of his own twenty-third century may be overruled by the ingrained traditions of his heritage. McCoy has complete confidence in the human brain. He is most comfortable with the human thought process and the insight it affords. He doesn't do things the hard way—he does them the *right* way. If that puzzles others, it probably amuses and even impresses Mr. Spock. So if the logical Vulcan is able to find a bit of gentle humor as he drills McCoy in the study of the Fabrini language, well, that's just fine. We understand. It's easy enough to see Mr. Spock tutoring McCoy, making the "illogical" human sweat over his work, coolly wondering out loud over his pupil's difficulty in mastering a concept. "Fascinating, doctor," the Vulcan might have said, "how intelligent humans such as yourself must wrestle with a language whose construction is founded upon simple logic. The fetters of your Anglo-American heritage, no doubt."

Yes, McCoy must have done his share of growing during those last two years. Too bad we'll never know.

But in many episodes we do see him grow. In fact, McCoy develops an entire philosophy as he examines the human creature in episodes like "Return to Tomorrow," "The Enemy Within," and "Bread and Circuses." McCoy, the keen observer, discovers that wherever he looks, he learns about himself. His personal and professional ethics are challenged in "Return" when one of the disembodied entities of Arret offers to make a deal: Kirk's life in exchange for McCoy's silence. The entity, Thalassa, decides that she wants to remain forever in the "borrowed" host body of Dr. Ann Mulhall. McCoy is incensed, and rejects the prospect of trading one life for another, announcing, "I will not peddle flesh!" Often McCoy's philosophy is apparent when he gives personal advice, as in "Enemy" when he reminds Kirk of the awful necessity for both the

driving and gentle sides of the human ego. But in many
cases, McCoy has his own harsh lesson to learn. During
the famous prison scene in "Bread and Circuses," he
seems unjust and overbearing as he chastises Spock for his
apparent emotionlessness. (Kirk, Spock, and McCoy are
under the death sentence—again. There is a great deal of
pressure. McCoy tries to thank Spock for saving his life;
it's like offering an overcoat to an icecube.) When McCoy
loses his temper, his cutting remarks bounce back at him.
He discovers that he is punishing others as a means of
dealing with his own pain. Spock acts like a mirror here:
His patience in the face of McCoy's rage shows superhuman understanding. Once the doctor sees this, a look of
painful self-admonition settles on his face. Another lesson
learned. In episodes such as this (and there are several of
them) it becomes clear that McCoy isn't merely examining
others—he is judging himself. He is continually refining
and remolding the man he sees in the mirror of friendship.
He is hard on others. He is hardest on himself.

That's how the myth evolves. He is hard on himself
from the beginning and we are never exactly sure why.
But whatever his dark, mysterious past may hold is unim-
portant—except that it stands before us as a broad, blank
wall. It is a slate constructed of time and space and uni-
versals; the story of all men. Those who feel the need may
write their secrets upon it.

But the past aside, it's the McCoy we *do* see who is important. He is filled with healthy human measures of self-
doubt, guilt, suspicion, and sorrow. He is admittedly
confused concerning his own place in the ever-expanding
universe of the twenty-third century. He approaches it all
with just enough humor and innocence to make the journey fun. And once in a while he slips and shows an embarrassed, barely disguised hope for genuine human
progress.

There is one element upon which all of McCoy's positive traits are based. It is his simple *unembarrassed joy* at
being alive. We see that joy in many episodes, from
"Shore Leave" to "For the World" to "Empath." It is
expressed in a variety of ways, from the light-hearted to
the serious. It is evident in every single episode in which
McCoy is able to find the humor and understand the
deeper significance of his own predicament. As the "coun-

try boy" and ship's physician, he stands for life. So if he does have a death wish (and it's only human that he should), it's not an unhealthily large one, for throughout Star Trek, life is McCoy's preoccupation. Kirk enjoys life too, of course, but he enjoys it as "the adventurer." McCoy enjoys life for its own sake. Kirk is the spaceman; McCoy is the "Earth" man.

It is easy to imagine that more than anything else, the good doctor longs to return to the kind of life he once knew: to the lush greenness and humanity of his beloved planet Earth. Of all the *Enterprise* crew, he is the one who is most easily pictured as the "homebody." He has just a touch of "the homesick Southern boy" about him and is easily imagined longing at times for the "green, green hills of earth." It's part of his myth, and it plays an important, if subtle, part in his impact as a character.

McCoy's love of life is most obvious in those episodes where he is enjoying a shore leave. But his *devotion* to life is most apparent when he is being "the doctor" of the ship. Whether he is treating a patient, or whether the entire *Enterprise* crew is in danger, the doctor can't help but let his opinions be known. ("I recommend survival.")

His all-too-famous "survival" statement is often misinterpreted as an indication that he is short-sighted, or even cowardly. And how far would the good ship *Enterprise* have gone had its captain not taken that advice again and again? Mr. Spock is wrong in "Immunity Syndrome" when he indirectly accuses McCoy of being so preoccupied with humans as individuals that he is not able to have empathy for the many. (The Vulcan-manned *Intrepid* is destroyed and Spock feels a moment of painful psychic empathy.) The "myth" which surrounds McCoy indicates that the exact opposite is true. Humanitarian though he is, he is often overly curt and harsh with individuals, even his patients. There are signs of this in "The Deadly Years" when he gruffly tells the ailing Mr. Scott that all he really needs is vitamins. He simply knows better than to "baby" a patient. He does feel for them, of course, but he tries very hard to keep those feelings to himself. It's something a doctor must do, not simply for the sake of his patient, but for the sake of his own sanity. So McCoy manages to build around himself a reputation for cynicism and crankiness which keeps much of the crew at bay. It's a defensive game. His close friends know his true nature—and play along with his need for isolation by ignoring and even toying with his mask of gruffness. In fact, they add to it with their playful taunting; even Spock has been known more than once to have tried to bring the doctor's steady simmer to a boil (as when he suggests that McCoy's medical technique employs the use of "beads and rattles").

But everyone is guilty; Kirk and Scotty also like to play games with Bones' quick temper. They are like children who fondle a loved but ill-tempered cat by rubbing its fur the wrong way; sometimes the cat bites, sometimes it purrs, and sometimes it just smoothes its ruffled coat and walks away. Bones is just as unpredictable.

Nevertheless, McCoy is completely devoted to his friends. For the sake of levity (and realism) the exchange of affection is carried off through quick-witted quips, jokes, and tauntings. It's a common human method for testing and displaying friendship. And myth has it that while McCoy is close to Spock and Kirk in a delicate, almost poetic way, he also enjoys a close, long-lived friendship with Engineer Montgomery Scott. The scenes in which the two men are shown together are few and short, but in the series' last episode, "Turnabout Intruder," the two are alone discussing the question of Kirk's identity (Janice Lester has taken over the captain's body). The scene becomes an important part of the McCoy myth as it is clear testimony that the two men are old and comfortable friends. It isn't a matter of Lieutenant Commander Scott "talking business" with Chief Surgeon McCoy . . . They are completely at ease with one another, and discuss the problem at hand with the casual openness of neighbors gossiping over the backyard fence; they are on the same level, somehow, like two men who have reached the end of a long road together. Of all the members of the *Enterprise* crew (Spock and Kirk included) it is Scott who can most easily be imagined adressing the ship's surgeon as "Leonard."

McCoy has certainly come down a long road since the apparently immature days of "Man Trap" and the carefree time of "Shore Leave." He has grown a great deal during his tour with the *Enterprise*. He begins (almost typecast) as the gangly, long-legged "boy from Georgia" who is more than a little bit "on the run" from some personal tragedy. He develops into the unofficious, if sometimes brooding, elegant Southern gentleman who chisels for himself an individualistic and down-to-earth philosophy of humanitarianism.

In those critical *Enterprise* years, Leonard McCoy turns the circle—from runner to discoverer.

The pivotal point where McCoy combines all that he has learned occurs in "The Empath." It all churns together here; he is doctor, officer, idealist, realist, gentleman, humanitarian, friend . . . and most of all, he is the lover of life. In "Empath," McCoy is most profoundly the Enemy of Death. He balances his capacities for logic and emotion more precisely than ever before, using his powerful emotions to give him the strength to do the logical thing. In "Empath," McCoy employs every facet of his character.

He is the noble knight protecting the fair damsel (Gem, the empath, whom the Vians are testing for her capacity for self-sacrifice).

He is the very frank, practical physician, who is keenly aware of the fact that Gem could not withstand empathic contact with an injured Spock (should the Vulcan be chosen to be the Vians' tortured guinea pig). On medical grounds, he overrules Kirk and Spock because he knows that it would be impossible for Gem to heal the superhuman Vulcan.

He is the officer, who considers himself to be the most expendable of the three.

He is the friend, who would prevent Kirk from making the decision which would haunt him for the rest of his days. (Kirk, as captain, is ordered to choose which of his two friends is to take part in the Vians' "experiment.")

Most of all, he is the human being, the sad comic and "fool on the hill" who finally rebels against Kirk's and Spock's ever-present desire to protect him. ("Not this time, Spock," he says with sad defiance as he renders Spock unconscious with the hypo-spray.)

In this scene the doctor is also the "confused" McCoy. He almost seems to stumble over his own motives as he goes about "convincing" Kirk and Spock of his own fitness for the gruesome task at hand. He is also very much the old McCoy we have known all along—frightened at the thought of death, bold in the face of it. He approaches the Vians with shy conviction, but once in their hands he shields his fears with an irreverent, sardonic tongue. "Get on with it!" he snaps, as they try to rationalize their cruelty.

So it happens that McCoy, the energetic lover of life, is given the opportunity to learn "the art of dying." He is brutalized to a point which becomes difficult for the viewer to bear—Star Trek's ugliest moment. It is, however, one of the most if not *the* single most significant moment in the McCoy myth. This is true for many reasons, the most important being that it allows us to see the strength of friendship McCoy shares with Kirk and Spock; for a brief time Kirk permits his commanding manner to completely fall away as he sits with his dying friend. In that instant, Kirk is overcome with the very natural emotions of love, sorrow, and childlike disbelief. He is like the child who had always supposed that his father would live forever. Mr. Spock, still quietly logical, becomes preoccupied with making McCoy comfortable. He takes over the physician's role, but he does not fight the slight tremor in his voice as he forces Kirk to face the reality of McCoy's certain death. McCoy responds to their affection just as we would expect him to—with just a hint of embarrassment, even humor, in his voice. There is an aura of satisfaction about him, a sense of accomplishment, an uncanny ease. He is heroic, but in a very realistic way. That is, he accepts his approaching death as a release from pain . . . as though it's something which has been a long time in coming. But he is also afraid, and wants his friends to be near. Kirk and Spock understand this, so their foremost objective is at any cost, to "go to" their friend.

"The Empath" may not overtly say anything about McCoy which it could not have said about the other two. But it is heavily symbolic, filled with subtle suggestions about the private character of the man McCoy. The writer of the episode (Joyce Muskat) consciously or subconsciously picked up on the many facets of McCoy's personality: his guilt, his determination, his love, his self-doubt, and his anger. And although McCoy is close friends with Kirk and Spock, "Empath" ironically showcases his own unique kind of loneliness. Here is McCoy at a time of ultimate decision, closer to Kirk and Spock than ever before—and more separate than ever before. Perhaps it's the closest we will ever come to defining his relationship to the other two.

The loneliness is important. It is an essential aspect of the McCoy myth, the secret of his success. The McCoy of "Empath" is alone in the way that many people come to be alone—he is a prisoner of himself. It all happens quite by accident. He is held separate from Kirk and Spock by virtue of their very affection for him. They have developed the annoying habit of protecting him. The captain and his first officer also share a military comradery which sets them apart from their essentially civilian-minded friend. It's no one's fault; it's just the way things are. It certainly isn't McCoy's intention to let himself be "sheltered." In fact, myth has it that one of the reasons he joined Starfleet was so that he might "prove" himself once and for all. But Kirk and Spock *do* shelter him because, on a subconscious level, he has come to represent to them what is best in humanity, what the *Enterprise* is all about. So they shield him.

As a result, a very subtle kind of separation comes about. It's very likely that McCoy misinterprets their attitude toward him to be one of a lack of trust. As we see in "Empath" and other episodes, he feels the smallest bit "shut out" and alone, like a little kid who has yet to make the team. He tries to compensate by volunteering for dangerous missions ("Empath," "Immunity Syndrome"). For command reasons, he is usually turned down. And so, imperfect human that McCoy is, it seems reasonable to assume that his determination to sacrifice himself in "Empath" involves a certain amount of revenge. Not to say that it's deliberate, but on a subconscious level McCoy could be getting even for all those times he had to stand aside. His motives are genuinely confused. In a way, he is punishing Kirk and Spock. At the same time, he is proving himself—to friends he considers to be his betters. He's out to make the team.

In one determined act he shows that his courage equals his love. For Kirk and Spock, it was an unnecessary display; his courage was never in question. Unfortunately, they never completely understood his need. The irony of this strikes home when Kirk instinctively admonishes Spock with the remark "Why did you let him do it?" It's all summed up in that one short phrase. Unwittingly, Kirk and Spock have forced McCoy's hand. They become his victims, like the confused parents of a rebellious, overly protected child.

The revenge aspect is minor, of course. It's a subconscious motive. But it is important to the myth because it saves McCoy from appearing to be a martyr. Martyrdom would have destroyed his impact as a character, not because it would have made him seem unreal but because it would have set him apart from the average man, denying him his universal appeal. He would have become typecast as a sentimentalist who sacrificed himself only for glossy-eyed ideals. As noble as that would seem, it's enough to make any self-respecting cynic transport to oblivion!

It has been established that the McCoy of "Empath" is a character who experiences a special kind of grand and poignant loneliness; what went on in his mind during that time, and during the period of recuperation afterwards will always remain a secret. Doubtless someone trained in psychology tried to get him to speak openly of his experience, his motives, and his innermost feelings concerning his ordeal. Pity the poor psychologist who drew that duty! It must have been a rough job . . . and a frustrating one.

The loneliness remains, then. It's a part of the man and the myth. It captivates the viewer with its uncomfortable realism. No answers or concrete explanations are offered in "Empath." It's the kind of episode which is either loved or hated. Its lack of clear-cut storyline leaves many viewers uneasy. It makes about as much sense as life, appearing to be more poetry than action-adventure—more Bradbury than Asimov. For those who seek absolutes, this episode will fail. It was not designed to make the audience comfortable. Rather it was constructed as a philosphical and metaphysical puzzle, employing concepts of religion, psychology, and humanitarianism. It is the closest Star Trek ever came to theater; an eerie, surrealistic play. It is a difficult episode to watch, but McCoy would be the first to point out the senseless cruelty it portrays is no fairy tale. It is a very real occurrence in our own unfortunate universe. And in our own century, on our own planet, we have no emotionless aliens to blame.

The ordeal on Minara II is generally believed to have been the most traumatic experience of McCoy's life, a fair enough assumption. Certainly there must have been emotional wounds which McCoy dealt with in his own private way. No man survives such an experience unchanged. "Empath" may be seen as a time of catharsis for him, and as the turning point or completion of a lengthy private quest. As a physician, he has now had the unique opportunity to experience total suffering (to say the least). As a humanitarian, he has been at once the victim and the conqueror of senseless cruelty. As a friend, he has been able to express his love—and perhaps repay a few debts. He has taken the part of "protector." And on the simplest of terms, but perhaps the most important to McCoy, he has reaffirmed his manhood. Dealing with that unnecessary but eternal question, he has "proved" himself to himself.

At last the circle is complete.

In the tradition of IDIC, McCoy's character evolves in its own special way—not through a series of steps or a linear progression of events, but as a combination of experiences which fall into place to make the whole man. He journeys through space, across the winding channels of time . . . just as do we all. He cheats the boundaries of his beloved Earth, with her motherly tendency to limit and define. In accordance with his holistic medical philosophy, the spirit makes itself whole. There is no reason to believe that McCoy's long Starfleet career was a conscious or deliberate time of testing. He was like any child, running long and hard from the confused and sinister dangers of the night. He tired, and stopped. And when he finally turned around for a look, we can easily imagine his surprise at finding that his own, fallible strength was enough.

McCoy's character is not so much "changed" as it is refined by the time of *Star Trek: The Motion Picture*. He returns to the *Enterprise* reluctantly, a picture of confident defiance. Of the Three, he alone likes and trusts himself. Whatever secrets the tall, lean civilian harbors about his secluded life on Earth, he'll be as free as ever with his professional opinions when dealing with Kirk. His chiseled face bears a degree of smug satisfaction as he leans heavily on the word "captain" when addressing the young admiral. Always the human, he is certainly not above saying, "I told you so.") It's a steady reminder of the enmity which may or may not have been resolved in the movie. Roddenberry's novel suggests that a split occurred between the two friends when McCoy refused to condone Kirk's promotion to admiral. Evidently the problem centers around each man's definition of success. To McCoy, success is a very personal thing, delicately intertwined with each individual's psychological makeup. It has nothing to do with the Old World misconceptions about prestige and personal glory. McCoy knew that Kirk was still too young and adventure-loving to be bound to an admiral's desk. As for the doctor himself, success has become an internalized thing; the need for glory and approval are long past. A few hard lessons have given him some simple answers. The lean, confident Southerner who returns to the *Enterprise* in *STTMP* is a man who is clearly at home with himself.

McCoy still protects himself, though. The myth and the man still stand together. He has his secrets. And no doubt he enjoys the eternally unsatisfied curiosity of a nosy, somewhat awe-struck crew. He keeps to himself much of the time with an almost Vulcan determination. At other times he boasts unmercifully of a grandchild. But when some brash, uninitiated young crewman is careless enough to gibe him with a "grandpappy" joke, McCoy responds with that devilish, intimidating snarl. And the good doctor will be certain to make a mental note of the crewman's face and name—not for the sake of revenge, but out of a kind of parental fondness as he thinks to himself, "Now there's an innocent if I ever saw one. Another damn baby in need of lookin' after!"

The circle does keep turning, doesn't it?

A LETTER FROM KATHY WITHEROW

Once again, a letter has arrived at our offices that is so thought-provoking, so characteristic of our readers and their feelings, that we felt it could only be done justice by presenting it in article form.

Kathy Witherow's letter is a very personal one. She shares with us her deepest inner feelings about Star Trek and what it means to her to be a Star Trek fan. But beyond that, Kathy offers some pithy and definitely uncharacteristic opinions about the movie, Trek articles, Gene Roddenberry, and Star Trek in general. You won't agree with everything Kathy has to say, but we assure you you'll enjoy reading it!

To Trek or not to Trek: that is the question. I am standing outside the local bookstore, wondering if any new Star Trek books have come out. "You swore off that stuff," I think to myself. "How much more can anyone say about a 1960s television show?"

By this time I am at the science fiction rack, giving it the old fisheye to make sure that there are no small children in the Star Trek section. The coast is clear and— great galaxy! There sits *The Best of Trek #3*! I snatch the book from the shelf, stick it under the crook of my arm, and slink off to the cash register. Then I sit up half the night reading. Confessions of a Star Trek junkie!

My affection for the series has waxed and waned over the years, but I have about decided that it will never go away. I thought that I could do without Star Trek until I was no longer able to pick it up on any of our twelve cable channels. Withdrawal set in. I skimmed through my paperback collection (already approaching galactic proportions), entertained serious thoughts of buying even the Fotonovels, and took to muttering, "Aye, aye, Captain Kirk!" in my sleep. Finally I decided to throw in with fellow addicts and subscribe to *Trek*. The isolation from other fans was killing me!

I belong to Second Fandom—First Fandom being those who recognized how great Star Trek was while it was still in production. It took me a little while longer, having seen mostly the third-season shows. (Don't ask what I was doing while the first two seasons were run; my memory is mercifully blank. Knowing me, I was probably watching whatever was on the other channel. Does anyone remember?) At any rate, I began watching Star Trek during the third season because it came on Friday nights at 10:00. This so-called graveyard slot was the big night for my little brother and me to pop popcorn and watch television till they played the national anthem. Being too young to date had its advantages, because it enabled me to see at least one season of Star Trek while it was still on.

It's hard to remember how I felt about the show back then, but it was more enjoyable than most of the action-adventure series we watched. There were many lovely moments in even the worst stories. There were exceptional stories as well, namely "The Tholian Web," "Turnabout Intruder" (chauvinism aside), and "The Empath." This last is my personal favorite from the third season. With little more than six characters and a lighted platform, it illustrated one of Star Trek's major themes: reverence for the lives of others, even above one's own life. However, most of the stories in the third season did not measure up to these, being about brain-napping, space hippies, and so forth. I remembered Star Trek fondly after it got canceled, but I was not yet an addict.

Then one day, hanging around the bookstore, I discovered James Blish's first collection of adaptations. The blurb on the back cover mentioned a "secretary to the Captain" named Janice Rand. Who the heck was she? Why hadn't she been in the third-season shows? I had to find out. I didn't learn what happened to Janice until years afterward, but it was she, the most forgotten character, who intrigued me enough to find out more about Star Trek. I bought the book and was fascinated by episodes that I had never seen. These early stories took place mostly on board the ship and were primarily about the people who made it fly. The situations were varied and realistic. I realized just how good Star Trek had been in the beginning and was heart-sick at having missed the first two seasons.

As if in answer to my prayer, the local television station began to show syndicated Star Trek reruns. They came on every weeknight at our suppertime, and I ate sitting sideways so I could see them. I've been basically glued to the set every time they've come on since then, taking time off for college, marriage, the working world, and a move to another state. I've never had so much trouble getting things done as the time when our cable channels were showing Star Trek on Thursday nights, Saturday mornings, and twice every afternoon! Right now they seem to be "Trekked out," though; I haven't seen an episode in about a year.

The aforementioned move to another state, more specifically Huntsville, Alabama, was another happy circumstance on the road to Star Trek addiction. Huntsville, otherwise known as Rocket City, U.S.A., is the home of the largest NASA installation in the country. A lot of the research and development for our spacecraft goes on right here at Marshall Spaceflight Center, not to take away from the other NASA laboratories, of course. You would be gratified to know how many people who work at Marshall like Star Trek. They appreciate anything that draws attention to what they are trying to do and presents it in as positive a light as Star Trek has.

To digress for a moment, I would like to share with you the reaction when the space shuttle came to Huntsville for launch-vibration tests. This story should interest Star Trek fans because it is about the craft that they campaigned to have named *Enterprise*.

The shuttle was due to arrive one Saturday morning, carried on the back of a 747 jet. (This was before its successful solo flight.) Everyone who could possibly find a way onto Redstone Arsenal was there to see it come in.

We drove in early and walked through the grass toward the airstrip, only to find that we NSIPs (Not So Important Persons) had been cordoned off into a large field. We were all the way across the airstrip from the reception area. Still, we crowded as close as we could get, hoping to see something. People who had binoculars called out that *Enterprise* was coming. There was much pointing and passing of binoculars. The jet flew in closer, and then the pilot did a marvelous thing. He made a low pass right in front of the crowd, almost over our heads. The *Enterprise* sailed by, almost bigger than life. Everyone was smiling and waving, and then there was a spontaneous burst of applause. There was such a feeling of pride, of being present at the beginning of such a historic program. The shuttles may explore the stars one day, and we, in a small way, will be part of that exploration.

So you can see that being a Star Trek fan in this city is not exactly a liability! I could hardly ignore the space industry; it's everywhere you look. I could hardly ignore it anyway, being married to a NASA physicist. Being around it every day just made it that much harder to wait for new Star Trek adventures to be published. I pounced on each new paperback like a starving wolf on a T-bone steak.

Not all of the new stories compared favorably with the episodes of the first season and a half of Star Trek, but at least they were something to tide me over during the dry spells. I especially enjoyed *Spock Must Die!* by James Blish, *Perry's Planet* by Jack C. Haldeman II, and *The Galactic Whirlpool* by David Gerrold. *Perry's Planet* is interesting for the theme it proposes—that total, enforced absence of violence in a human culture makes it incapable of defending itself. This has not been a very popular viewpoint over the last few years, with all the concern for disarming our global superpowers.

The Galactic Whirlpool should be admired for the realistic way it portrays the *Enterprise* crew contacting a less-developed and hostile race. A contact team doing the legwork while Kirk directs from the ship is definitely more plausible than his beaming down to an unknown planet with all his most valuable officers and getting trapped, as happened so often on the show. The contact team is not only more believable, it gives the Unseen 400 something to do and allows us to meet many of them. Last, but not least, *The Galactic Whirlpool* brings back Kevin Riley, whom I have always liked!

As for the *New Voyages* volumes, I thought the stand-out stories were "Ni Var" by Claire Gabriel, "The Winged Dreamers" by Jennifer Guttridge, "The Enchanted Pool" by Marcia Ericson, "The Sleeping God" by Jesco von Puttkamer, and "Marginal Existence" by Connie Faddis. I did not see any of the animated episodes, usually being out of town on weekends, but I read the Alan Dean Foster adaptations. With the exception of "Yesteryear" and "The Albatross," I found them curiously uninvolving and rather predictable. My reasons for favoring all of the stories that I have mentioned is that they are the most consistent with the best live episodes and could have been made as such.

The most exciting news of all was the announcement of the movie. Gene Roddenberry came to town some months before it premiered and packed the Von Braun Civic Center. Both blooper films and the original-length pilot were shown. After than, Mr. Roddenberry answered questions and talked about the motion picture. At this stage of the game, Stephen Collins was slated to play a younger Vulcan character named Xon and negotiations were still going on to get Leonard Nimoy to play Spock. Some smart aleck asked Mr. Roddenberry why the *Enterprise* flew to warp 15 in one episode when it was stated in a previous episode that the ship would shake apart at warp 9. Mr. Roddenberry replied that no one expected a television show to be perfect and that it was silly to dwell on such trifling errors. I wish I could remember his exact words because it was a very effective put-down. The audience cheered, and that was the end of those type of questions.

It was interesting when Mr. Roddenberry brought up the subject of *Star Wars*. He knew that the Star Trek fans were concerned that this and other recent space movies would be a difficult act for *Star Trek: The Motion Picture* to follow. Everyone got really quiet to hear what he thought of *Star Wars*. When he said, "I liked *Star Wars*," then and only then did everyone cheer! He went on to say that the Star Trek movie would be just as exciting and definitely different from any preceding film.

Finally there was something to look forward to—the *Enterprise* would fly again! I was in Trek Heaven. Summoning all my meager writing talents and typing prowess, I sent a letter to Paramount with my comments and suggestions for the picture. I had at long last reached the letter-writing stage that Mary Jo Lawrence described in her touching article in *The Best of Trek #2*, "A New Year's Revolution." (It had me laughing, sighing, grumbling, and saying, "Uh huh, uh huh!") My letter-writing career didn't last long, though.

After I had finally gotten up the gumption to write the very first fan letter of my life, I received the form letter in which Mr. Roddenberry reams out the fans (whoever *they* were) for accusing him of not liking Mr. Spock and not wanting him to be in the movie. At this particular time it was uncertain whether Mr. Nimoy would agree to play Spock, and apparently many fans were unfairly blaming Mr. Roddenberry for Spock's absence. I am the first to admit that my letter may have been redundant because I wasn't aware that so many other fans had been saying exactly the same things (upgrade the women's roles, no miniskirts, no superficial love affairs, etc.), but at least my letter was cordial and supportive. That form letter was like a slap in the face, no matter how many times I told myself that it was just the latest bulletin that an overworked studio mail handler was stuffing into thousands of envelopes.

My enthusiasm for Star Trek took a nosedive. The fan following was just too large, beyond my comprehension. Everyone publicly connected with the show received a tremendous volume of mail; there just wasn't room for those who had awakened late to its appeal. I had toyed with the idea of finally subscribing to a fanzine, but gave it up. I stopped watching the reruns and even stopped collecting paperbacks.

I wasn't foolish enough to let the movie get by me, however. The whole town seemed to be on pins and needles waiting for it to come out. The theater that it was coming to had a sign posted weeks in advance—the premiere date was even worked out as a stardate. The science fiction magazines were full of tantalizing snippets of information. The paperback version of the movie hit the stands a month before the movie opened, but I wasn't about to read it yet. That would have destroyed the freshness of seeing the picture. At any rate, by the time *Star Trek:*

The Motion Picture arrived, my enthusiasm had built back up enough for me to want to see it.

Having read both Mr. Irwin's basically positive review and Judith Wolper's basically negative review of the movie in *The Best of Trek #3,* I would now like to put in my two cents' worth. The two reviewers covered the film's strengths and weaknesses pretty thoroughly, so I will try only to elaborate on some of the points that they made. I have to agree with Ms. Wolper that the film was a letdown; waiting for it to come out was more exciting than viewing the final product. I disagree with Mr. Irwin's opinion that the movie's major flaw was making too many changes in the ship just for the sake of making changes. The film's major flaw was its failure to sustain action.

The beginning was absolutely electrifying; the Klingons were engulfed by huge sprays of energy from a mystery source. (They were finally speaking Klingonese, too.) Kirk came on the scene, willing to do anything to get the *Enterprise* back, ruthlessly shunting his protégé aside. Outpost Epsilon Nine was destroyed in the same manner as the Klingons. The ever-temperamental transporter malfunctioned, killed two people. Decker met his old flame Ilia again. The launch sequence over, the ship plunged immediately into the wormhole. This was one of the most effective scenes in the film; the visual and voice distortion conveyed an urgency lacking in the movie in general. There was even a quick cut to Captain Kirk putting on his seat belt—no more people bouncing all over the bridge!

If things had boiled along at this pace throughout the picture, *STTMP* would have been a satisfying film. Unfortunately the main problem came early on: the $42-million pause. All action stopped and dialogue was kept to a minimum. The characters stopped and stared reverently at the special effects, complete with grandiose music. All those scenes said to me was: "See how much money we spent?" The first instance of this was the sequence in which we were introduced to the refitted *Enterprise.* We saw it from every angle as Kirk and Scotty approached. Since we had waited ten years to see the ship again, I can understand if not completely forgive the long look.

But V'Ger! The cloud was supposed to be a width eighty-two times the distance from Earth to the sun, and I felt as if I had traveled it a centimeter at a time. We saw the outside of V'Ger as the *Enterprise* flew over it; endless vistas opened up on more endless vistas. We saw the interior of V'Ger when Spock penetrated its data-storage area—more endless vistas. And what did we actually learn about V'Ger's appearance? It still looked like a cloud to me. The only effective visual inside V'Ger at all was the images of the objects that it had reduced to data patterns—its home planet, the Klingons, Epsilon Nine, and Ilia—the only recognizable images that we were given up to the revelatory scene.

This latter scene was moving, but slow. The camera seemed to crawl from the *Enterprise* hull to the core of V'Ger. Kirk and his men were awed by their discovery of Voyager 6 almost to the point of falling into a trance, their lines coming few and far between. I would think that the opposite would have happened—that they would have been so excited at finally discovering V'Ger's identity that they would have all been talking at once. Then finally we observed the transcendence of Decker, the Ilia probe, and V'Ger until practically the last molecule has disappeared. This grand finale could have been less lingering or more varied visually.

In all of these scenes the focus was on the special effects. They were dazzling and original, but they were not the subject of the picture. Special effects fascinate me more if the focus is not on them but on the character interplay and the plot. One of the more successful scenes, the scene in which the plasma-energy probe roams the *Enterprise* bridge, is an example. A blinding column of light and energy materialized and prowled among the bridge crew. It shocked Chekov. Spock thwarted it from draining the ships computer banks, so it attacked him. Then, seemingly distracted, the probe examined Ilia. Whoosh! She disappeared. Her tiny tricorder fell to the desk, the only thing left behind. In this tense scene we not only saw a terrific special effect, we empathized with the characters and watched the plot advance. Other gripping special-effect scenes were the destruction of the Klingon ships at the beginning and the plunge into the wormhole.

If the V'Ger footage had been trimmed, then what should have been added? Mr. Irwin says in his review that the time would have been better spent on developing story and characters. I would like to discuss this further. For one thing, more plot elements from Mr. Roddenberry's book version could have been included so that we did not have to read the novel to find out what went on in the film. I suppose that was the intention, but a film should be able to satisfy viewers on its own.

We learned what happened to Spock before he returned to the *Enterprise,* so why not a flashback to Kirk's confrontation with Admiral Nogura? It could have been inserted as Scott was ferrying Kirk to the ship. A confrontation would have shown us what Kirk went through to regain command and given us a better idea of what had happened to him since the end of the five-year mission. Some mention could have been made also of why McCoy left Starfleet and what he had been doing in the interim. A few members of the crew might have voiced their opinions about Kirk's walking over Decker, their captain of two years. The crew's viewpoint was entirely neglected, aside from Kirk's old hands. Speaking of old hands, Uhura, Christine, Sulu, Scott, Chekov, and Rand could have been given more to say and do. It is a tribute to the actors who play them that their characters are loved so much by fans, because we haven't seen much of their personalities aired on Star Trek. How did Christine feel about being near Spock for the first time in two years? Had she gotten over him or not? A brief reunion scene between her and McCoy would have established that she bore him no ill will for taking over her job. And how did Janice feel when she found herself on the same ship with Captain Kirk again after all these years? (Bless them for bringing her back anyway!) The lack of background for Decker and Ilia's romance has already been mentioned by Mr. Irwin. I also wish that they had made some attempt to explain the reason for her oath of celibacy. It didn't have to be explicitly stated; perhaps two crewmen could have been overheard talking about it, one warning the other that if Ilia broke her oath with an Earthman, he would no longer be satisfied with any but Deltan woman. All these things couldn't have been crammed in, of course, but even a few of them would have made the film more interesting.

A minor quibble: When a short circuit caused the transporter to malfunction and kill two prospective crewmen, Captain Kirk took the controls away from both the transporter chief and the chief engineer. This is silly.

Kirk had not set foot on the *Enterprise* in two years, much less operated the revamped transporter.

I don't quarrel with many of the changes made from the old ship to the new ship. They had to recreate the *Enterprise* from scratch anyway, so why not build something new? I have to confess to a nostalgic twinge for the gaudy colors of the old uniforms, but most of the new ones were pleasing enough. Kirk's uniform, the security guard's getup, and the spacesuits were terrific, but the form-fitting coveralls of some of the men looked like Dr. Denton's without a drop seat. But hurray for the pants on the crewwomen! Now I don't have to wonder if twenty-third-century women get runs in their pantyhose.

The Great Klingon Metamorphosis is harder to swallow. After reading Leslie Thompson's article, "The Klingons (?) In *STTMP*," I tried my hand at a solution. I think that the new gang is the illegitimate offspring of the original Klingons and the warlike humanoids in Mr. Roddenberry's series pilot, *Planet Earth*. Anyone who remembers this show should spot the resemblance. What happened was that the old striped-shirted bunch got trapped in an alternate universe—that of *Planet Earth*. The Klingons "got acquainted" with some of the militaristic humanoid females in typical Klingon fashion. They found these ladies so well endowed with Klingon virtues (love of combat, bad temper, sneakiness, greed) that they brought a few of them back to improve the breed when they finally stumbled into the Star Trek universe again. Oh well, at least it explains the ridges on their heads!

I also propose a solution as to where V'Ger went after it "united with the creator" and disappeared. It went off to find the Organians because it was too embarrassed to associate with us carbon-based units anymore.

I won't dwell at length on the handling of the individaul characters in *STTMP* because Ms. Wolper and Mr. Love have already analyzed them to my satisfaction. But I think that the portrayal of Captain Kirk deserves special mention. At the beginning of the film he was desperate, uncertain, and ruthless (showing much of his wolfish side), and most of all he was vulnerable in a way that we had not seen since the very first season of the television series. It was not until midway through the film that he regained his confidence. This vulnerability is essential to the Kirk character because it keeps him from becoming just a strong hero figure whose actions are justified no matter what. (This was one of my main gripes about the third-season shows.) At no time during the movie or the novel did I think to myself, "This is not what Captain Kirk would do." This was due in no small part to the fact that Gene Roddenberry was back at the helm—glory hallelujah and long may it last!

So much for what *Star Trek: The Motion Picture* was and could have been. I guess every fan has a long list of criticisms. Maybe the reason we criticize Star Trek so minutely is that we want each aspect of it to dovetail with our personal view of the Star Trek universe. When it isn't all things to all fans, some of us get upset. My problem is, when I know that Star Trek has been darn near perfect at times, I want to let the people in charge know what could be done to bring new stories closer to perfection! My criticism is not motivated out of a desire to attack Star Trek, but from a desire to see it reach its fullest potential. Fan criticism is just the cross that Mr. Roddenberry has to bear for giving the television audience a show that was "too cerebral"!

Now Paramount is waffling around about making a new Star Trek production. If the *Enterprise* does fly once more, I hope that it is in made-for-TV movies scheduled every few months or so. This format would free it from the hassle of a weekly series while retaining the special intimacy of television. I think the same people would watch Star Trek as watch current popular shows such as *Lou Grant*, *M*A*S*H*, *WKRP In Cincinnati*, and *Barney Miller*. After all, Star Trek pioneered the arrangement that is so important to each of these shows: a large, very diverse cast of characters who work together and try to treat each other like family.

Until the day Star Trek returns to the airwaves, however, there is nothing to feed my addiction except the fan publications. Fortunately I have been able to lay hands on *The Best of Trek #2* and *#3*, so whenever I need a Star Trek fix, I reread them. Besides the articles I have already mentioned, I have enjoyed Leslie Thompson's brief looks at Kirk's and Spock's careers, the Mysteries, the Roundtable, and Mr. Irwin's "Jim's Little Black Book." I am one of those readers who is more interested in the characters than the hardware in science fiction, but I plowed through Richard van Treuren's "On Ship-to-Surface Transportation" nevertheless. Boy, am I sorry I did! He pointed out inconsistencies in the transporter that I had never imagined, and they still bug me. Oh well, like real life, Star Trek is full of inconsistencies. We have the technology to reach the moon but not the technology to completely cure cancer. Mr. Irwin's Star Trek parody was a delight, though. I laugh every time I read it.

I just couldn't resist writing (finally) to tell you how much I have enjoyed your paperback collections of *Trek* articles. I especially respect your practice of publishing writers with opposing viewpoints, as in the case of the movie reviews. I look forward to receiving your magazine; and since you actually *want* to hear from fans, I will try to work up an article from an idea that has been knocking around in my head. In the meantime, good luck answering your mail—handling all those letters must take truly Vulcan dedication!

At last I have received my first issue of *Trek*! Your request for letters from readers for a special issue inspired me to haul out the mighty Smith-Corona and drop you another line. It continually amazes me that someone actually *wants* an avalanche of Star Trek mail. Your special issue has probably gone to press by now, but I'm going to send my opinions along anyway.

I think that the letter special is an excellent idea, because Trek Roundtable was the section of your magazine that I enjoyed most. It is always refreshing to read a letter from someone who just cannot control his or her enthusiasm for Star Trek any longer and writes for the very first time to share experiences, sometimes after many years of being a fan in secret. I was especially touched by Mary Rottler's letter describing how she has tried in vain to put Star Trek behind her. My Star Trek books have never quite made it out the door either, even though I periodically entertain the thought of carting them all down to the used-book store. It would be a wasted effort because in six months' time I'd be out collecting them again.

You asked what readers liked least about *Trek*, but I really can't find much to dislike! I would just like to see more on aspects of Star Trek that have never been covered in *Trek* to my knowledge, such as the paperback novels of new adventures. No one has hailed them as great science fiction literature, but they come out regularly and stay on the bookstore shelves for a long time. That means that a lot of people are buying them, myself included. I'm the first to admit that some of them leave a lot to be desired, but that is no reason to totally ignore them. They are at least as good as the worst television episodes of Star Trek ("Spock's Brain" leaps to mind), and they are certainly better than the comic books, which you did cover. How about a series of reviews of these paperbacks and some interviews with their authors? It would be interesting to find out how they sold their stories to a publisher, how the book was edited, and generally what is involved in publishing a Star Trek novel.

There also seems to be an unstated editorial policy against publishing original fiction submitted by readers. Is there some legal reason that this is so? I assume that it is because you are professional writers yourselves and might be accused of plagiarism if your work ever showed any similarities to material sent to *Trek*. Whatever the case, could you please explain your position in the magazine? I know from the Roundtable that other readers are wondering the same thing. If there is no reason not to print fan fiction, how about it?

(Editor's Note: We feel that only those publishers licensed by Paramount have a legal and ethical right to publish fan fiction.)

A regular feature that I would enjoy seeing added to *Trek* is a fanzine exchange column with capsule summaries of other current Star Trek fanzines. This wouldn't necessarily be free advertising; surely the other fan editors would reciprocate by mentioning *Trek* to their readers. The caving club newsletter that we subscribe to provides a newsletter exchange, and it gives readers a much broader outlook by telling what other groups are doing.

For me, the big question in your reader survey was "Where do you think Star Trek should go from here?" Certainly not right back where it came from! Civilization-of-the-week shows have not fared well recently, as *Buck Rogers in the 25th Century* and *Battlestar Galactica* have shown. I think that Star Trek should return to television on a weekly basis if possible, with a slightly altered format. I would like to see Star Trek become a sort of *Lou Grant, M*A*S*H,* or *Hill Street Blues* set in the future. Each of these shows is about *all* the people who make an organization work, from the decision-makers in the top echelon to the lowly people who work the streets or empty the bedpans. Yes, they have their big stars, but the focus shifts constantly from them to the supporting characters. Thus we know Billie Newman, reporter, as well as we know Lou Grant, city editor. Another characteristic of these shows is that there is action throughout the stories, but the focus is on what happens to the characters. This is what the best Star Trek stories emphasized all along. The *Lou Grant* and *Hill Street Blues*-style format, which I will call reality-drama for lack of a better term, is much more suitable for Star Trek than its original action-adventure format.

You might argue that early Star Trek was very similar to a reality-drama, and you would be right. The oldest episodes managed to generate quite a lot of human drama between battles and monsters. During the first season we peeked into Janice Rand's boudoir, saw Sulu calm a nervous "plant," and groaned as Kevin Riley sang, "I'll Take You Home Again, Kathleen." Unfortunately there was less and less of this as the series went on, until we were left with Kirk, Spock, McCoy, and the weekly guest star(s) doing practically everything. *Star Trek: The Motion Picture* continued this practice. Although Mr. Roddenberry had his reasons for doing the movie this way, I would hate to see Star Trek return to television with the same format.

I am confident, however, that the supporting characters will get more attention if Star Trek gets back on the air. After all, how much better can we get to know Kirk, Spock, and McCoy? Something pretty drastic would have to happen to them for us to be surprised. (And that's an interesting possibility, too.)

Applying the reality-drama format to a new Star Trek, we could begin to see what goes on in the parts of the ship that were rarely shown in the old series. The staff in each department could be fleshed out and developed further; Scotty's engineering team, the research lab staff, the security division, and the maintenance crew, etc. A planetary contact team as suggested by David Gerrold in *The Galactic Whirlpool* would also be an excellent idea, serving both to introduce new faces and to add to the action element of the show. Knowing a few faces in every department would make the idea of a 430-person ship much more believable.

Branches of the Federation that have only been hinted at in the past could be brought in from time to time as well. Kirk could be the speaker at an Academy function and we could see what life at the Academy is like. The brass could drop in occasionally to give us glimpse of the goings-on at Starfleet Headquarters. Some of the paperback authors' ideas have great story potential too, such as Vonda McIntyre's border patrol in *The Entropy Effect* and Kathleen Sky's Special Security Division in *Death's Angel* (although in the latter case, less similarity to the Nazi SS would be welcome).

The reality-drama format could encompass new worlds as well as new areas of the ship and the Federation. The crew of the movie *Enterprise* contained many more aliens than previously, and developing them would provide other points of view in addition to Terran and Vulcan. I would love to have the same knowledge and feel for Tellarite and Andorian culture as I do for Vulcan culture.

You also asked readers, "If, eventually, new actors are cast as Kirk, Spock, etc., who would you choose to play these parts and why?" I have to say that as surely as Johnny Weissmuller will always be everyone's favorite Tarzan, William Shatner will be the only Captain Kirk, Leonard Nimoy will be the only Spock, and DeForest Kelley will be the only Dr. McCoy that people will accept. The producers will squeak by if the supporting parts are recast. However, if the roles of Kirk, Spock, and McCoy are recast, I flat out don't think that Star Trek can be successfully revived. You can replace actors, but you can't replace chemistry. If the original three stars could not be used, Star Trek would be better off with new actors in completely new roles rather than trying to find another Kirk, Spock, and McCoy.

Ideally, a new series would contain a balanced mixture of old and new characters. The *Enterprise* is so closely associated with the old stars that I hate to lose them, but at the same time I think that the show would benefit from several new faces. In addition to new personnel in the various departments, there should be a younger group of of-

ficers aboard who are clearly in training for the positions
of the old veterans. They may live longer and work longer
in the twenty-third century, but they will have to retire
someday.

While we are still discussing the new characters, I hope
that the next time the *Enterprise* ships out there are one or
two gay crewmembers aboard. Maybe that will satisfy all
the fans who insist that Kirk and Spock's relationship has
nowhere else to go.

On the "What would you do differently?" question, I
would, in addition to slightly changing the format, alter
the Star Trek universe a bit for a new television show. The
Enterprise should continue to discover new life and new
civilizations, but what if the Federation is slowly eroding?
What if the Prime Directive is somehow abolished by
pressure groups who would benefit from its not being enforced? What if the Organians have had enough of keeping the détente between Terrans and Klingons and inform
them that their fate is in their own hands from now on?
What if the Klingons want to normalize relations with the
Federation? Any of these situations would alter the Star
Trek universe to reflect the fact that it is growing and
changing, give our heroes more issues to deal with, and
give them more things to fight for or against.

"Almost two years later what are your feelings about
the Star Trek movie?" I was disappointed in it when it
came out and regretfully must say that I haven't come to
like it any better. I say this after viewing it several times
on the cable subscription channel. *Star Trek: The Motion
Picture* just goes to prove the old saying that bigger is not
necessarily better. Even the title is too long, and downright
pretentious.

"What does Star Trek mean to you?" It is difficult to
put into words just what Star Trek means to me personally, but roughly it means two things. First, it is a fantasy
world that I can escape to when the real world is too
bleak and boring. Just as often it is an irritating reminder
that I have not outgrown the need for fantasy and makes
me feel that I should take up "adult" concerns like pursuing a career, raising a family, or improving my mind.
Sometimes I wonder what can possibly come of such a
strong attachment to a television show that was canceled
so many years ago. Then I remember that the movie was

made because of the fans' devotion, so perhaps there is something to be gained by being a fan after all. Who knows, maybe with continued effort we can make the *Enterprise* fly yet again!

OF SPOCK, GENES, AND DNA RECOMBINATION

by Jennifer Weston

There have been many articles concerning the facts about Spock's conception and birth, but few (if any) have ever examined it from the standpoint of new and current breakthroughs in medical science. In the following article, Jennifer Weston briefly explains these techniques and extrapolates how they could be used to conceive such a startlingly successful Vulcan/human hybrid—our Mr. Spock.

In 1978, *TV Guide* published an article by author/astronomer Carl Sagan on the subject of the general lack of scientific accuracy in network television programs. Of Star Trek in particular, Sagan complained that many of its premises "fly in the face of what we know of molecular biology and Darwinian evolution" and cited Mr. Spock's half-human, half-Vulcan ancestry as an example. The chances of hybridizing life forms from different planets are, Sagan contended, worse than those of crossing "a man with an artichoke."

Irrefutably, Star Trek did stray from dissertation-perfect accuracy in nearly every episode, but Mr. Sagan should be the first to admit that this does not render a story devoid of any merit. After all, much of his earliest interest in outer space was sparked by Edgar Rice Burroughs' "John Carter on Mars" series of novels—which postulate that one can be transported to the Red Planet by staring at it and wishing oneself there. I am, however, somewhat surprised at the example Sagan picked. As a man with a reputation for giving serious consideration to unconventional scientific ideas, he must know that it *is* theoretically possible to cross a man and an artichoke. Or, for that matter, any other pair of DNA-based organisms. The method is the currently developing, and highly controversial, new technology known as DNA recombination.

Another very readable scientific essayist, biologist Lewis Thomas, explains the process this way in *The Medusa and the Snail:*

"The only living units that seem to have no sense of privacy at all are the nucleated cells that have been detached from the parent organism and isolated in a laboratory dish. Given the opportunity, under the right conditions, two cells from wildly different sources, a yeast cell, say, and a chicken erythrocyte, will touch, fuse, and the two nuclei will then fuse as well, and the new hybrid cell will now divide into the monstrous progeny."

Dr. Lewis exaggerates somewhat; there are presently insurmountable chemical obstacles to deriving a complete organism from greatly diverse nuclei. However, gene-splicing techniques *have* induced many simple life forms to accept pieces of genetic material from related organisms, thus developing genotypes with the desirable traits of more than one species (and lots of in-jokes about "designer genes"). Such techniques were what brought about the recent development of a permanent hoof-and-mouth vaccine, and, many agricultural researchers hope, will soon bring about the production of higher-protein, disease-resistant crop plants. If the geneticists continue as they are (i.e., if their present theories are correct, and if no one commits such an abuse of the technology that public opinion turns strongly against it), then we may even see a less ludicrous version of Sagan's plant-animal hybrid before this century is over. An organism capable of deriving substance from both eating and photosynthesis could be a boon to world food production. The development of new organisms for many more specialized purposes can become ever more efficient as geneticists learn more and more about what DNA codes can do, and how to best utilize them. (This, incidentally, is one of the great practical arguments for preserving endangered species. The extinction of a plant or animal represents the irretrievable loss of a genetic storehouse whose potentials we are only now learning how to use.)

In the Star Trek universe, progress was, no doubt, slowed by backlash against all genetic research in the wake of the Eugenics Wars. Nonetheless, by the Enterprise's century the recombinant technologies may well have become sophisticated enough to feed the Earth from two hundred square kilometers of farmland, to produce pets and houseplants to order, and, just possibly, to achieve a viable splicing of Vulcan and human DNA.

Everything we currently know about genetic reproduction indicates that the chances of Spock's being conceived in the usual way are, literally, astronomical (touché, Dr. Sagan). To explain why this is so requires a brief review of terms.

In Star Trek fandom, *gene* usually refers to Roddenberry, but in biological lingo it's defined as all the genetic information controlling an organism's traits. It consists of a coded sequence of nucleotides in a DNA molecule, the latter being shaped like a spiral staircase with nucleotides forming the steps. A single long DNA strand, combined with a few other proteins, makes up a *chromosome*. All chromosomes exist in cell nuclei in *homologous pairs*—which means that each member of every pair was contributed by each of the organism's parents.

Every DNA-based species has its own characteristic number of pairs, and its own characteristic distribution of traits among the pairs. For example, a normal human being possesses twenty-three chromosome pairs; genes for facial features are included on the eighteenth pair, genes affecting mental capacities on the twenty-first pair, etc. The less complex life forms (everything from reptiles on down) can tolerate variations on their normal arrangements. But among mammals, anything more or less than a complete chromosome set will produce an imbalance of gene products, and result in physiological abnormalities ranging from the neglible to the lethal, depending on the size and location of the extra/missing piece.

In all higher organisms, sexual reproduction (i.e., that involving exchange of genetic information) is accomplished by the use of *gametes*—cells containing exactly half of the genes necessary to form a complete organism. Mammalian gametes (egg and sperm cells) are created by *meiosis*—the specialized type of cell division unique to oocyte cells in female ovaries, and spermatogonia cells in male testes. Meiosis consists of two stages. First, as happens in all cell division, every chromosome replicates (makes a copy of itself). Next, instead of the whole cell dividing, the chromosomes line up in their homologous pairs and undergo *crossing-over*—a breaking off and exchange of chromosome pieces. (The purpose of this is to diversify the gametes, and thus the offspring.) The oocyte/spermatogonia cell divides after this, and each daughter cell divides in turn, but in this second division no chromosome replication occurs. Instead, one member of each homologous pair is contributed to each of the third-generation cells, resulting in a precisely *complementary* distribution of genes in the gametes.

This is why, when the same species of sperm and egg cells fuse, their nuclei meet to form another complete set of genes, and cell division to form an embryo can commence. But a meeting of gametes from diverse species cannot achieve proper complementation, for even if their chromosome number is the same, the distribution of traits on them will not be. The fertilized egg either will not be able to effect division, or, if it does, will survive only until the differing genes begin producing their conflicting chemistries, at which point the growing embryo will be spontaneously aborted. (Purebred embryos with large chromosomes missing or extra chromosomes will usually miscarry for the same reason.) This is an example of a *reproductive isolating mechanism*—one of the devices nature uses to ensure that species will diversify rather than assimilate, thus allowing new ones to evolve constantly. This is the ultimate reason why organisms separated by as much as a taxonomic genus are generally unable to hybridize. The only exceptions are species with a recent common evolutionary ancestor, such as the horse and donkey, which may be bred to produce mules.

So to return to the question of how reproductively successful a Vulcan-human mating would be, Carl Sagan's assessment is, if anything, too optimistic. Even if one subscribes to the theory that all humanoid life in *Star*

Trek's universe has a common origin, any two who have specialized enough to evolve different blood salts (sodium chloride vs. "quite different") and metallic bases (iron vs. copper) have to be more genetically diverse than any two vertebrates on the planet Earth. So the only logical conclusion is that Spock is a product of DNA recombination technology.

But Fandom's romantics need not protest that this reduces Spock's conception to a mere mechanical event— quite the contrary. It indicates that his parents wanted a child very, very much, for it must have required all the resources of a DuPont-sized laboratory and a small army of geneticists. Sarek's and Amanda's chromosomes had to have been charted in painstaking detail, then just enough of the genes isolated and spliced to make a complete set—a nightmarishly intricate task due to the minuscule size and vast numbers of genes (and totally impossible using twentieth-century technology). But evidently, twenty-third-century science can read DNA as well as warp through space.

And an immense amount of trouble was obviously saved by the fact that it was not essential to line up everything in homologous pairs. Since we've seen Spock pass himself off as a full-blooded Vulcan, and he has many Vulcan physiological traits (pointed ears, green blood, etc.), it is evident that the recombiners utilized many of Sarek's genes in the already-paired form, and presumably used Amanda's contribution in the same way. In both cases they probably used the more advantageous traits so as to produce *hybrid vigor* at its most refined. This would explain why Spock has frequently been known to display the best of his heritages.

Once a set had been isolated and the chromosomes combined to make a single nucleus, it was a comparatively easy matter to implant the nucleus into an egg cell whose original chromosomes had been removed, then allow the cell to gestate normally in a placental environment. *Placental environment* because it is obvious that Spock could not have spent his prenatal life within Amanda's uterus. A fetus receives its blood components directly from its mother's circulatory system, by way of *villi*—projections from the placenta into the maternal circulatory system. Since the recombiners gave Spock genes that determined his hemoglobin would be copper-based (perhaps it was seen as essential to the development of his Vulcan abilities), that precluded any possibility of the fetus' being carried full term in a human womb, where only iron is available. Putting a sufficient level of dissolved copper into Amanda's blood would have been fatal to *her*. It is conceivable that Spock was gestated in the uterus of a Vulcan surrogate mother, an idea with interesting dramatic possibilities. But it is more probable that the hybrid zygote was implanted in an artificial placenta—another item which might have become possible before the year 2000. There the geneticists could closely monitor all chemical developments and correct any incompatibilities before damage was done.

Again, that needn't have reduced the event to cold impersonality. One can imagine the laboratory staff growing ever fonder of their charge, and when the day came to remove the baby, all gathered around in relief and joy as Spock drew his first breaths and everyone realized he was going to make it.

Indeed, every technician involved has a right to feel proud, for Spock is a magnificently viable specimen, strong of limb, keen of sense, intelligent enough to earn (from the sound of him) a dozen science degrees. (And gorgeous too, but that's a subjective opinion.) But almost certainly, he is also subject to that infamous characteristic of hybrids—sterility. In the case of the mule, this phenomenon results from the fact that it has fifty-one chromosomes from its donkey father, and fifty-two from its mare mother. Even this slight deviation from complete homologous pairing is sufficient to prevent its oocyte/spermatogonia cell nuclei from effecting crossing-over, so the second division is never accomplished; no gametes are formed. Spock, whose chromosomes probably lack any vestige of pairing, is in a geometrically worse situation as far as parental possibilities go.

Does this mean that Sarek and Amanda can never look forward to bragging about their grandchildren? Not necessarily. For if the Federation has sufficient genetic technology to create an interplanetary hybrid, it may not require much more to bring about a viable three-species cross—a "tribrid," so to speak. You can picture the scene: Spock standing close to his lady love (of whatever planetary origin), their eyes burning with intense feeling as he tenderly takes her hand and guides her up the broad staircase and into the sumptuously appointed genetics laboratory. . . .

But that's another story.

(Editor's Note: Ms. Weston holds a bachelor's degree in environmental science, and is presently working toward a masters in museum science with emphasis on natural history. References for this article include Biological Science *by William T. Keeton,* Genetics: Human Aspects *by Arthur and Elaine Mange, "The Gene Machine Hits the Farm" by Ann Crittenden, and the aforementioned works of Carl Sagan and Lewis Thomas.)*

HOW AND WHY VULCANS CHOOSE THEIR MATES

by G.B. Love

G.B. doesn't write very many articles, but when he does, they're doozies! In this outing, he tackles one of the most obscure and controversial aspects of Star Trek: the Vulcan mating rituals. It's a difficult subject to write an article about—no matter what you say, zillions of fans are going to vehemently disagree. But G.B. has covered the ground so thoroughly and with such fealty to statements made in various episodes that it is hard to dispute his conclusions. See if you agree.

Of all the concepts presented in Star Trek, perhaps none is as interesting and continually fascinating to fans as Spock's homeworld, Vulcan. There is something about Vulcan: its strange society based on logic and the suppression of emotions, its graceful people, its history of warfare and unending strife ended forever by the Reformation. It appeals to the imagination in a way which cannot be denied. When we think of Vulcan, we become psychologists, sociologists, historians, geneticists, and archaeologists. We want to *know* about Vulcan. We dig, we interpret, we imagine. Vulcan is an idealized mirror of our own world and the problems which our differing peoples have in living together; and above all, we wish to know how we may make our lives as peaceful, as constructive and as *interesting* as those of the people of Vulcan.

Much has been written about Vulcan in fan circles. Much more remains to be written. Every subject from the eventful first meeting of Spock's parents to Vulcan prehistory has been discussed in great detail. Unfortunately, much of what has been written and theorized does not agree with the facts given in the series; and even worse, much of this has been accepted as "gospel" by a number of fans. Primary among the mistaken impressions are those about the manner in which Vulcans choose their mates, the marriage rituals, and the mechanics of *pon farr.*

This article will attempt to explain why and how Vulcans make the very important decision of choosing a marriage partner. But first, we should look at our own marriage and courtship customs and their development. For without a basic understanding of how our customs work, it is very difficult to fathom the "alien" customs of Vulcan.

In our twentieth-century American society, we have perhaps a greater amount of freedom in choosing a lifemate than in any other time or society in history. We all know the rituals: dating, courtship, proposal, ceremony, honeymoon, etc. And restrictions on whom we choose to marry are imposed only by own personal beliefs: We can choose whom *not* to marry as well. As a sociological custom, arranged marriages are defunct in our country and time.

But the practice of arranging marriages is still alive and thriving throughout much of the world. Even in the more "modernized" nations of Europe, it is very difficult for a young person to marry "outside of his or her station"; and in many cases, to marry without parental approval is unthinkable or even illegal.

Throughout the history of man, the practice of arranged marriages has been the norm. It is an old axiom, but a true one, that parents want their children to have a better life than they have had. Arranging for a marriage partner is perhaps the most important manner in which a parent can assure that a child will not marry someone "unsuitable," someone of lesser class, wealth, education, etc. These arranged marriages not only perpetrated class-oriented societies, but to a great extent they assured that wealth and power would remain in the hands of a very few. Money marries money; and for thousands of years it was very true.

But it was not just the upper class or the wealthy who had arranged marriages. The custom pervaded every strata of society. It was often felt desirable for a child to mate with another from the same village, from the same economic class, from the same religion. Some of these arrangements were made when the children were very young, others not until childbearing age. Other marriages were not so much arranged as "steered"—young people were not allowed to socialize with anyone outside of a select group and had no choice but to choose a mate from that group. And even in the middle and lower classes, parental approval was required for a marriage to take place, so it was very difficult for a couple to marry when either set of parents did not approve.

In other societies, it was common practice for a young man to "purchase" a bride. Again, this purchase required the approval of the father, for it was from him that the young woman was "bought." And if the father was wealthy, there was little chance for a poor young man to "buy" the bride, so again economic standing dictated and limited choice of mates. And as wealth often determines class standing, it was uncommon for a wealthy young man to purchase a poor woman as his bride. More often, he would take her as a mistress, and another, more "suitable" woman as a wife, in order to keep wealth within the upper class.

Such were the customs all over the world until relatively recently in our history. Indeed, many of these customs are still being practiced with regularity throughout the world. It is only our free society and our economic opportunity which has allowed the western nations to break away from these ancient practices. It is obvious that as wealth and class lines are blurred or dissolved, the need to perpetuate them by arranged marriages is negated.

But what then of Vulcan? Surely, Vulcan is a completely class-free society, for our own human history has taught us that freedom for all is the only way in which all may remain free. And to deny basic rights to any person because of the circumstances of birth is completely illogical. Why then has the practice of arranged marriages remained in Vulcan society?

To begin with, we must look back thousands of years to the time before the Reformation. Vulcan was a wild and inhospitable planet. It has been implied that the race did not evolve on Vulcan itself, but was "seeded" there in pre-history by a vastly superior alien race. Amid the difficult survival conditions of the arid and almost barren planet, it is not surprising that Vulcans were warlike, extremely violent, primarily emotion-guided beings. If nothing else, there would be a constant battle for possession of the scarce supplies of water and green-growing areas.

Even with this constant strife, however, the innate intelligence of the Vulcanoid enabled technology and social norms to develop at a rate comparable to that on Earth. We may even assume that international and interpersonal relationships were much like those of humans, although more violent and less based on reason, for Spock says that if Surak had not united his people through logic and peacefulness, his race would have destroyed itself, whereas Earth peoples did not.

Two facts point to Vulcan's having had a highly developed technology at the time of the Reforms: The Vulcans who left the planet and later formed the Romulan Empire had to have spaceships to do so; and Vulcan nations obviously had atomic weapons (or their equivalent) and thus faced the ever-present threat of total world destruction. (Perhaps a limited nuclear war did break out during the Reforms, for Spock is unsure of the origins of the Romulans, so records of their flight must have been destroyed.)

So we can see how difficult Surak's task must have been. Many fan writings have idealized Surak roaming among the "tribes" of Vulcan and preaching his gospel of logic—a Christ figure reforming the savages with love and logic, and having them turn their swords into plowshares. It is a romantic vision, but an incorrect one.

Surak was faced with the problem of reforming a highly developed society, and his enemies would not have been sword-wielding hordes, but entrenched bureaucracies and power-hungry individuals. From his absolute refusal to fight in "The Savage Curtain," it is apparent that Surak taught the techniques of passive resistance. This was probably something entirely new in Vulcan history—a person *refusing* to raise a hand against his fellow man—and to a people obviously tired of constant strife and the continual threat of destruction, it must have been enormously appealing.

It is to be noted, however, that Surak's teachings did not require his fellow Vulcans to *eliminate* their emotions—only to *control* them. Logic was not unknown on Vulcan (for no society can advance technologically without the application of it), and Surak postulated that this same logic which had been used so efficiently to build weapons and cities should now be used to *reason through* problems, rather than reacting emotionally to them. It is likely that the reverence in which logic is held on Vulcan in Star Trek's time is an offshoot of that original philosophy; the more logically and reasonably one can consider, the more efficiently he can perform. One would also suspect that perfection of individual logic and its application is a Vulcan's way of channeling the need to achieve and compete with his fellows in a peaceful and mutually beneficent way.

Why then, one may ask, does it seem that the customs of arranged marriages and family hierarchies still exist on Vulcan, when such customs appear to be more atavistic than logical? Certainly we would expect a Vulcan to respect and revere an ancestor, elder, or family member if that individual deserved respect. And just as certainly we would expect both Vulcan males and females to choose mates who would be mutually acceptable in all ways—biologically, intellectually, and so on.

However, that does not seem to be the case. Spock tells us that his marriage to T'Pring was arranged by their families when he was about seven (she was apparently the same age); and at that time they were bound not only by the mind touch, but by law and tradition. No matter how logically and reasonably their respective families decided that Spock and T'Pring would be suitable for each other, the extreme youth of the two would absolutely preclude any consideration of their desires in the matter.

And that such binding of children would be legally enforceable years later is evidence of a family-ordered society. When law and custom declare the wishes of a family (whether it be parents, elders, or a group decision) to be binding on an individual in that family, it is obvious that to the Vulcans the entire sociological basis for such action is as a means of preserving and protecting the family unit.

It is fair to assume that one of the major problems faced in pre-Reformation times was the breakdown of the family unit, and the corresponding relaxation of morals and cultural norms. Vulcans apparently consider it highly logical to nurture the nuclear family, as well as to honor and revere ancestors and the aged.

So we see that the title of this article is somewhat incorrect: In reality, it should be "How and Why Vulcans Have Their Mates *Chosen for Them*"; for if the practice of arranged marriages is common to all of Vulcan (and we must assume it is, for we are told it is both *custom* and *law*, and Vulcan is a completely unified planet), then the engaged couple has no say-so at all in the matter. Indeed, they are so young at the time of the first bonding that they probably have very little idea of the full implication of the act.

In a society (like that on Vulcan) where law and custom are designed to protect the family unit, we usually see very strictly defined social divisions—classes, almost a caste system. But such systems, as noted before, are illogical. So for such a system to exist on Vulcan, it would have to be a system in which class structure is based not on birth or wealth, but on achievement. This *is* logical. The honoring of great successes in any field of endeavor is an affirmation of the quality of the race as a whole. Even here in our own society, we have awards for outstanding individual achievement—Nobel prizes, Oscars, Pulitzers, scholarships, athletic trophies, Hugos. There are literally thousands of "prizes" awarded each year to persons who have contributed to their field in an outstanding way. The awards are a way of saying, "Well done." This is even more true on Vulcan, for in their society of controlled emotions, the acknowledgment of one's peers is the greatest tribute that can be earned. And it follows that the more honors given to a family unit, the more honored the individual members of that family will be.

We are told that Spock's family is among the oldest, most revered, and most honored on Vulcan; we can assume that T'Pring has equally impressive lineage. So the fact that these two families arranged for their children to marry is not an indication of snobbery, but instead, of a conscious desire to strengthen the lineage by having two outstanding lines joined. It is simple genetics, and quite logical.

But genetics are not enough. If such "marrying into" continued over a long period of time, the consequences of interbreeding would catch up in the most harmful ways (for example, the hemophilia of the royal European families). The logical Vulcans would realize that a certain amount of "fresh blood" is not only desirable, but necessary, both for the avoidance of inherited recessive tendencies and for the general improvement of the race as a whole. So other criteria must come into the decision-making process.

As most Vulcans seem to take up the work of their families, their acquired interests would be fairly predictable. Spock's family is composed of scientists and diplomats; so must be T'Pring's family. Although each Vulcan has complete freedom of choice in his work and life-style, it is obvious that that freedom is not often exercised, if Sarek's anger at Spock's refusal to follow in his father's footsteps is any indication. When skills and knowledge can be passed down from one generation to the next in a specialized field, in several generations' time the youngest generation will have a wealth of knowledge and skills literally learned from birth. It would make for a quite efficient and smoothly operating system, a logical system. And it would logically follow that intermarriage with another family or similar or identical indoctrination would only serve to strengthen the system.

We can also assume that the heredity of Spock and T'Pring was carefully checked to ensure that they would be able to bear healthy, strong, and highly intelligent children. (This would be done with every pairing, of course.) As the choosing of a lifemate is one of the most important decisions made in one's life, it would be (to the Vulcans) too risky to allow it to be left to something as untrustworthy and illogical as emotion, *especially* to the overly emotional young. So years before the burgeoning onset of adolescence, a future mate is coolly and logically chosen for each child.

We must assume that Vulcans have normal sexual stirrings, even to the point of physical yearning. The attachment of T'Pring and Stonn was hardly that of two cool intellectuals—they were obviously in love and wanted each other sexually. It is just this normal attraction of the male and female that Vulcans seek to avoid by bonding the children when they are very young, long before the onset of puberty and its accompanying sexual pressures. Vulcans don't feel that youth is wasted on the young—they feel that youth is wasted, period. And without the proper guidance and control, the young are liable to choose a partner who is totally "unsuitable."

Although a particular Vulcan may not be especially happy with the mate chosen for him, in the vast majority of cases, the children will accept the logic of the decision as they grow older. The actions of T'Pring were an anomaly; for the average Vulcan, personal preference—especially emotional preference—is the last consideration. It would seem that Vulcan would be full of unhappy marriages, but such is not the case, for most couples quickly discover that their shared interests and life-styles bring them close together. And as the family and continuation of family is paramount in Vulcan affairs, any Vulcan would work very hard to make his or her marriage work. And all but a very few obviously do.

So we can see that the choosing of mates on Vulcan is done in the same logical, reasoning manner as all other facets of Vulcan life and work. But not logical at all is the manner in which the marriage is performed and consummated. In the ritual of *Koon-ut-kal-if-fee*, the last remaining vestiges of Vulcan's violently emotional prehistory are acted out in a strange ceremony.

We are told that in ancient times, Vulcans battled for their mates. Of course. So did humans. It is perhaps the strongest yearning of man to take a mate and sire children to perpetuate the species. And in a precivilized society, the female was always taken by force, whether it was through rape or by battling and killing another male for possession of the female. The eventual abandonment of this practice was one of the first steps toward civilization, a step which moved man above the other animals in his world.

But the Vulcans, having achieved suppression of emotion, have to pay a price. That price is a regression into the depths of animallike behavior at the time of strongest emotion—the time of mating. (It is not within the purview of this article to discuss the seven-year cycle, but it is logical to assume that if mating takes place only every seven years, the emotional pressures at that time would be extreme, to say the least!) But the ever-logical Vulcans took pains to couch this unavoidable and necessary outburst of emotion in elaborate ritual, thereby ensuring at least a measure of control and a minimal disruption of daily life for those not directly affected. So was born the *Koon-ut-kal-if-fee*, the time of marriage, the time of challenge.

We can assume that these rituals predate the Reforms by many, many years. For the Vulcans to have achieved a sophisticated civilization, there could not have been battling in the streets for possession of women. It is likely that the rituals were originally created for the sake of privacy. But after the Reforms of Surak had spread across Vulcan, and the principles of logic and IDIC had been accepted, the Vulcans must have discovered that the violent emotions of mating were impossible to control. Then the practice of arranged marriages must have been inevitable, for only in that way could a measure of logic be brought to the proceedings. With the introduction of logic, control of the inherent Vulcan mind powers must have grown, and the practice of *bonding* a male and female would have been an excellent way of ensuring that the chosen couple would be forced to mate with each other at the proper time and in the proper place. Too, the time of *Koon-ut-kal-if-fee* would remain as a constant and vivid reminder of the consequences of emotionalism.

As Spock is a hybrid, his reaction to *pon farr* may have been different from those of the average Vulcan male, but we may still use his experiences as a guide to the effects of *pon farr*.

As has been pointed out, a male and female are brought together at about the age of seven. We may assume there is a ceremony of sorts, even though Spock does not say so, for every facet of Vulcan life seems to be couched in ritual acknowledgment of the past and of family. The children touch minds (perhaps the first mind meld for each, as an initial experience would be the most lasting and memorable) and a linking is formed between them. They have become "tied" to each other. This linking is probably only broken by death of either partner . . . surely neither Spock nor T'Pring desired it to last or permanently affect them. Apparently it cannot be broken by choice; once formed, the linking inexorably joins the two children together throughout puberty and young adulthood. (Again, we cannot go by Spock's experience, for he was much older than one would expect a person to be for "marrying age." Still, no one on Vulcan deemed it necessary to make any comment about Spock's first *pon farr* being late.)

At the "proper time," each partner feels a mental "tug" which requires them to meet at an appointed place and join in marriage. This is the final bonding, a total joining of minds, much stronger and closer than the initial joining, formed when they were children. Also, we have seen in Spock's case, great internal sexual pressures—both psychological and physiological—build up to the point where if one of the individuals cannot physically be present for the ritual of marriage and consummation, he or she will die. The male seems to be the most affected by these pressures, but the female must also abide by them, or the entire system simply would not work. If this were not the case, then T'Pring would not have needed a champion to battle Spock. Were she unaffected, all she would have had to do was take a short vacation off-planet at the time of Spock's *pon farr*. He would have died in agony and she would have been free.

When both have appeared at the appointed place, the ceremony of *Koon-ut-kal-if-fee* begins. Officiating at the ceremony is an elder. It is not clear whether the elder is a member of either family; nor is it clear if the elder is always a woman. One would suspect that it is always a woman, for a Vulcan female would probably be less affected by the heightened emotions rampant at such an event. If a challenge is offered, it is the men who do the fighting, and even a logical, controlled Vulcan would be hard pressed to keep from getting excited when in the presence of such unfettered violence.

The ceremony seems to be a simple one. Although we did not see Spock and T'Pring's go through to a conclusion, it was apparent that T'Pau intended only to speak a few words over them, join them in a marriage bonding, and then let nature take its course. There would hardly be time for anything else, for when it is time for the bonding to begin, the male is deep in *plak tow*, the "blood frenzy," and is totally prepared to take his mate or fight for her.

Such a state is hardly conducive to a long-drawn-out ceremony or a festive reception afterward!

We have explicitly seen what happens in that rare instance when the female refuses the marriage and challenges. It is total battle to the death, and to the victor go
the spoils. This adage is perhaps responsible for the chal-
lenging female's becoming "the chattel and property" of
the victorious male, but more likely this is a penalty imposed on recalcitrant females to discourage them from is-
suing the challenge. The emotionalism of this time is
upsetting and embarrassing enough to Vulcans without
having any number of intended marriages regress into
battles to the death. It is likely that a female such as
T'Pring would lose all rights of citizenship and in effect
become a "nonperson"—an outcast of society and, worse,
of her family. Such a penalty would make any woman
think twice about "giving it all up for love."

Many fan stories have woven highly romantic versions
of the male Vulcan dragging his new wife off into the
wilds and having his way with her through the conclusion
of *pon farr*. Most likely, the two are conducted to a place
of complete privacy where the marriage is consummated
with a minimal amount of discomfort and disruption. It
would not be logical for it to be otherwise.

Once the *pon farr* has run its course, the two will settle
down and begin married life, much as couples do on
Earth. We may assume that Spock's case was rare; most
couples probably have ample opportunity throughout their
lifetimes to get to know one another and form mutual interests in preparation for their married life. And although
pon farr occurs only once every seven years, it is not beyond the pale to assume that Vulcans share a healthy, ac-
tive, and completely normal sex life with their partners.
Whatever the reasons for *pon farr*, such a state is not
likely to be conducive to childbearing, the health of either
partner, or the success of a relationship. The manner in
which Spock's parents, Sarek and Amanda, look at each
other and touch each other is very caring and very sensual. It is quite difficult to imagine such a relationship's
growing without a certain regular amount of sexual activity.

So we have seen that although Vulcans have very little
individual choice about whom they are to marry, the en-

tire system of arranged marriages and the rituals of linking and *Koon-ut-kal-if-fee* works to the advantage of both the individual and Vulcan society as a whole. It is a completely logical system, and why should we be surprised by that?

THE DOOM 'N' GLOOM MACHINE

by Kiel Stuart

Kiel Stuart is back with another of her hilarious Star Trek parodies. This one, however, is a bit different. Told almost completely in dialogue, it takes full advantage of the familiar speech patterns of the Enterprise crew, with just a slightly weird twist. To enjoy it fully, hear the voices of our heroes as you read. That is, if you're not laughing too loud!

"Sorry, captain," said Communications Officer Uhorta, a frown of concentration creasing her false eyelashes. "I know the urgent message for help came from the Starship *Big Dipper*, but I don't know where it be."

"Keep trying," murmured Captain Jerk, engrossed in a game of solitaire.

"We're entering system Pennsylvania 6-5000, captain," added Lieutenant Lulu, "but there's no sign of life." He looked puzzled; it was a popular system with good subways and cable television.

"Look," said Uhorta, "there be the *Dipper*."

"I see it too," said Lulu, "But it's not doing anything. Wonder why?"

Science Officer Shmuck rose from his viewer. "The ship appears to be dead."

"Well, then," said Jerk, rising and stretching, "I guess we can turn around and go home now."

Shmuck headed him off at the lift. "Had we not better ascertain what happened to the ship? And where Commodore Snicker and the crew went? I would suggest that you, captain, beam aboard her with a landing party, leaving me"—Shmuck paused to rub his hands—"In command of the *Enteritis*."

Jerk glowered at him. "All right, all right, Don't touch anything while I'm gone. And leave the cards alone." He turned from the lift. "And no turning tail until I get back, understand?"

Jerk beamed onto the derelict ship with Chief Engineer Snott and Lieutenant D.W. Washburn. Materializing on the Big Dipper's bridge, they saw no sign of the crew.

Immediately all business, Snotty pulled Washburn along: "Let's see if there's anything left tae drrink at th' bar."

Left to his own devices, Jerk soon accidentally stumbled into a broom closet, where he discovered Commodore Snicker slumped in a chair, drooling gently. Jerk shook him vigorously.

"Gloob," said Snicker. "Wacka wacka."

"Get your teeth out of the scenery and tell me what happened," snapped Jerk. "Where's the crew?"

"Booble gleeble," answered Snicker. "They're on the third planet."

Jerk backhanded him. "There is no third planet!"

"There isn't?" blubbered Snicker. "Uh, oh . . ." He clawed at Jerk's lapels. "Yokka ibble! It . . . it . . . bogey men and scarey monsters! Ukto bobo jeepy tutu!"

Jerk, knowing fully well that Starfleece uniforms didn't have lapels, decided that something must be wrong with Snicker. Brushing him away, Jerk pulled out his walkie-talkie.

"Washburn, did you find out what's wrong with the ship?"

"Yes, sir. It doesn't work."

Jerk pressed a hand to his temple. "Lemme talk to Snotty. Snotty, what's the matter with this ship?"

"Ach, captain, it appears that th' antimatter turbothruster mechanism reacted wi' h' cross-circuit willie generator unit, an' caused a shorrt in the hyperpseudoflex monitors."

"Hmmm, ship not working, eh? Could an energy-ener-vation Vanillium field do all that?"

"Sure, why not?"

"Wonder what could generate a field so powerful," mused Jerk.

Snicker raised his head. "Neeka blork. If you saw it, you'd know. It *eats* planets . . . it's . . . it's . . . with a great big . . . and a giant . . . and a massive . . ." He slumped. "It's real big."

Jerk adjusted his walkie-talkie to call Schmuck.

"And it puts out a beam of pure Vanillium," interrupted Snicker.

Jerk paled at this. "Shmuck," he said, "what's going on with the *Enteritis*?"

"I am unable to raise Starfleece Command due to heavy subspace party lines," replied Schmuck. "The computer banks have discovered that the threatening entity is a giant Hoover—the last relic of a race of oversized door-to-door salesmen. It is tremendously destructive, designed to con-sume planets, starships, and stubborn pet hairs. And it is headed . . ." He paused for a music sting. ". . . for the most densely populated sector of our galaxy."

Sounds like trouble, thought Jerk. "I suppose it was only a demo model, but someone goofed up."

"Stick your theories," said Snicker. "What are you going to *do*?"

"Well, first," snapped Jerk, "I'm gonna get you off this ship before you eat any more scenery."

After he had had Snicker beamed up, Jerk got a hail from Shmuck. "We have the machine on visual here. It would appear to be pursuing the *Enteritis*."

"Oh, gosh," interrupted Lieutenant Lyle. "Transporter's out all of a sudden!"

Shmuck ordered, "Take evasive action, helm."

"What about the captain, Snotty, and Lieutenant Wash-burn?" chirped Lyle.

"Oh, I am sure they will manage somehow. Besides, if they needed aid, they would contact us."

"Captain," said Snotty, "Th' communications boarrd ha' joost gone out, an' so ha' yon walkie-talkie."

"This could mean trouble," said Jerk.

"Mebbe Ah ken get th' impulse engines gaein'." Grabbing a screwdriver, drinking it quickly, then picking up some tools, Snott scurried away.

"Belay evasive action!" belched Snicker as he reeled onto the bridge. "We're gonna get that thing."

"You have my orders, Lieutenant Lulu," said Shmuck, trying to ignore Snicker pounding on the back of his head with a belaying pin, as he yelled, "Belay, belay!"

"Dashdongdedadblast, Shmuck," snorted the commodore, "That thing killed my crew! We've gotta get that thing!"

"How come whenever there's a thing out there and we don't know what kind of thing it is, somebody always call is a 'thing'?" asked Dr. McCrotch, as he sauntered out of the lift.

The entire bridge crew groaned. Shmuck turned to Snicker: "You sent your crew to the third planet after the first and second had been eaten, so I would say your negligence killed the crew," Shmuck pointed out, barely concealing a smile.

"I'm senior officer here and I say we fight. So there! Yokka pook pok." Snicked shoved the Vulgarian aside, and lowered his ample beam into the command chair.

"Shmuck!" cried McCrotch, raging within at the small size of his part in this episode. "Do somethin'!"

"Certainly doctor," answered the Vulgarian, breaking into a spiffy fox trot.

"No!" screamed the Doc, "I mean *do* somethin'!"

Shmuck halted in mid-dip. "Well, Commodore Snicker could be relieved on a Section Eight."

"Sounds good t' me," said McCrotch. "I'll jess get a straightjacket down heah . . ."

"You will also be asked to produce evidence," added Shmuck.

"Now y'all know Ah don' got no evidence," whined McCrotch. "All Ah know is that he looks mighty crazy t' me."

"Doctor," ordered Snicker, "get off the bridge." He wriggled about in the chair, flinging a Bronx cheer in the direction of the departing McCrotch. "Okay, let's get that thingy," he ordered, gloating over Shmuck's defeat. "Throw a couple of Ashcans at it, see what happens."

"Captain," panted Snotty, "Ah got impulse power." The *Dipper* gave a huge shudder. "Clutch is kinda stiff, though."

The Ashcans did indeed have an effect on the giant Hoover: It turned to chase the *Enteritis.* "Oh, oh," said Snicker. "Fire fizzers!"

"We can't," said Lieutenant Lulu. "The Vanillium field is causing a continuous-loop Doppelgänger power drain!"

"Commodore," observed Shmuck, "it could be a prudent move to take a hike right about now."

Snicker's face twitched. "Geeba geeba. Maintain course and launch Blockbusters."

The Hoover liked these. For dessert, it had Deflector Shield #5.

"Sir," warned Shmuck, his ears twitching slightly. The commodore ignored him.

"Yocka bork! We gotta get it! One more try with the Blockbusters!"

"Commodore," said Shmuck, "if we don't veer off, then you *are* crazy, and I shall personally sign the Section Eight."

"Blugdug," gibbered Snicker. "Veer off!"

"Too late!" reported Lulu. "The thing's sucking us in!"

"Waaaggghhh!" screamed Jerk. "Whaaat the flibbitygib is Shmuck doing with my ship. I told him not to touch anything!" Leaning forward to get a better look, he accidentally tripped the Dipper's Forward switch.

Attracted by the Dipper's motion, the Hoover turned away from the *Enteritis.* "Snotty!" cried Jerk, "How do you put this thing into reverse?"

"Yahoo!" cheered Snicker as the Hoover turned away. "Now we can finish it off when it's not looking! Fire torpedoes!"

Shmuck sank into his chair and opened a bottle of Mylanta. Clearing his throat, he spoke. "Satisfied? Now we've lost warped drive and all deflectors. We can maintain a small margin away from the Hoover for only seven hours. The Hoover can refuel itself limitlessly. We cannot destroy it. We cannot even run away now. Good work." He downed the bottle of Mylanta and began to open another.

"Mugdug," said Snicker. "We'd better get after it for real then." He adjusted his tricorn hat and inserted a hand into his coat.

"Sir," said Uhorta, "Scuse me, but I got ship-to-ship communications now."

"Shmuck!" Jerk's voice booming from the speakers cut her off. "Are you out of your Vulgarian skull? Get my ship away from that thing!"

"Snicker here. Just relax, Jim. Gwish froop. We'll kill that thing in a minute or two."

"What happened to Shmuck? Did he fall out of a port-hole or something?"

"I assumed command according to regulations."

"Take your regulations and stuff it! I wanna talk to Shmuck!"

"Anything you have to say," puffed Snicker, "will be said to me, click forp nobble."

"I have only *one* thing to say to you," snarled Jerk. "But this parody will be printed in a family magazine, so I can't. Shmuck, take over!"

The overwrought Snicker swelled visibly, and he ripped a bit of upholstery loose with his teeth. "Muggle wiffle," he barked, eyes rolling, fat quivering. "You can't take command, Shmuck, and you know it. You wouldn't dare." Clouds of steam poured from his ears.

"Get the net," Shmuck instructed Security. "And a certain amount of police brutality would not be amiss." They dragged Snicker off.

"Shmuck," said the captain, "slip on a pair of ear-phones, willya? Private conversation." The alien complied, eyebrows skittering up as he heard the captain's instructions. Removing the headphones, he whispered something to a Security goon. Ignoring the question marks hovering in the air, he sat down.

Aboard the *Dipper*, Jerk also sat, whistling and buffing his nails.

"Mr. Shmuck," cried Lulu, "one of our shuttlecraft has taken off!"

"Oh, really?" said Shmuck, and continued to peruse his latest copy of *Scientific Vulgarian*.

"Come in, shuttlecraft," called Uhorta. "Who be there?"

"Yokka biggle!" There was no mistaking that obese howl. "Two guys on the goon squad clubbed me over the head and *stuffed* me into this tin can!" shrieked Snicker. "I'm headed directly down the Hoover's throat, and someone poured Crazy Glue all over the controls and I can't budge her! Yikka bibble ing! I insist that you return me to the ship *at once*!"

"Sorry," said Shmuck pleasantly. "Wrong number."

Snotty grabbed at the captain's shirt. "Captain! Ah dinna believe it! Ca ye nae see whut is gaein' on wi' tha shuttlecraft?"

"Oh, my," said Jerk. "It seems that Matt Snicker has become a kamikaze pilot. Tsk, tsk, what a shame."

"Gobble, gabble, gibble," moaned Snicker, tearing at the walls of the sturdy craft. But it soon became clear there was no escape. "Ah, jeez. Might as well cop an Emmy on the way out." His eyes rolled like greased golf balls, his hair stood on end. Flames shot from his nostrils as he bit huge chunks from the control panel. He was at the pinnacle of swinging from the chandelier, upside down, when the Hoover sucked him up.

"Dear, dear," said Jerk. "There goes a perfectly good shuttlecraft—I mean, a cherished old companion-at-arms."

Shmuck hailed the captain. "Commodore Snicker did not perish in vain," he confided.

"Too bad," murmured Jerk. "But what do you mean?"

"The explosion generated by the shuttlecraft when it was ingested *did* slow down the Hoover's motor, but it was not powerful enough."

"Oh?"

"If a starship, armed with a nuclear warhead, were to be driven down its throat . . ."

"Oh?"

"Piloted by you, of course, since the *Dipper* is destined for the scrap heap anyhow . . ."

"Now wait a minute . . ."

"And it will, of course, involve a hair-raising bit of accurate transporter work, but nothing could possibly go
wrong."

"Hold on there . . ."

"Of course," Shmuck said casually, "if you were successful, you would no doubt win a medal and get all manner of prerequisites."

Snotty broke in eagerly. "Captain, me an' Washburn
could rig a relay detonator, an' all tha', so ye could hae th'
glorry all t' yersel'."

Jerk sighed. "Ohhh, what the heck."

The transporter threw a fit as soon as Snotty and Washburn beamed aboard the *Enteritis*.

"Ye'll hae t' stand by, captain, while Ah chase oot t' engine gnomes," called Snotty. "Theer, it's fixed noo."

"Good," called Jerk, throwing the switch. "Beam me
aboard now."

"Captain!" wailed Snott. "Ma transporter's gone agin! It
must ha' been the lollipop Ah stuck in there!"

"Twenty seconds to explosion," added Shmuck help-
fully.

"Beam me aboard or you won't get any Christmas
bonuses," warned Jerk.

"Captain, Ah'm tryin'," panted Snott.

"Mr. Snott," said Shmuck, "Stop setting off those smoke
bombs and try reverse phasing of the psychobabble generator." He continued his thoughtful countdown. "Fifteen,
fourteen . . ."

"Yatta muggle wump!" cried Jerk.

"Six, five . . ." said Shmuck.

"Try it now, Mr. Lyle," barked Snott.

"Four, three . . ." called the Vulgarian cheerfully.

The Hoover's powerful suction engulfed the *Big Dipper*.
It shuddered, coughed clouds of dust, and ground to a
halt, its plug pulled for good.

"Snotty," called Shmuck from the bridge. "Did you get
the captain?"

"Aye, sir, all safe an' soond, we did."

"Oh." The Vulgarian sounded distinctly disappointed.

Jerk fumed his way to the bridge and pried the reluctant Shmuck out of the command seat.

Taking his usual position, Shmuck asked, "Shall I enter

into the log that Commodore Snicker gave his life in service above and beyond the call of duty? He did, after all, give us the idea that led to the Hoover's destruction."

"Who?" asked Jerk. "You mean Matt Snicker, the notorious, unstable lunatic who lost his entire crew and started this whole mess? Naaah."

"I understand," sniped Shmuck, "that he has a son, Will, who's in Space Cadet Academy with a minor in Theater. Got very good reviews, too."

"Oh, shut up," said Jerk, rummaging about for an aspirin.

SON OF MORE STAR TREK
MYSTERIES—SOLVED!

by Leslie Thompson and our readers

The letters keep coming in, and our five-foot stalwart keeps coming up with solutions to those nagging Star Trek mysteries! By the way, Leslie is anxious for all of you readers to pose more mysteries for her. She's happily planning "The Bride of More Star Trek Mysteries—Solved!"; "The House of More Star Trek Mysteries—Solved"; and "Abbott and Costello Meet the Son of . . ." We think you get the idea.

Here we are again with another installment of what is beginning to look like a never-ending series. I've been told that mystery-solving has become one of the favorite convention pastimes, holding a high place of honor in late-night funfests of filk-singing, trivia, and X-rated story readings! And judging from the amount of mail we've received posing mysteries and solutions, it seems to be true.

One typical letter is from Rita Clay, of Denton, Texas. Rita writes:

"A running series for television must, of course, leave room for errors due to lack of time, but Star Trek never *had* that many. For the most part, the 'flaws' that fans notice (after the umpteenth time of viewing an episode) are minimal and may not be flaws after all. I've taken a little time to go over some of the 'eye catchers' that I've noted recently. (Yes, I'm one of those who is on my umpteenth time!)

"With all due respect to Gene's creativity and continuing genius, there are just a few things that I've simply *got* to ask!

"Did you ever notice that the turbolifts seem to always be there when they're needed? You have never seen Kirk waiting to catch an elevator, have you? I wish my building had those. Many times you've also seen someone disappear on the bridge lift to be followed *seconds* after by another person. Just how can that elevator be in two places at once—in the same shaft, yet?

"Well, I've figured it out like this: The lift system of the *Enterprise* operates on a float basis. Several 'cars' come and go on request—tilting, rising and falling—even in the same shaft. This is possible when one car slows down to sidestep another, much as they slow to change tubes. A ship as large as the *Enterprise* must have a multitude of criss-crossing tubes interconnecting the many areas of the ship. I doubt that one car would even be able to find another, much less run into one. That many cars also allow for one to be close at hand whenever it is needed.

"Still, I have the horrible vision of Kirk stepping through a door—and falling down an empty elevator shaft!

"The question of consecutive cars on the bridge can easily be explained. The bridge is the most strategic area of the ship, and thus must always be accessible. Given this, it is logical to assume that several cars always remain near for heavy traffic (ta-da!).

"While we're on mechanical operations, let's look at the phasers—the ship's phasers, to be specific. A slight inconsistency prevails: Exactly who controls the phaser banks?

"In 'Balance of Terror,' we see the *Enterprise* under attack and preparing to fire in defense. But—oh no!—the order to fire is delayed in operation. We then see Spock, in the phaser control room, fire the weapon at the last minute. All well and good, but we also have a multitude of times when Sulu or Chekov *directly* fires the phasers by the touch of a button or two.

"Wait a minute! I'll give you one or the other, Gene, but not both!

"This flaw cannot be explained away by other than dramatic necessity in "Balance of Terror." That particular episode was also early in the series, so we can explain the later changes as Kirk's efficiency—once having no phasers is enough; let's wire control directly to the bridge. That takes care of that. (I think?)

"A few more questions and I'll let you draw your own conclusions.

"Did you ever notice the colors painted on the *Enterprise* corridors? (Yes, there are colors.) They just "happen" to be red, white, and blue—or do they? I seem to remember in "Omega Glory" where Spock was drawing a parallel between the cultures, and made the remark, "It was like the great confrontation on Earth, but this time the other side [the communists?] won." That leaves the United States as the basis for the Federation—so why not red, white, and blue? (Gene, did you do that on purpose?)

"There is one thing that I would like to know from Nichelle about our dear communications officer: How did you have such long nails and manage to push those buttons? I have long nails and they definitely do not go with buttons. (I have someone else do the button-pushing for me.)

"And did you ever think that the ship's computer voice sounded a bit familiar? You're right. It *did* sound a lot like Majel Barrett. Well, we can't explain that as Leslie did with the look-alikes in Chapel and Number One—sisters? Leslie, I'll leave that one for you.

"There are plenty of other mysteries. Ever wonder what happened in the alternate universe of "Mirror, Mirror?" Terrible to leave us hanging. (Gene, even a Vulcan couldn't get away with that!) It's enough trouble to keep up with one universe at a time, I know, but still . . .

"Consider next the masterful engineering feat of transporting *all* those tribbles into the Klingon ship *all* at once. Not detracting from Scotty's genius, but how *did* he do it? Transporters only take a limited mass, and there were *tons* of tribbles.

"How about some speculation? How about a few thoughts bandied about? How about some *answers*?

"And what of Lazarus?"

Gee, Rita, thanks a bunch. What of Lazarus, I really can't say, but I'll have a try at some of your questions.

First, let's have a look at the solutions Rita offered. Her idea of a large number of "floating" turbolift cars is a good one. I have always just assumed that the cars were able to move in either direction simultaneously, and that they "stacked up" awaiting passengers much as taxicabs line up at the airport to wait their turn. The floating system postulated by Rita, however, is superior, as it allows cars to move to a needed area quickly, and without stacking up.

True, it would seem the bridge is an important area for the lifts to serve . . . but if it is so important to get people on and off the bridge quickly, why is there only one lift door on the bridge? Actually, it is not all that important for access to the bridge in an emergency situation. The lift cars appear immediately one after another there because they do so all over the ship.

And Jim Kirk will never fall down a shaft. Not only does it make sense for the lifts to have a safety device which would prevent the doors from opening if no car is present, but as captain, Kirk has his own personal lift car that "follows" him around! Well, it is actually not one specific car, but the ship's computer always makes sure that a car is available to Kirk (and probably Spock, McCoy, and Scotty too) wherever he may be on the ship.

Ever notice that when Uhura and Sulu want Kirk, they immediately know where to call him up on the intercom? Apparently, Kirk wears some sort of small transponder somewhere on his uniform that allows the computer to track him anywhere aboard the *Enterprise*. When he's needed, someone on the bridge simply instructs the computer to buzz him on the nearest intercom. (Much as our present-day "beepers" only work when they are near a telephone, Kirk's transponder will only work in the confines of the ship, so the device is useless to track him on the surface of a planet or aboard an alien ship. And again, we can assume that other important officers have transponders as well.) It would be a simple matter for the computer to constantly track the signal and keep a lift car nearby for immediate use.

In the matter of phaser banks, Kirk would have made sure that control of the phasers was rewired to the bridge

. . . if he had needed to. In "Balance of Terror," we see that the phaser control room is a place where the deadly weapons are *readied* for firing. Even at this time, it was either Sulu or Chekov who did the actual firing. What Spock did in the control room was engage the final readying sequence and allowed the order from the bridge—the firing of the phasers—to come about. What Kirk probably did was make damn sure that a computer backup was put on the readying sequence, one that couldn't be overcome by phaser coolant fumes.

As mentioned above, Chekov occasionally fired the phasers, although we all know the main firing controls are on the helm side of the console. Again, more redundancy. Kirk and Scotty realized that the helmsman could be knocked out of action and valuable life-or-death seconds could be lost before someone else could get to the firing controls and operate them. So they put in a backup on Chekov's board. (And apparently other redundancies as well. We see the two often interchange functions—Chekov will engage the engines, Sulu plot the course. They must be a *very* efficient, almost synchronized team.)

In any case, you can be sure that Kirk took full advantage of having the best science officer in the fleet and the best engineering officer in the fleet to make his ship as foolproof as possible. That's probably one of the major reasons why he was the only commander to bring his ship back intact from the original five-year mission.

The colors of the corridors are probably just coincidence. True, the United States won the "great confrontation"—but anyone even passingly familiar with nuclear-war scenarios knows that no real "winners" would result from such a conflict. What obviously happened in Star Trek's history is that all of the nations of Earth, having been devastated by the explosions, radiation, and perhaps even germ warfare, called an immediate halt to the conflict, threw out the leaders (on both sides) who led them into the conflagration, and banded together in a world government with the rebuilding of civilization the number-one priority. Having worked together for the good of all in an emergency, the nations realized that they could do so permanently. And so the United Earth, the forerunner of the United Federation of Planets, was born.

As to the fact that Kirk recognized the Preamble to the

Constitution in "Omega Glory"—heck, *I* didn't remember it, and I wasn't raised in a world federation! We can assume that the United States still exists in Star Trek's time, as well as many of the other nations extant today. We were told that Uhura is a native of the United States of Africa, and Chekov proudly speaks of "Mother Russia." Kirk, probably about twenty years removed from History 101, understandably had a little trouble remembering the Preamble . . . especially as his only "memory jogger" was the bastardized, pig-latinish chant of the Yangs. (What would have been impressive is if *Spock* had known the words!)

Nichelle isn't around right now, so I'll have to take a stab at answering the all-important fingernail question. Gee, I don't know, I have long fingernails, and I type a lot. Could be that by the twenty-third century, scientists will have developed a fingernail polish made from collapsed neutronium or something tough like that?

The ship's computer voice was that of the actress Majel Barrett right enough, but it was not Christine Chapel who did the original voice printing that the computer used. It was, of course, her sister, Number One, whose cold, emotionless, already computerlike voice was the print for the Enterprise's computers. As Number One served for some years on the *Enterprise*, it only follows that she would be available for the tapings when the audio units were installed on the ship's computer.

What happened to the alternative universe of "Mirror, Mirror" is not just a mystery—it is another series. And one, I'm afraid, that we will never see. But don't discount Spock 2—if he's only half as smart and resourceful as his "real Star Trek" counterpart, he will manage to find a way. True, he may not personally be able to overthrow the Empire, but he will certainly get the ball rolling . . . and if the alternate-world Kirk has even a spark of our Jim in him, then Spock 2 won't be working alone!

Remember that the *Enterprise* has many more transporters than we were ever shown: at least three more "beaming rooms," several emergency personnel transporters, and a number of cargo transporters. The cargo transporters should be able to carry quite a large load on their own. The real problem of transporting several tons of tribbles to the Klingon ship is the amount of energy involved. It is a wonder that Scotty didn't blow every circuit on the ship!

And he probably would have, had he sent them all over at once. But he obviously did not. Directing the transporter beam to cover the entire area of the ship is a relatively simple matter, as is directing it to only lock in on and transport tribble life forms. What most likely happened is that he sent them over in batches, albeit very quickly, beginning with the unoccupied areas of the Klingon ship. Once he had to place the beasties where they could be seen by the Klingons, he already had most of them over, and being scared of the tribbles, the Klingons were in no shape to work up a defense. They're probably lucky they survived at all!

Ellis Cambre of Gretna, Louisiana, wants to know if the primary hull of the *Enterprise* is indeed detachable and capable of independent action. Yes, Gene tells us so in *The Making of Star Trek*, and although we never got a chance to see this happen, it makes sense. For (as Ellis points out) if the primary engines were about to explode or intruders had taken over the nacelle and engineering hulls, the largest portion of the crew and the most sensitive departments and sections would be able to move clear and take appropriate action.

The only solution to this mystery is the happy thought that things never quite got bad enough for our boys to have to take such a desperate action. For although we know that the hulls can separate, we do not know if they can effectively rejoin. It may be a one-time-only, last-ditch maneuver to be taken only when absolutely nothing else is possible. And as we were told that the hull (once separated from the nacelles and engineering hull) could only operate on impulse engines, the separation probably could not be made during warp without disastrous consequences. While such a maneuver would be fascinating to see, let's hope we never do see it—for it would probably mean the death of our beloved *Enterprise*.

Eric Elliot (no address) is obviously a sadist, having sent me a list of eight very tough mysteries to solve. Okay, Eric, I'll give it a try . . .

1. In "Charlie X," why were chefs preparing the food, instead of just using a selector?

Ahem. This is one of the toughest kind of mysteries, those that stem from throwaway lines placed in an episode for purposes of humor, color, or technical gobbledegook. One can only assume that on board the *Enterprise*, there is a department whose duty it is to see that the food selectors are programmed, operational, and well stocked. By "stocked" I mean that a large selection of dishes is listed in the computer banks, available to crewpersons. When a meal is ordered up, the computer ties into a transporterlike beam, tells it which item to rematerialize, and that dish is recreated within a compartment from which it is taken by the crewperson and happily devoured. (As the "food" is made from nonorganic, highly nutritional minerals, vitamins, etc., the patterns can be utilized over and over again. The raw material for the fresh meals is probably—ick —the remains of the last meals, and Surak knows what else!)

The person(s) in charge of all this activity probably have a title something like "Chief Officer in Charge of Food Disbursement," but Kirk and everyone else probably finds it easier to refer to them as "chefs." The turkey remark was probably an example of Kirk's occasionally black humor, for the quality of Starfleet's food (like all service food, no matter how good it may be) is probably unendingly derided by the troops. It's a soldier's right to gripe even when the griping is unjustified and in good humor.

But we can also assume that the *Enterprise* has a small but extremely well-stocked galley, where crewpersons can cook specialty foods for recreation. Most likely, Nurse Chapel uses it to lovingly prepare Spock's *plomik* soup.

2. In "The Enemy Within," why wasn't the shuttlecraft used to get Sulu and the others off the planet?

Easy enough. The upper-air turbulence of the storms on that icy planet was so strong that a shuttlecraft would have been risking destruction to venture into it. As it would have been foolish to almost certainly lose more lives in a futile attempt to rescue Sulu and Co. in that way, Kirk and Spock did not even consider it.

3. Why did Pike ("The Menagerie") and Kirk, in

"Where No Man Has Gone Before," have only two stripes on their sleeves?

The basic uniforms changed after the events of "Where No Man" (remember, although this episode aired *after* some others, it is generally accepted to be the first) and someone, somewhere, decided that captains should have the extra, broken stripe. We cannot know for sure, but perhaps only starship captains have the extra stripe, as a mark of their exalted status.

4. Why were dilithium crystals called "lithium crystals" in "Mudd's Women?"

Again, an instance of the ship's being upgraded. Somewhere along the line, a scientist discovered a way to double the load capacity and life of a lithium crystal; e.g., a *di*-lithium crystal. The term was quickly taken up as accepted usage by everyone, and that's what they were (correctly) called from that time on.

5. Why do the people of Eminar VII have the same phasers and communicators as Klingons?

Form follows function. To perform correctly and efficiently, there are just so many ways a communicator, or a phaser, or a typewriter can look. As to the shape of the items being almost exactly like the Klingons', it is one of those strange coincidences that pop up in Star Trek (and in real life) once in a while. But if you would like a pat solution, okay. Let's assume some time before the *Enterprise* crew made planetfall on Eminar VII, a Klingon crew wandered along. Having less luck and smarts than the Federation stalwarts, they were quickly dispatched and their weaponry and technology was adapted to Eminarian use.

6. In "A Taste of Armageddon," Scotty refused to lower the screens, yet Fox beamed down. How?

Obviously Scotty, in a tricky situation *vis à vis* the stuffy diplomat, decided to risk briefly lowering (or more likely, forming a "hole" in) one of the screens and letting him beam down. As the ship was not under actual attack, it would have been possible for him to do so.

7. In "City on the Edge of Forever," it is stated that Edith must die in a traffic accident to set things straight. Yet the reason why she was crossing the street was to go to a movie with Kirk. If Kirk was never there, she

wouldn't have crossed the street, and wouldn't have been killed—but she was. How?

I've been dreading the day when someone would finally ask this question. I *hate* time paradoxes! Okay. As Kirk had little or no knowledge of that time, he probably couldn't have cared less which movie he saw, and left the choosing of it up to Edith. Edith chose the Clark Gable film, and was obviously looking forward to seeing it. So it is likely she would have gone to see it that night even if Kirk had not been there, and would have left just late enough to be hit by the truck as, worried about missing the start, she hurried across the street. It is not stated anywhere in the episode, but it may have been the first night the film was showing, and Edith wanted to see it right away—or the *last* night it was showing, in which case it would be even more important for her to hurry.

As with all paradoxes, the explanation is as full of holes as the occurrence, but the fact that Edith would go to see a movie is more likely than—for instance—that she would be prevented from rushing in front of the truck by the appearance of McCoy in front of her. That would really be a paradox, for short of shoving her out in front of a speeding vehicle, it would be very hard to make the accident come about as it was meant to happen.

A much more serious, and confusing, paradox is what the heck was Edith doing going to see a Clark Gable movie in *1930*? At that time, he was a few years away from stardom, and hardly more than a bit player, much less the "king." So here it is, *Trek* readers, the solution to one of the greatest Star Trek mysteries of all: Edith, having more than a little inspired insight into the future (she predicted space travel and the uniting of mankind), was especially receptive to the undeniable charms of the young Clark Gable. She knew that he was destined to be big star, and in her mind, anything with him in it was "a Clark Gable movie." The movie she and Kirk were on their way to see was probably *Dance, Fools, Dance*, a Joan Crawford film which included Gable's first featured role for MGM. Edith, had she not been such a fervent and effective social worker, would have made a great talent scout.

8. Why was Starfleet sometimes called "Space Fleet Command," "Space Command," and "Star Command"?

Aside from these connotations being verbal shorthand, it

is likely that specific orders came from specific echelons of Starfleet, and that those sections each had a coded designation. It is a fact of life that each little bureaucracy has its need to aggrandize itself with a fancy-sounding title.

Chantal Guadiano, of Seabrook Texas, writes in to wonder why Sarek and Amanda were not present at Spock's "wedding" in "Amok Time." She points out that if the matriarch of Spock's clan (T'Pau) officiated, then Spock's parents surely also would have been there. Chantal surmises that the reason they weren't present was the chance of an emotional scene from Amanda—especially if Spock was killed.

However, up until the time T'Pring challenged, the ceremony was going as planned, so Sarek and Amanda had no way of knowing beforehand that Spock would even be in a battle. And after living for many years on Vulcan, it is highly unlikely that Amanda would allow her emotions to get the better of her in public—even at her son's wedding. So I'm afraid that there is another explanation for Spock's parents' absence, a more logical one:

Spock and Sarek were still not talking to each other at the time of Spock's *pon farr*, so it is unlikely that Sarek would have attended the marriage even if it had not come about so unexpectedly.

And we still know very little of the rite; perhaps parents do *not* attend. Perhaps Sarek would have come out of duty, but he and Amanda were off on a diplomatic mission at the time. Or Spock, either because of his stubbornness or in his agony, simply did not inform them. (We can assume that T'Pring, feeling the time nearing, made the necessary arrangements with T'Pau.)

Or it could have been common knowledge that T'Pring was going to challenge. Surely, she and Stonn had to meet sometimes (they fell in "love" with each other), and it would have been noted. I doubt that Vulcans gossip, but the fact that T'Pring was acting illogically and disgracefully would have gotten around. T'Pau seemed to know the challenge was coming—she specifically asked Spock to ensure his human companions would not interfere in whatever happened. In such a case, Chantal could be correct in part. Sarek probably wouldn't have attended, but Amanda would have—unless there was a very good chance she would have to see her son die.

Chantal also wonders why, if Spock and T'Pring were "mentally linked" when they were about seven years old, and if *pon farr* occurs every seven years, it didn't first occur to Spock when he was fourteen. Or twenty-one. Or twenty-eight.

Although *pon farr* occurs every seven years, it is not necessarily every seven years from the time of the first linking. We are never told how much time passes between the linking and the first *pon farr*. In Spock's case, it seemed to have been about thirty years, but as a half-breed, he may have been an exception to the rule. It wouldn't be illogical to assume that full-blooded Vulcans have their first *pon farr* at around age twenty-one. Spock didn't, so he assumed (and hoped) he would be spared it completely. (If poor T'Pring had been sitting around for ten years without sex, and not knowing if her "marriage" would *ever* be consummated, it's no wonder she took up with Stonn!)

In response to another of Chantal's questions, T'Pring looked younger than Spock because she was a full-blooded Vulcan. Spock, being a hybrid, has apparently inherited normal human aging patterns, and so *looked* like a man in his middle to late thirties, while T'Pring, barely more than a schoolgirl by Vulcan standards, appeared considerably younger. (This could be another reason why the first *pon farr* was so long in coming. As Vulcans are much longer-lived than humans, it is possible that their life cycles are longer as well. So a Vulcan's puberty may last from his early teens until his late twenties. Spock didn't go into *pon farr* until T'Pring was ready.) As we have established that Spock ages faster than full-blooded Vulcans, his puberty was over quicker as well. This could have had a lot to do with the disagreement Spock had with his father, for when Spock was about eighteen or nineteen, and grown, Sarek may have considered him still a child, and therefore was very much opposed to Spock's leaving for Starfleet.

And many readers have wondered what happened to Stonn's intended mate. Although it is possible that he chose to release her in favor of T'Pring, it is more likely that she was killed in an accident some time before. And in the time before he could be joined with another Vulcan

female, he and T'Pring became involved. It is obvious that
he, Spock, and T'Pring are all contemporaries, about the
same age, as Spock greets Stonn as someone whom he
knows. (It is understandable under the circumstances that
Spock isn't more friendly.) Since they were about the
same age, Stonn wouldn't have yet had a chance to go
through his first *pon farr* either, and when T'Pring was
ready to bear children, Stonn would have felt some stirrings from his attachment to her, even though they had
not been linked. Although his fires wouldn't have been
nearly as great as Spock's, it does explain why he acted so
emotionally at the ceremony, and why he was so anxious
to battle Spock.

More letters here about the "double identity paradoxes":

Lisa Jones (no address), who says she is only ten years
old and loves my "stories" (thanks, Lisa!), offers an explanation as to why sisters Christine Chapel and Number
One had such different personalities. Lisa says:

"Number One is about thirteen years older than her sister. (Obviously, she didn't look any older than Christine
on a film that was supposed to have been made thirteen
years before, did she?) So the baby got all the attention,
and she became tight and upset. Things were worse when
Christine was four. Number One was seventeen, and
Christine was always showing off and pestering her. She
was as miserable as ever and remained unemotional for
the rest of her life."

Well, I tell you, that sounds like an acceptable solution
to me. We've all known someone who has repressed at
least part of his or her emotions because of an unhappy
childhood. It is not too farfetched to assume Number One
did so to an extent that bordered on the psychotic, and if
such is the case, she and Christine would probably not
have had anything to do with each other. And that would
explain why we never heard Christine speak of her sister
or why no one ever referred to the resemblance between
the women during the events of "The Menagerie."

On the same subject, Denise Bird of Payson, Utah,
seems to have caught me with my continuity down. She
point out that in "A Brief Look at Spock's Career" (*Best
of Trek #3*), I stated that Number One was born on a

planet where names were very personal and secret. And if the two were sisters, then why the name Christine Chapel?

Not wishing to go around hearing everyone call her a number as her less emotional sister did, Christine simply chose a pseudonym for use in her Starfleet duties. Although the name has no obvious double meanings or symbolism, it may to her. And looking so very much like her sister, who was probably renowned in Starfleet, Chapel (upon entering the service after the apparent death of Roger Korby) wanted to make doubly sure she had her own identity. It could have been that Christine was a pet name Korby had for her, and she continued to use it in memory of him. Had we seen any intimate scenes of the two together, we might have heard Korby use her real name. And here's a question for you readers: Has she told it to Spock?

Denise also offered an intriguing explanation for the resemblance of Trelane and Koloth.

"In the case of Trelane, it would be silly to think that this child was in trouble for the first time. It seems to me he has probably caused mischief among other races—anyone with a two-year-old of their own would know that. I would suppose that at one time he played among some Klingons, or even just spent time peeping—at which time he had seen Koloth. Later, when wishing to take humanoid form to play with the *Enterprise*, he borrowed freely from Koloth's form. When you don't look like anybody to start with, you may wish to save time and energy by looking like someone else."

Good solution. The fact that Kirk (who had had dealings with his enemy Koloth previous to "Squire") didn't recognize the form could be due to the more human facial features of Trelane and the fact that Kirk had other things on his mind than trying to remember whom Trelane reminded him of. Even if Kirk had made the connection, it wasn't worth mentioning, for it would have done nothing to help them get out of their plight.

Denise also offers an admittedly more prosaic explanation for the resemblance of Sarek and the Romulan commander from "Balance of Terror." The similarity of the Vulcan and Romulan races increased the possibility that there could be two men of extraordinary likeness.

Patsy Brautigan, of New Orleans, Louisiana, has a some-what more involved explanation, however. She postulates that the Romulan ship in "Balance" was actually from a parallel dimension, and somehow wandered over to ours when making the thrust into Federation space. She states that this would make the resemblance less amazing. Her evidence is that the Romulan ship is quite different from those used in later episodes; they used an "invisibility shield" and in later episodes (notably "Enterprise Incident") the cloaking device was touted as a new weapon. Also the behavior of the Romulan warriors in "Balance" was subtly different from that of the Romulans in later episodes.

Well, it *could* be, but I doubt it. We are told that Romulans began using Klingon ships and weaponry under their mutual-defense, nonaggression alliance, so that ex-plains that. And the cloaking device may have been a vast-ly improved model of the invisibility shield, one which did not require nearly as much power and could be used for a longer time or while in battle. And the behavior of the Romulans was not so much different—it was only the commander, a man tiring of war and conquest, a man more disposed to the philosophical side of life, who was noticeably different. As he was the focus of the episode, it is easy to make Patsy's mistake and assume *all* of the Rom-ulans in that episode were of the same bent.

And while the events of "Balance" are never directly re-ferred to by Romulans in later episodes, it is obvious they know of them. They consider the *Enterprise* to be their number-one target, from a standpoint of both information and revenge. So the original ship must have come from "our" Romulan Empire, not from a comparable but differ-ent Romulan Empire in another dimension.

Denise also wonders, if Vulcan males are betrothed at age seven, does that make Amanda Sarek's *second* wife? "What happened to the first, the one he was bonded to? And if he did have a first wife, does that mean that Spock might have some half brothers or sisters?"

This has long been an object of discussion, and I am surprised it has not surfaced in these mystery funfests until now. Popular opinion holds among fandom that Sarek did indeed have a first wife, a Vulcan bondmate, but that she died many years before he met and married Amanda. Whether or not the first wife had any children is usually the hottest part of any such discussions. Some fans seem to think it would be grand if Spock had brothers or sisters; others feel the idea wouldn't be a good one at all. I'm afraid I can't really offer a solution to this mystery. There just aren't any clues to work with. And I feel that it is something better left to each Star Trek fan to decide for himself. More than likely, it will lead to a story—so write it!

Steve Aprahamian of Columbus, Ohio, wants to know why Uhura (as fifth in command) was overlooked in "Catspaw" and assistant chief engineer Vincent De Salle put in command.

Uhura is indeed fifth in the *chain of command*, as per Starfleet regulations. The order goes: Kirk, Spock, Scott, Sulu, Uhura, chief navigator (a position Chekov never officially held), and various department heads in the *command* chain (not ship's services or sciences). Order of ranking is decided by officer's rank, position, and seniority. Therefore, those rankings after captain and first officer could change. For example: When Pike commanded the *Enterprise*, Spock was third in command, even though he was science officer and not included in the above listing. When Gary Mitchell was aboard, he was third in command, his position and rank being equal to Spock's, but having less seniority. Scotty is currently third in command, for even though he is not in command services, his seniority precludes his serving in a subordinate rank to Sulu or Uhura. A good rule of thumb would be if an officer serves regularly on the bridge, and is the head of his or her respective department, that officer is in the immediate chain of command.

So then why was DeSalle given command in "Catspaw"? Well, as the ship was in immediate danger of being damaged by the tricks of Sylvia and Korob, it would make sense to have an experienced engineering officer in charge. Too, Uhura would have been more valuable staying at her position where she could continually attempt to contact Kirk and the others while still directing and coordinating emergency ship operations. We can assume she does this no matter who is in the center seat. But the main reason that DeSalle was put in charge is that he had obviously only recently gotten his promotion to assistant chief engineer, and it was felt that he needed the experience of command.

Steve also wants to know why Spock, with his great psionic abilities, was not affected by the energies in the barrier at the galaxy's edge.

True, the episode stated that those with the greatest psionic abilities were the most affected. Mitchell had greater latent abilities than Dehner, so he began to evolve before she did (and apparently to a greater extent). So on the surface it would be logical to assume that Spock, whose mental abilities are great, would be affected first and to a greater extent than Mitchell. Or if he did not begin to mutate, his mental openness to the energy's effects should have left him dead, like the nine others on the *Enterprise* at that time. (True, it is not specifically stated that the nine are killed by the energy—they could have been injured in the gyrations—but it is strongly implied.)

A possible explanation is that Spock, being trained in the use and control of his psionic abilities, was able to resist the effects of the energy. But we never saw him get the "shock" as Mitchell and Dehner did, and even if he got an offscreen buzz, he was obviously the least affected on the bridge—he continued his reports through the worst of it, and leaped immediately to take the controls when Mitchell passed out. Had he been, even unconsciously, fighting off the energy's effects, his behavior would have been at least slightly off.

So why didn't Spock feel the effects of the energy? Well, we know that a Vulcan's internal organs, blood, and endocrine balances are all radically different from a human's, so it is only logical to assume that the convolutions and synapse patterns of a Vulcan brain are vastly different from those of a human brain. Since we saw that the energy—whatever it was—had no effect on Spock, it follows that the energy can affect only a *human* brain. Spock's brain, even though it houses great psionic abilities, was simply too different from Mitchell's or Dehner's to undergo the same metamorposis.

But another question arises: Why didn't Spock, with his knowledge and experience in these matters, inform Kirk of the fact that he wasn't affected? The information *could* have led to some form of treatment or control for Mitchell.

Two explanations are possible for this mystery: First, Spock says in "Dagger of the Mind" that his mental abilities are personal and private, so much so that he could not suggest using them on another. (He later changed his attitude, but this was probably due to a "loosening up" caused by his frequent use of the meld and other powers in the humans' presence.) So he would have been reticent to bring the subject up. We know he *would* have, however, if it could have saved the situation. Apparently, Spock logically realized that his own psionic abilities were so different from the Mitchell-mutate that mentioning them would not help matters. Indeed, had he done so, it could have given Kirk false hope for saving his friend Mitchell. Spock had a hard enough time convincing him to abandon Gary as it was.

Second, Spock could possibly have been affected by the energy, but to a much lesser extent and with a delayed effect; again because of the alien configuration of his brain. In later episodes, we see Spock's mental powers seemingly grow in strength and variety, so it is not too farfetched to assume that the energy at least enhanced his native psionic powers. Has anyone ever wondered *how* Spock was able to feel the death cries of several hundred Vulcans across thousands of miles of interstellar space in "The Immunity Syndrome"? Or how the mind of T'Pring was able to call to his (and vice versa) across an even greater distance? A call which was designed by heredity and tradition to go to a mate who was—at the very farthest—on the same planet? Perhaps the sheer distance between him and T'Pring was why Spock hoped he would be spared the travail of *pon farr*.

So it is not out of the realm of possibility that Spock *was* affected by the energy, and that his powers of the mind are now far beyond what they were (and would have been) had he not gotten the exposure. And remember, when he was among the Masters, only Spock was able to sense the presence of V'Ger . . . so his powers, if not his emotional control, must be greater than even theirs.

Anthony Smythe, from right here in Houston, Texas, has several questions about *Star Trek: The Motion Picture*. I've been quite surprised that more questions haven't popped up concerning the movie, for it was full of inconsistencies with the series and unexplained mysteries. This is an invitation, folks!

But to get to Anthony's queries: His first question asks why Kirk, who is a full-fledged admiral at the beginning of the movie, is referred to throughout (after he takes over the ship) as "captain" and even wears captain's braid on his sleeve.

You'll remember that when Kirk took command from Decker, he told Decker that he would have to take a temporary reduction in rank to commander. So it could have been possible that Kirk too had to take a "temporary" reduction in rank. It could even have been one of the penalties Admiral Nogura placed on Kirk for insisting that he be given back the *Enterprise*.

Simple enough. Kirk was reduced in rank back to captain, and would logically enough wear captain's braid. But wait . . . isn't there a rank *between* admiral and captain? A rank which we have seen individuals hold and *still* command starships? Yes; Matt Decker, for example, was a *commodore*. So why, even if Kirk did have to take a reduction to command a starship again, wasn't he reduced to commodore instead of captain?

The only possible explanation is that Kirk did not actually take a reduction in rank at all, but was still technically an admiral (his official rank would be rear admiral) throughout the events of *STTMP*. He could have been acting under orders to wear captain's uniform and stripes as a ruse of sorts. After all, no one had any idea of what the Intruder really was, and if the ship was captured by unfriendly aliens, a Kirk disguised as a captain would not be as valuable a prize as an Admiral Kirk. Starfleet, as we have seen on many occasions, is not above this sort of slightly paranoid subterfuge.

More likely, however, is the fact that Kirk *chose* to dress and act as a captain rather than as an admiral. Not only would it have eased the transition of power as much as possible, but the members of his old crew would be much more comfortable around him without the psychological barrier of "admiral" to contend with. Had we seen any sort of confrontation or diplomatic dealings with aliens, Kirk would have correctly identified himself as "Admiral James T. Kirk, in command of the United Federation of Planets Starship *Enterprise*." But for a number of reasons, not the least of which is the fact that he still thinks of himself that way, he prefers to be *Captain* Kirk. And I think most of *us* prefer it that way, too.

Anthony also wanted to know why the shuttle that delivered Spock to the *Enterprise* was named *Surak*. "Surely," he states, "the Vulcans would not place the name of their most revered historical figure on the prow of *any* ship, much less a shuttlecraft that is little more than a glorified tug!"

I agree. Vulcans most certainly would not bandy around Surak's name. But it must be noted that the craft in *STTMP* was much more than a typical shuttlecraft. It was quite large and obviously had warp-drive capabilities, for it not only caught up with the *Enterprise* after she had been in warp, but it reached the general area of Earth's solar system from Vulcan in (at the most) two days. Most likely the *Surak* is the top-of-the-line Vulcan craft, one used exclusively for the highest officials involved in peaceful diplomatic missions, and therefore the only ship which would be honored with the name *Surak*. The arrival of the *Surak* at any function would be a mark of Vulcan's respect, for they would consider that his spirit travels with the ship.

Okay, if that's the case, then what the heck was Spock doing on it, zipping around space on what was (at that time) little more than a personal whim, and aiming to meet a mysterious entity which would most likely fight? Hardly a mission of peace.

Three factors would have contributed to the unusual use of the *Surak* for such a mission. One, the high standing of Spock's family and his own outstanding record. Two, his powers of persuasion, which could have convinced his superiors that the possible gains in knowledge would be worth the use of the ship. And three, the fact that Vulcans honor, cherish, and truly love their Earth brothers. As the Earth was in danger, and Spock's telepathic contact with the Intruder could help alleviate that danger, it was only logical to supply him with the fastest craft available—the *Surak*.

Anthony also wonders why it would be necessary for Ilia to take an oath of celibacy and file it with Starfleet. If she could not be trusted, then what was she doing in a responsible position on a starship?

Apparently, the effect of the pheromones emitted by a Deltan are so strong that humans are constantly attracted to one of the opposite sex. Fan fantasies aside, it is unlikely that one sexual encounter with the highly skilled Ilia would make a "love slave" of any of the crew. Her oath is a protective measure against plain old human nature. If any member of the crew *was* having relations with Ilia, the constant attraction of others would inevitably lead to jealousy and resentment. And men being men, even in Star Trek's time, we know what that leads to—violence.

So the oath requiring a Deltan to be celibate is simply a way of avoiding unnecessary—and probably unavoidable—trouble. (Y'know, it's lucky Mr. Spock is celibate, or the same kind of trouble would probably crop up with female *Enterprise* crewmembers!)

Another mystery Anthony wants explained is why, when Spock states that V'Ger has been trying to contact Earth with a simple binary carrier wave signal, Kirk spins around and says, "Radio?" in the same tone of voice we would say, "Tin cans and string?" As the term "subspace radio" was used in just about every television episode, Kirk should hardly be so amazed.

Apparently, the term "subspace radio" is just a handy description of whatever communications system Starfleet uses, just as they would say "a mile" when all measurements are made in metrics. Kirk's astonishment was clearly due to the fact that V'Ger was communicating with *radio* waves as we know them, a method of communication which would be quite primitive and virtually obsolete by Star Trek's time, and definitely *not* the sort of communications anyone would expect from the supremely developed V'Ger.

Anthony's last question concerns why a weapons station would be added to the bridge, and an extra officer be assigned to man it full time. This harks back to the earlier discussion of phaser control. Just as Kirk, Spock, and Scott would have made sure that phaser power was routed through the bridge, so would Starfleet have learned the lesson. The weapons control station is a modification which incorporates *all* control of the ship's weaponry into an area on the bridge which can be in direct contact and under observation by the captain and his executive staff. And as for an extra man being needed to staff it, most likely it would free several crewmembers from duty below-decks. We know from "Balance of Terror" that at least two men manned the phaser control room, and perhaps many more were working behind the scenes. So not only is having a station on the bridge safer, it is more efficient.

That's all the mysteries to be covered this issue. But as always, all of you are invited to challenge your over-worked correspondent with new and tougher ones . . . as well as your own solutions to them. Thanks again to all of you who have written, even those who have submitted duplicate mysteries, for there is nothing more fun than making this thing we love much more real and involving. Star Trek not only lives, it *exists!*

THE CINEMATOGRAPHY OF
STAR TREK

by Michael D. Klemm

Television is a visual medium. To quote Flip Wilson, "What you see is what you get." How a scene in a film or television show is shot, directed, lit, etc. has the most direct bearing upon its final success. In this article, Michael Klemm looks at the cinematographic elements that made Star Trek so outstanding in this vitally important area.

A film topic that many people often take for granted is the cinematography employed in the making of it. What most people don't seem to realize is that a film can have a terrific story and the greatest actors in the world, but if it is poorly directed and photographed, the result is a boring film.

One of many factors that contribute to Star Trek's greatness is the fine direction evident in many of the episodes. Television is notorious for putting shows together hurriedly, the main problem being that barely a week of production time is devoted to each show, and this strict deadline has to be met. Such deadlines tend to stifle a director's creativity, and he is often forced to settle for less than he would like.

On the other hand, a lot of careful planning goes into

the filming of a good movie. Alfred Hitchcock used to draw up a storyboard of every intended shot in his shooting script before he even started filming. Steven Spielberg did the same thing with his recent hit *Raiders of the Lost Ark*.

Because of the time and expense involved in this sort of preparation, it is impossible to so thoroughly prepare a television shooting script. Such care cannot even be given to the actual filming. Often the director is forced to improvise on the set. Film editing, perhaps the most tedious stage of filmmaking, is often hastily done.

But despite all these limitations, the makers of Star Trek still managed to produce shows that were visually as well as dramatically interesting. Although the results were not as polished as they could have been given more time, they were often outstanding for a television series.

The director is the person responsible for what you see on the screen. He must decide where to place characters in each scene, and more important, how it is to be filmed. This is often a joint effort between the director and the cinematographer. Will the characters be in long shot or close-up? A low camera angle or a high one? Deep or shallow focus? Harsh or soft lighting? Will the camera move or will it remain stationary? And how will the final footage be edited?

When a director just places the camera on the set, films, and does nothing else, the result is nothing more than a filmed stage play. Effective use of the camera, lighting, etc. is what distinguishes a good film from a bad one. Since preparing a storyboard is usually out of the question, a master setup is often used to get the required footage. In this way, scenes are shot in long, medium, and close shots so there will be a variety of each to choose from when it comes time to edit the film.

The Star Trek series was fortunate in that it had many fine directors who knew how to work within the restrictions of television. Among these was Joseph Pevney, Marc Daniels, Ralph Senensky, Vincent McEvccty, and John Meredyth Lucas. Behind the cameras were Jerry Finnerman and Al Francis.

Undoubtedly, one of the reasons so many Trekkers identify with Captain Kirk is William Shatner's fine acting ability. But this ability is enhanced by the way in which he is filmed. For example, whenever Kirk is in trouble or has a decision to make, the camera moves in for a close-up, allowing us to see the full range of emotion on Shatner's face. Would we empathize with him as fully if he were seen in long shot at the far end of a huge set? Similarly, in "City on the Edge of Forever," a close-up clearly shows Dr. McCoy's cordrazine-induced madness when he leaps forward on the bridge, and when he enters the transporter room. A more controlled feeling of madness can be suggested through the use of an extreme close-up, such as the shot of Lenore's eyes when she aims a phaser at Kirk in "Conscience of the King," or Spock's nervously drumming fingers in "Amok Time."

Conversely, a long shot is often used to put some distance between the viewer and the actor. A long shot is used when a landing party materializes on a planet in order to establish the setting. Such a shot can also give us a sense of isolation or alienation. For example, in "This Side of Paradise," we see Kirk enter the empty bridge in extreme long shot and we immediately know he is alone aboard the ship.

A medium shot photographs the actor from shoulder or chest high. It is usually used when the camera alternates between speakers in a stretch of dialogue.

But by varying the angle of the camera in a medium shot, the audience's perception of the actor can be changed. Captain Kirk seems to be a dynamic character because we often see him filmed from a low camera angle. Such an angle makes a character appear stronger, more powerful, and sometimes even dangerous. A good example is the shot of Spock attacking Kirk in "This Side of Paradise." Seen from Kirk's floor-level point of view Spock is very menacing, as he holds a metal bench over his head.

On the other hand, a high-angle shot makes the actor look weak and helpless. In the reverse of the above-mentioned scene, Kirk lies on the floor, raising an ineffectual hand against the rage of Spock. It is an uncharacterisitc position for the captain to be in, and the drama and our involvement with it is heightened.

A good example of how all three medium shots are used to enhance characterization are those of Trelane in "The Squire of Gothos." When Trelane has Kirk cornered, he is shot from a low angle, emphasizing his strength. But when Kirk breaks Trelane's sword, the camera moves to eye level. Trelane has now lost the upper hand; he and Kirk are on a more equal footing. Then when confronted by his parents, Trelane is shot from above; now he is a weak little boy, deprived of his former strength and about to be disciplined by his parents.

A "bird's-eye view," where the camera is placed over the set pointing straight down, makes the objects being filmed look small and insignificant. This was done in the opening of "Arena," when the landing party materialized on Cestus III and found it destroyed.

When the camera trades places with one of the actors and we see what *he* sees, we have a "point-of-view" shot—a subjective camera angle. Such a shot makes us identify with the actor to a great degree, as in the cuts from Kirk staring dumbly at the ceiling to the whirling neural neutralizer light that is the cause of his torment. It is as if we were in the chair. In "Devil in the Dark," director Joseph Pevney uses the point-of-view shot to great effect. In the early scenes, we see attacks on the miners from the Horta's point of view, a common type of shot in "monster" movies. Later, however, when we realize that the creature is only trying to protect its eggs, the same type of shot allows us to identify with the Horta rather than with the humans. It has now become the pursued, they the attackers. Emotions such as fear, paranoia, insanity, etc, can be effectively communicated by the use of a subjective camera angle. In "The Tholian Web," a fish-eye lens gives us a totally alien, distorted view of Spock through the eyes of the temporarily insane Chekov.

Also interesting is the way onscreen objects are positioned in the film frame. A director may arrange elements within the frame much as a painter does, with the most important elements being given emphasis by placement. For example, in "This Side of Paradise," as Spock approaches one of the spore plants, it is in the foreground directly in front of the camera, seemingly dwarfing the Vulcan. By this placement, we are warned that the plant will pose a danger to Spock. As he moves closer to it, the sense of danger heightens. A character may also be given a sense of alienation by placing him or her away from others. A perfect example of this is the beautifully framed shot in "Miri" where we see Kirk, McCoy, and Janice Rand grouped together on the right while Miri is set off alone on the extreme left of the frame. Without anything being said, we can immediately see that she is not part of the group. She is unnecessary and alone. Characters can also be "framed" within the frame to illustrate isolation, helplessness, or inner turmoil. In "City," Edith Keeler is first seen framed by the stairs leading to the cellar; Kirk and Spock were earlier framed by the oval opening of the Guardian of Forever. Gary Mitchell is framed by the doorway of his cell in "Where No Man Has Gone Before"; in "Dagger of the Mind," Spock's arms form a frame around Dr. Van Gelder's head during the mind meld. By compressing the area which the frame shoots, and showing people in a cramped space, a feeling of claustrophobic tension is conveyed—as in the scenes inside the shuttlecraft in "The Galileo Seven," or Captain Pike's cell in "The Menagerie."

The camera may also be tilted to one side or the other (this is known as a Dutch Tilt shot) to give a feeling of imbalance or mental distortion. In "Wink of an Eye," the distorted time sense of the accelerated Scalosians is nicely illustrated with a Dutch Tilt. When Kirk drinks his drugged coffee, the movement of the others is seen in slow motion while the camera slowly tilts until the set is seen at a noticeable angle. When the action returns to the others, the camera is at a normal angle, and it tilts again when the scene cuts to Kirk and the Scalosians. A point-of-view shot is often filmed with a Dutch Tilt and a fish-eye lens to give an eerie and effective feeling of disorientation. A Dutch Tilt is also effective in conveying fast action, such as a chase.

Lighting can also be used effectively to heighten the drama of a scene. In "The Enemy Within," the violent half of Kirk is bombarded with harsh lighting (often from underneath) which makes his features sharp and evil-looking. The mild Kirk is filmed with soft lighting, blurring his features slightly and giving an impression of benign friendliness and familiarity. The same kind of soft lighting was usually used on women to enhance their feminity, but lighting is just as often used to highlight the features of a

person's face and give him a much stronger appearance. Such was the case when Kirk was harshly lit by a single light on an otherwise darkened transporter panel in "This Side of Paradise"—as was the Romulan Commander in "Balance of Terror," the Organians in "Errand of Mercy," and the Keeper in "Menagerie." In "The Enterprise Incident," harsh lighting was used to bring out the strength of the female Romulan commander, blurring her feminity and giving her a much more forceful veneer.

Often the dramatic impact of a violent scene can be heightened by *not* showing the violence. When the children in "Miri" begin beating Kirk, the camera moves to a medium shot of a young girl looking down at the violence and giggling. When the Black Knight spears McCoy in "Shore Leave," we see a close-up of the doctor's anguished death scream. In "A Private Little War," Tyree is seen from a low angle with a rock raised over his head. We know without the violence being shown that he has been bashing in the head of one of the men who killed his wife. The anguish seen on his face as he is moved to violence is more striking than the actual violence itself could have been.

Much can also be told by the way in which transitions between scenes are made. One device is the fade-out, where the screen fades to black. This is usually used in television to indicate the end of an act, but is occasionally used to indicate a very long passage of time or to give particular emphasis to a character's inner turmoil or decision-making. Used more often is the dissolve, where one image fades out while the following one fades in. It usually indicates passage of time or distance. The standard way to bridge scenes is with a direct cut, where two pieces of film are simply joined together, and a scene "cuts" to another scene. Action in cuts is simultaneous or quickly consecutive.

An interesting aspect about cutting is that transitions between scenes may indicate a time duration of minutes, hours, days, years . . . even centuries! Everyone remembers the shot in Stanley Kubrick's brilliant *2001: A Space Odyssey* where an ape throws the bone used as a tool for the first time up into the air, and it suddenly becomes a rocket flying through space to the moon. Thousands of years passed between one frame of film and the next.

The soundtrack can also connect one scene to another. In "Errand of Mercy," we cut from Kirk speaking to Ayelborne in the bugged council chamber to Kor in his office listening in on them. It is the continuation of Kirk's voice that connects the two scenes. Kirk's log entries are often used to connect scenes, fill in lapses of time, and provide us with information we have not been shown.

The editing of a film or television show—the selecting of shots, transitions, etc.—contributes greatly to its success. For instance, in *Star Wars* the fast-paced editing helps to keep us interested. The same is true of Star Trek. The action flows quickly and smoothly, allowing for as much story as possible to be crammed into the one-hour episode. When Kirk decides to beam down to a planet, the action immediately cuts to the transporter room or even to the planet itself.

Effective editing is a hallmark of Star Trek. A few outstanding examples: In "Arena," Kirk vanishes from the bridge and Uhura screams. Then there's a quick cut to the evil Gorn. We immediately know the danger Kirk will face. In "Day of the Dove," there is a cut from Kang to Mara's torn dress. We immediately know of his suspicions. In "Errand of Mercy," Kor states that even he is under surveillance, and we see a shot of the camera monitoring his office. In "The Deadly Years," there is a series of cuts from Chekov to the dead body to the landing party as they hear his scream of terror. "Conscience of the King" opens with a shot of Anton Karidian holding a knife poised to strike. We quickly learn that he is only acting on stage, but it is effective in startling us as well as symbolic of the man he eventually is revealed to be.

Most episodes ended with a shot of the *Enterprise* in space heading off to its next mission, but a beautiful example of how disregarding this convention heightens the dramatic impact is seen in "City on the Edge of Forever." After the landing party has beamed back to the ship, the camera lingers on the Guardian. The ending would not have been as depressing—or as memorable—if the majestic *Enterprise* had been shown receding into the distance.

In closing, it must be noted that Star Trek was only one of dozens of television shows in the sixties which had outstanding direction, editing, cutting, and cinematography. Compare Star Trek or any other show of its era that was made with care and love to some of the current atrocities on television and you will definitely notice a difference.

TREK ROUNDTABLE—Letters from our Readers

Robert Walsdorff
Green Brier, Tenn.

I've enjoyed the latest edition of *Trek* magazine, as I've enjoyed all of them. It never fails to amaze me how many varied and interesting articles *Trek* can find to write about for just one subject. This letter is written mainly in response to your request for letters to include in an all-new magazine devoted solely to letters from your readers. I felt I should limit my letter to just the topic of the movie, for to answer all the questions you asked would probably make the letter too long.

Watching *Star Trek: The Motion Picture* was like paying a visit on old friends. It was pleasurable, comfortable. Everything and every moment of *STTMP* was enjoyable, but something was missing. It wasn't that anything there was poorly done; it was what *wasn't* there that made the motion picture a little disappointing.

Perhaps my expectations, like those of all Star Trek fans, were a bit too high. I didn't enter the theater wondering how good the film might be, as I usually do with movies. Instead I was hoping for a masterpiece. I left satisfied and disappointed. Satisfied because all the original cast members were there, looking and acting the way they should, and the storyline and atmosphere were clearly within the "world" and philosophy of the Star Trek I knew and loved. The changes were only minor ones, as far as I was concerned; the essential elements of Star Trek were not changed. I was disappointed because probably Star Trek's greatest strength was in its scripts, which were so original, involving, well structured, exciting, dramatic, thought-provoking, imaginative, and unique. It seemed like those who made *STTMP* thought of everything but a plot. While it is true that the novel based on the movie clarified many of the dangling ends of the film and added much more detail to the plot and the background of the characters during the intervening years, most people who have seen the movie have not and will not read the novel. They will judge *STTMP* only by what was presented on the screen.

What is most disturbing about this is the effect it may have on Star Trek's future. The budget of the film was so enormous that it would have to appeal to a larger audience than just Star Trek's strongest supporters to make a profit. My fear was that if the film flopped, most likely that would be the end of Star Trek. If Star Trek is to continue it must be now while conditions still make it possible. My hope was that *STTMP* would be just the beginning of new Star Trek stories and not the culmination of the saga. *STTMP* seemed too weak to do that. I still hope I am wrong. While it is true that the film is really much more complex and better than it appears to be at first, as several excellent articles in Trek point out, the fact still remains that the general public only saw it once and most people have judged it by what appears on the surface and on first impressions, and that isn't overly impressive.

Still, I think the public will give Star Trek another chance. It still has an enormous reputation, and while most people, like me, found *STTMP* lacking, very few hated it, and the film, while not perfect, was far from disastrous and in no way damaged Star Trek's reputation or appeal. I'm sure that if a good follow-up film should be made, the public would come en masse to see it, and not stay away because of the flaws in the first film.

I hope that if a new film is made all of the original cast members will be in it. If any are not, it would be better to drop the characters from the film than to get any other actors to play the parts, even if such included all the regulars. The actors are so closely identified with their roles that no other actors, no matter how talented, could ever be accepted as the characters. If Star Trek must be done without the original cast members, it would be better to have all new characters set in the Star Trek world. By that I mean that the new characters would be on the Starship *Enterprise* in the same time period, the Federation would still exist, as would the various peoples who inhabit the Star Trek world, and the philosophy would remain consistent with the original Star Trek as should all elements of Star Trek's "world." To me, that would be the only acceptable alternative other than discontinuing Star Trek altogether. Naturally, doing Star Trek with all the original cast members is what I would really like to see again.

I hope that if there is a new movie made there will be more concentration on the characters and dramatic situations, rather than special effects. Special effects were never one of Star Trek's strong points, but it hardly mattered. I didn't need to see everything to believe it! For example, I did not need to see the ship full-size to actually believe it was that big. In *STTMP* we see modern-day Earth and Vulcan, but the moments are too brief. I can understand as far as Earth is concerned, since the possibilities of what it may be like three hundred years or so from now can be so varied that few would accept any one individual's interpretation. Still, the imaginative possibilities are great, and this an area that could possibly be explored. Less demanding but just as interesting would be to really see more of Vulcan. I'd like to see that in a new film it if could be integrated into the plot naturally. I would also like to see possibly more background information of what occurred to the various characters in the intervening years. Most important, though, is an interesting story involving the main characters in a dramatic way, and a story that isn't just a reworking of an old series plot, yet is consistent with what has been presented before as far as Star Trek's world is concerned.

That is really demanding a great deal, but Star Trek has accomplished a great deal before, achieving a standard that no other television series has ever reached. It is my belief and hope that Star Trek can and will do it again.

Mrs. J.H. Syck
Bellefontaine, Ohio

I've just finished reading *Trek* 18 from cover to cover (nonstop!) and I must tell you I have never read in one place so many of my own feelings and opinions about Star Trek. (Could that possibly be why I enjoyed it so much?)

I am a thirty-seven-year-old housewife who, as Mary Rottler said so elegantly in her Roundtable letter, has tried repeatedly to talk myself out of my singleminded devotion to ST (and particularly to Bill Shatner).

All to no avail. My husband and sons tease me but I simply reply that they have the same reaction to a football game or boxing match so why shouldn't I be allowed the same freedom? Live and let live. (See how well I'd fit into the twenty-third century?)

I would love to see *Trek* print at some time a complete list of Star Trek novels and books. I think I have all of them ("The Price of the Phoenix" and "Entropy Effect" being two particular favorites). My books were collected over the past several years, but it was strictly a chance situation; one book mentioning another, a line in a magazine. Someone coming to ST only now would surely find such a list invaluable.

I am presently living in a very small town and have no one to share my views with or whom I can have read my ST stories for helpful criticism. (Although I really write for my own amusement, my husband keeps asking when the great American novel will be finished!)

Beth Carlson's "A Woman Looks at Jim's Little Black Book" was very insightful. Kirk probably appreciates women more than anyone can know; he's simply realistic and accepts the fact that personal relationships take a back seat to the fate of the galaxy. He could hardly feel otherwise and hope to fulfill his mission.

I found "A Letter from Judith Wolper" very interesting and well thought-out. Again, a very exact representation of my own feelings, especially in regard to the motion picture. It was a disappointment (which didn't keep me from seeing it fifteen times); however, I saw a great deal more in it after reading the novelization by Gene Roddenberry, and I place a great deal of the blame on the film editors (obviously not ST fans) who chose special-effects scenes over those which focused on characterizations and "the friendship."

Which brings me to the final article I wanted to comment on—"Friendship in the Balance" by Joyce Tullock. This article presented to me in black and white exactly why I love Star Trek so much—the friendship. The love—yes, love—these three men have for each other is, to me, the essence of Star Trek. This "greater love has no man" personified in them gives me a hope for the future of mankind (a lot to lay on a television series, I realize). Perhaps that is why my favorite episode is "The Empath." How wonderful this friendship is and what a magnificent thing if all men in the twentieth century could learn to accept each other as these do. I will cherish the article always.

I apologize for rambling on so, but as I said, I really have no one with whom I can share my feelings and have them understood.

I must also add that I would go anywhere, anytime, to see Bill Shatner. He is just the most fantastic actor. People have asked him about being typecast as Jim Kirk—well, I think it is the other way around—Kirk is very much Bill Shatner!

Denise Habel
Holy Cross, La.

I've been a Star Trek fan for about six years on and off. I'm eighteen years old and live on a farm in eastern Iowa. I write poetry and stories and read . . . all the time I read.

It's hard to believe, looking at my overflowing bookshelves (a row and a half devoted to pure Trek), that I ever disliked reading. Now it seems that if I don't have a book with me, part of me is missing! My room is flooded with paperbacks; SF, fantasy, horror, adventure, etc., I'm practically on a first-name basis with all the librarians in the area, and I frequent the bookstore so much they ought to make me a permanent resident.

But how did all of this happen? How, in a few short years, could I have gone from a typical unconcerned kid to someone who reads constantly, has learned to write— and *loves* to write—poetry and an occasional story? Someone who has come alive to this world and all its possibilities both in the present and—especially—in the future.

Well, you can blame it on my grandpa—and Star Trek. A long time ago (it seems like) and far, far away from my present condition, my grandpa bought me a book at the local K-Mart. A book that (unbeknownst to me then) marked the turning point of my life, one that would change it forever. If you haven't already guessed, it was a Star Trek book; number nine of the James Blish series, to be exact. One story was all it took to hook me, and the rest proceeded to haul me irresistibly into the thoroughly "fascinating" world of SF (and most especially Star Trek) fandom.

After that it was like an explosion. I grabbed all the Blish books I could find and started watching Star Trek on television. (Mainly, the shows I'd never seen, of which there were quite a few. Where I'd been before I don't know. Maybe Outer Mongolia.)

That first explosion left a kind of fire in me, and an urge to read . . . and read . . . and read! It was like suddenly discovering a whole new universe. I started rushing hither and yon, begging and borrowing money to buy books. (I was only in grade school at the time and the only money I had was from birthdays and Christmas.) Even so, I soon had all the Blish books, including his one novel, *Spock Must Die!* Then came the drought. No more new Star Trek books. The shows on only late at night. The animated episodes still a year or so away. It was like starting a fire, only to have it abandoned to be washed out by the rain.

My enthusiasm waned, and though I still bought a lot of SF and fantasy books, Star Trek to me was dead. Empty spaces left by its passing slowly were filled in with other things. But there was an ache inside that nothing could ever erase. Months and then years went by, and Star Trek came to brighten up Saturday-morning programming. But it couldn't brighten up my life; the necessary vital spark wasn't there. Even the brilliant Alan Dean Foster adaptations of the animated shows failed to revive it.

I loved Star Trek and the picture of a golden future it painted so well, but I realized that maybe it was time to move on. After all, who really cared about a television show that was dropped years ago? (Silly me!) Maybe I was the only one who had cared so much. Those few shows were so beautiful, so good, that there must surely have been others who noticed, who cared. But it didn't appear to be that way. It seemed as if I was all alone.

I was ignorant at the time of the true scope of Star Trek fandom—the conventions, clubs, fanzines; indeed, of the simple fact that there *were* others out there who cared. Hundreds and thousands of others.

Maybe I would have moved on after all if it hadn't been for one thing: that beautiful day I entered my favorite bookstore and found, sitting on a bottom shelf, a Star Trek book! It was *Star Trek Lives*, and I soon realized, boy, does it ever! My first response was pure joy. Here was proof at last that there were others who felt the same way about Star Trek as did I. I was not alone! My second reaction was envy. Look at all this great stuff I had missed and was missing! Conventions, clubs, parties, souvenirs, fanzines, parties, stars, parties. (Yeah, I *love* a good party!)

That old flame, never really extinguished, was fired up again. The books flooded in again. I began haunting the bookstores more than ever. (When is the new shipment coming in? Next week? Oh well, see you then.)

The next few years come back to me in a haze: learning to write poetry, seeing *Star Wars* three times, being able to recognize Star Trek and SF authors by their work, seeing *Close Encounters*, never missing a Star Trek show (even if it meant staying up late nights to do so), seeing *Empire* six times, and finally writing to the Welcommittee. They sent me names and addresses and soon I was being initiated into the wonders I'd only read (and dreamed of) before.

I bought some fanzines and was soon building up the nerve to send in some of my own poems and stories. Wonder of wonders, they liked them! This spurred me on to try more of this new hobby—writing. (At the moment, I'm working on my fourth story, with several others, including a novel, in the planning stage.)

After that, the ball really started rolling. One of my poems got chosen to be published. *Spin Dizzie* accepted more of my work, including a new project of mine, a Star

Trek filksong. And finally, Star Trek came to my favorite institution, the movie theater!

Now that I look back, I can see how Star Trek put me where I am today—a high school graduate bound for college and a possible career in English. It gave me my dream of someday being a poet or possibly a writer. Star Trek made me more aware of life and all its joys more than anything had before. With only the simple power of its people, its stories, and most important of all, its ideas.

It hasn't been easy. My family and friends consider me a little nuts for being so involved in "just a TV show." But Star Trek is more than that to me. It's a promise. The hope of a bright new tomorrow just waiting for us to make it happen. I love you, Star Trek. You've made me cry, made me laugh, made me glad to be alive. But most of all, you've opened my eyes to the true magic of fandom. And if it takes a little work to be a part of that magic . . . so be it! I'm having far too much fun not to ever quit. Thank you, Star Trek. And thank you everyone who is involved in it and cares enough to help other find it.

P.S.: This started out as a simple letter to your magazine, but as you can see, it ended up more a story of how I found Star Trek. (Or how it found me.) You might call this a love letter to Star Trek, and it probably is. Nothing in this world has affected me more than ST and somehow I just had to say that. Thank you and keep on *Trekin'*!!!

Mark C. Henrie
Mt. Carmel, Pa.

I just finished reading *Trek* 18, and I must say that I was once again most pleased with this magazine. It truly deserves to be "the mouthpiece of Star Trek fandom," for nowhere else can one find articles of such an intelligent nature. I constantly tease my older brother, who is a *Star Wars* fan, that he and his people will never come close to the intensity of Star Trek fandom. *Star Wars* is transitory; Star Trek is definitely not. Several years ago, in my opinion, it was *Trek* that brought our favorite television series out of the realm of popular culture and put it into an honored place of immortality. I must say a thank you to G.B. Love and Walter Irwin for the part they have played in propelling Star Trek fandom to a level above any other science fiction production past, present, and, most likely, future. I must, however, warn you to keep your guard up against mediocrity. Only by accepting the *best* material will you be able to continue as the most intelligent fanzine currently in publication here on Terra.

Well, enough of the seemingly mindless praise. I have only a few comments on this specific issue. First of all, kudos to Eleanor LaBerge for an excellent article which exemplifies all I stated in my opening paragraph.

Next, in Judith Wolper's exceptionally long but well-written letter, the first point she makes is that Star Trek somehow serves as a balance between idealism and realism in regard to war. Now, I must admit that my political philosophies tend toward the hawkish end of the spectrum, but I see ST making a much different point. For me, the crew of the *Enterprise* exhibited idealism in excess of realism, and I believe that was meant to be. It is a sign of how good the writing of the episodes was that a divergence of opinion such as this can exist. Surely, the theme of many an episode was pacifism and how it is at times good and bad. Actually, it tries at many junctions to illuminate the Morality of Pacifism and the Morality of War. As in many episodes, both sides of the issue are given a fair shake, but what I must take exception to is Ms. Wolper's basic premises. Clearly, Star Trek dealt with the Morality of War in idealistic terms which should be, but of necessity cannot be, applied to our all too real world. The world of Star Trek fandom consists of idealists partially because those who wrote the episodes were dealing with ideals.

Well, I'm already going overboard, so I must say good-bye. But just one last comment: I must say that I enjoyed Uhura's background history.

Jeff Scott
New Market, Ontario, Canada

I have recently completed reading *The Best of Trek #3* and I have got to admit it is the best Star Trek book I have out of (my) assorted Star Trek reading material.

However, there were a few things said about *Star Trek: The Motion Picture* that were rocks that broke the horta's back. For the past year I have been hearing about how badly *STTMP* was done. Well, I just want to say that I loved it. Actually, I don't think I could have not liked it. I was brought up on Star Trek by my older brother and was a member of a Star Trek club for three years (until it folded). Several years ago, when I heard about the movie, I, as a young Trekkie in the making, was so excited I thought Star Trek would never die. I started losing hope, though, after about the third delay, and the rumors of cancellation of the movie didn't help my optimism. It wasn't until a year before *STTMP* was released that I read a positive report. In this report I saw scenes from the movie. Which brings me to the point of my letter:

People have continually been criticizing the changes made and the plot. Well, at first I was surprised and a bit mad about the changes, but I started thinking about it and it all made sense.

First of all, the Klingons: The complaint was about the change in appearance, but who says they changed? Now, let's pretend for a moment: Suppose we are all Klingons, watching a terrific show called *Star Wreck*. On this show, the villains are humans, but we only see white humans on the series. Later, a movie is made of this series, and instead of white humans, we see black humans. Would we Klingons complain that the producers "invented" these new types of humans? I rest my case.

Now consider the uniforms. Stop for a moment and get a picture of yourself taken ten years ago. Are you wearing in it what you are wearing now? Of course not. Styles are going to change as long as there are styles. At least we are rid of those shirts that rip apart at the slightest tug.

Then comes the design of the *Enterprise*, changed almost completely from the *Enterprise* we all knew and loved. However, look at the space shuttle that was recently launched. Does it look anything like the Apollo craft? Not at all. You have to give those twenty-third-century engineers a little bit of credit; they want to progress whether we twentieth-century onlookers like it or not. This applies also to the change in the transporter effect. Considering that most, if not all, of the mechanisms have been changed, it will affect the energy beam, even if it doesn't help the actual performance.

So you see, with a little imagination, it all makes sense.

128 THE BEST OF TREK #5

Steve Aprahamian
Columbus, Ohio

I have with much pleasure read the new *Best of Trek #3*, and many of the things in it moved me greatly to write.

A comment I have concerns some of the writings about *Star Trek: The Motion Picture*. It seems that people just don't understand the ending. In Lynn Adams' article, "Parallels in *STTMP* Vs. the Series," she states at the end of the article: "After Decker's sacrifice, V'Ger dissolves itself into nothingness. Although not quite as dramatic as Nomad's death (see The Changeling), the result is the same" (p. 60). Also, in "A Letter from Judith Wolper," Wolper states, ". . . we never did see what happened to V'Ger. Just because Decker and Ilia joined with V'Ger doesn't necessarily mean that V'Ger was rendered harmless" (p. 89).

Vejur (to use Roddenberry's spelling) was only "harmful" because it wanted to unite with its creator. It would stop at nothing within its power to accomplish this goal. Vejur was a child. It had knowledge but no use for it. Roddenberry states in the *STTMP* novel: "Vejur was almost capable of traveling into these higher dimensions . . . [but] Vejur was trapped here in its present dimension of existence. . . . It was so completely and magnificently logical that its accumulation of knowledge was totally useless" (pp. 217-18).

When Decker and Ilia merge with Vejur, it obtains many human and Deltan characteristics, including creativity, drive, curiosity, and the abilty to use the vast knowledge to travel to higher dimensions of existence, not to "dissolve into nothingness" as stated. The result is *not* the same as Nomad's death. Decker, Ilia, and Vejur were *reborn* into a new type of entity; an evolution of the human race. As Spock says at the end: "We witnessed a birth—perhaps also a direction in which some of us may evolve" (p. 250). Evolution is *not* the same as death!

Another thing that really surprised me was people's comments concerning Kendra Hunter's "Characterization Rape" (*Best of Trek #2*). Judith Wolper and Mary Phelan in their letters to *Trek* almost seem disgusted by the idea of a homosexual relationship between Kirk and Spock.

Phelan states that Kirk's saving Spock from *pon farr* via homosexuality "may be somewhat possible but highly improbable . . . the social mores of his [Spock's] race would forbid it" (p. 76). Wolper states: "In the mainstream of our society, there is only one relationship in which sex is acceptable . . . between a man and a woman" (p. 87). Hunter contends in her article that after Spock would be saved via homosexuality with Kirk, Kirk "allows the seeds of guilt to form and grow until they not only destroy the relationship but the man himself" (*BOT #2*, p. 82).

Why do people assign our prejudices to the future? One would imagine that in the future there would be no restriction placed on what consenting adults may do when no harm is done to anyone. The people who are offended by homosexual relations between two consenting adults are of the same mentality as those who are offended by relations between two different races. When "Plato's Stepchildren" was broadcast in 1968, the network took a lot of static about Kirk's kissing Uhura. A white man kissing a black woman—"disgusting." In the thirteen years since then much has changed and now interracial marriages can be shown on television without any static whatever. In the two hundred years until Star Trek's time one can imagine much more of the same mentality.

In the *STTMP* novel, Kirk "himself" comments about this very subject. He states: "I have no moral or other objections to physical love in any of its Earthly, alien, and mixed forms." He also states, ". . . I have always found my best gratification in that creature *woman*" (p. 22). It only seems logical to assume that many others would have no moral or other objections, so why should it be "improbable" or make Kirk feel so guilty?

Some of the comments in Rebecca Hoffman's "Vulcan As a Patriarchy" (*BOT #3*) also need reply. In it she used as a suggestion for patriarchy the conversation between Sarek and Amanda in "Journey to Babel" after the incident about Spock's "teddy bear" which he was fond of as a boy. She quoted Sarek to Amanda: "You embarrassed Spock this evening. Not even a *mother* may do that. He is a Vulcan" (p. 171). This is not, as she states, an unlikely restriction in a matriarchy. It is more unlikely in a patriarchy. The "not even" implies that the mothers have a certain independence to do much to their children. But as

Sarek says, *not even* a mother (implying that she may do many other things) is permitted to embarrass a Vulcan child.

She also states in her article that "a woman's cycle . . . is controlled by lunar influences. On starships birth control is necessary . . . to regulate a woman's cycle. For without the lunar influences, those cycles become totally out of kilter" (p. 172). I don't know where she got her information, but if a woman's cycle were controlled by lunar influences as she states: (1) Every cycle would be totally predictable just as are tides, which *are* affected by lunar influences. The fact is, "The absolutely regular cycle is so rare as to be either a myth or a medical curiosity" (J.S. Hyde, *Understanding Human Sexuality*, p. 73). (2) All women would have a cycle at the exact same time—only when the moon is right—which is just not true. The fact is that the cycle has *nothing* whatsoever to do with lunar influences, but is affected by hormones. This is the reason that birth-control pills are capable of providing a woman with a regular cycle, since the pills regulate the hormone levels. It shocks me that in this day and age a woman can still think that a cycle is dependent on lunar influences.

My last comment concerns Larry Nemecek's letter in the Roundtable and his comments on "The Alternative Factor." He stated that "the writer did not understand the nature of antimatter, for he apparently believes that only a hunk of matter and its exact physical double in antimatter can set off the gigantic annihilation" (p. 75), but then states that "any antimatter coming into contact with any *matter . . . will* cause the blow" (p. 75).

I agree with his beliefs that the author did not understand the nature of antimatter but it seems that Nemecek understand it even less. In *Elements of Physics*, a text by G. Shortly and D. Williams, antimatter is discussed: "Quantum mechanics requires that every particle have an antiparticle. . . . When a particle collides with its antiparticle, the pair undergoes annihilation" (p. 944). Note that the pair annihilate each other, *not* the entire universe as implied by the story and by Nemecek. An antiparticle is "identical but opposite" to the corresponding particle. For example, the electron has an antielectron, which is called the positron. They both have the exact same mass, but the electron has one unit of negative charge. The positron (antielectron) will not annihilate the entire universe, or anything else for that matter, when it comes into contact with other matter, e.g. neutrons or protons. Particles only react with their antiparticles and will only annihilate *each other*, releasing energy.

There has been speculation by physicists (Williard Libby and others) that a major matter-antimatter interaction has already taken place on Earth. In 1908 in northern Siberia a meteorite caused extensive damage, and the physicists feel that the meteorite "may have consisted of antimatter" (Shortley and Williams, p. 946). It would also be very, very illogical to allow starships to be run on matter-antimatter engines, as we have been told they do, if when they met the entire universe would annihilate. It just would *not* be worth the risk!

I feel that I may have been slightly nitpicky, but Star Trek means a lot to me and I feel if people write, they should think about what they write and maybe do some research on their own. Star Trek is a learning and entertainment experience, and although the shows were not always perfect, that does not mean we shouldn't try to be as accurate as possible. Thank you for this opportunity to write and air my thoughts.

Rowena Warner
Louisville, Ky.

I am one of the rejuvenated Trekkers, having let my interest wane during the seventies and having it rebound with twice the fervor on January 18, 1980. On that fateful day I was perusing my local bookstore and came upon a copy of the novelization of *Star Trek: The Motion Picture*. I remembered my earlier interest, so I decided to give it a try. That night about 8:45 I began page one with slightly less than tepid enthusiasm. At 9:30 P.M., January 18, 1980, I was a renewed, rejuvenated, reactivated Trekker. I began watching the reruns and bought all the Star Trek and Star Trek–related material I could find. All of this lent fuel to my passive interest in astronomy, and I began purchasing books by such authors as Asimov, Einstein, Sagan, Clarke, Nichols, etc. This in turn led to an investment in a small telescope. So I now, literally and figuratively, have stars in my eyes.

It turns out January 18, 1980, was the most expensive day in my life. I am now debating on figuring up exactly how much I have spent on ST and my related hobby (help, I need Spock!) and sending bills in porportionate amounts to all the individuals connected with Star Trek. Gene Roddenberry would receive the largest bill, Leonard Nimoy slightly lower, William Shatner and DeForest Kelley equal and only slightly less than Nimoy's. The rest of the cast, technicians, directors, writers, etc, would get slightly lower bills. I wouldn't miss a person, because, after all, every one of them was involved in this conspiracy to get me to expand my horizons and open my mind to new knowledge, new ideas, the true meaning of IDIC, the value of friendship, and the curiosity, love, courage, and stubborness of mankind, whether in the twentieth century or the twenty-third century. Congratulations, ladies and gentlemen: your conspiracy succeeded far better than you will ever realize. But keep an eye on that mailbox!

I would like to express my opinions and raise some questions.

1. I have come to the conclusion that Vulcans do not quite suppress their emotions as much as they want us to believe. Take for instance, T'Pau. She did not seem a bit surprised that Spock introduced Kirk and McCoy as his friends. She even made the comment that Spock chose his friends well. Obviously, friendship is an emotional attachment. What about T'Pring? We all know the woman was crazy, but you had to admit she had guts. She felt love or passion for Stonn, and just the same as bragged to Spock that she would have Stonn one way or another. Speaking of Stonn, what about his emotional outburst when T'Pring chose Kirk as her champion? That was like a sudden thunderclap on a sunny day.

2. I have read many opinions regarding the crew's behavior in "The Galileo Seven." I believe, as many do, that all that insubordination was a bit hard to take. Granted, the crew probably knew they could get away with more with Mr. Spock than they could with Captain Kirk, but that was a bit much. My biggest disappointment was Dr. McCoy. He might tell Mr. Spock his heart was put together wrong, but he would never discuss Spock with another crewman and he would never publicly side against

Spock, inciting insubordination. This is not the Dr. McCoy I have grown to know and love.

3. I would like to make a brief comment concerning "Turnabout Intruder." Like most Trekkers, I consider that definitely not one of my favorite episodes. However, I think the "moral of the story" was important, although it was so cleverly disguised as to be almost indistinguishable. I think it pointed out the fact that each of us, irrespective of sex, race, or culture, has limitations. We must recognize that fact and accept it. These limitations become a fault within us only when we try to blame them on imaginary exterior forces. Dreams are necessary to each of us, but when those dreams are unobtainable, we must release them before they become a nightmare.

4. Much has been written in connection with the Kirk/Spock relationship, but one aspect of the friendship I find interesting is Kirk's reactions. For a man known for his open display of emotions, he does a good job of hiding his affection for Spock. At times he suppresses his emotions more than Spock when it comes to displaying that affection or concern. In "Operation Annihilate," when Spock was attacked I was almost shocked by Kirk's rather harsh, "Spock, are you all right?" It seemed more like a command than a plea. I don't really feel he is doing this so much in deference to Spock, but more because he is reluctant to admit this friendship to himself. We all know Kirk's attempts to avoid any lasting relationships with women, but I think this carries over to any type of relationship; perhaps because his past friendships—Gary Mitchell, Garrovick, and Janice Lester—all ended disastrously, with him being personally involved. I get the feeling part of him accepts Spock's friendship, but especially in times of danger, part of him shies away because he is afraid of another disaster and doesn't want to be hurt again.

I'm afraid I have gotten quite carried away, but I have never had a chance like this before. It seems that once I got started I couldn't stop. Thank you for doing what you are doing so well.

Carole Parisi
Portland, Me.

I have never had the opportunity to peer into an issue of *Trek* magazine, but one day during a sojourn in a bookstore I came upon some most fascinating items: the *Best of Trek* series. Naturally, being true to my title as Trekker, I quickly snatched them off the shelves. (I hastily point out that I paid for them as well!) Now, not very long after that, and halfway through #3 (amazing that I'm putting it aside long enough to write this), I am pleased to say that I have truly enjoyed each wonderful feature; especially the parody "Command Decision Crisis," which had me laughing till nothing short of the end of the story or a Vulcan nerve pinch could've stopped me.

These *Trek* books are a true blessing to adventure-seeking Terrans like myself. I am sorry to say, however, that there has been a lamentable lack of features written about my personal favorite, Engineer Scott.

Mr. Scott's character offers 1,001-plus possibilities for exploration, and I hope this will cause someone to investigate them. I would do so myself were it not that my time is so greedily demanded by the university at which I am a senior art student. Painting being my major study, this "creator" is now in the process of completing a life-size (or slightly larger than life-size) oil painting of Mr. Scott.

Before closing my communication, I would like to ask you two questions:

1. This one's been bugging me for a while. Is G.B. Love male or female? I ask because I'd love to think one of the editors is a woman. I say, equality in all fields, but especially in Star fields!

2. I once read that Mr. Scott is second in popularity only to our beloved Mr. Spock. Yet since that time I've heard many things that would prove otherwise; that Captain Kirk and Dr. McCoy have more of a following. Could you solve this mystery for me?

Editor's Note: In the various pools we've run and judging by the mail we receive, Kirk and Spock are tied for "most popular," just as they have always been. McCoy is always a strong third, and Mr. Scott usually finishes fourth, but is occasionally supplanted by Uhura support-

ers. We hope your disappointment at this news will be somewhat assuaged by the appearance of a Scott biography in this volume. G.B. Love is a male. A quick glance at the table of contents of this volume and the previous four will quickly tell you that women contribute almost half of the articles we run. And women have always been in the vast majority on our subscription rolls. So fear not, Carole, the ladies have always been an integral part of Trek . . . and we trust they will continue to be.

Pam Jenkins
Long Beach, Cal.

I just finished reading *The Best of Trek #3.* It was *great!* I especially liked the articles about Spock's career and "The Klingons (?)" by Leslie Thompson. *However,* my all-time favorite from *BOT #3* has to be "Command Decision Crisis"! I *loved* it! I laughed so hard that halfway through page three of the story, I looked to the end of it to see how many pages were left—I was not at all certain that I would be able to take it! (Gasp) *Seventeen more* pages? I nearly "passed out" at hearing Spock referred to as "Skunk." And the "sight" of "Skunk" *sidling* into a room and "stropping" his tongue was almost more than I could handle. My overall impression of the parody was that it could also have been titled "More Lines We'd Like to Hear." By the way, I do hope your parody was not a criticism of "The Enterprise Incident," as the "Rumbleon commander" has a lot of friends out here, *me* included.

However, I do have some "nitpicking" to do. (It seems that letters to *Trek* are *always* doing that, doesn't it?)

In [Walter Irwin's] article on "The Other Federation Forces," you made the statement that the *Enterprise* "landed" on Rigel VII. As we all know, the *Enterprise* never landed *anywhere!* One must only hope that your unfortunate use of the word referred to the orbit of the *Enterprise,* rather than an actual *landing* on the surface of the planet.

Although I am fond of all the Star Trek characters, the articles in *Best of Trek* (#1) and #2 dealing with Mr. Spock are my very favorites. (I'm female, and *everyone* knows what women think about Spock! Those NBC execs had to be men!)

Ken Janasz
Leavenworth, Kan.

Thank you, Joyce Tullock.

There has been something bothering me about *Star Trek: The Motion Picture*, and your article, "Friendship—in the Balance," has solved it for me. You see, I never could really understand why McCoy was brought back. Surely Roddenberry wouldn't do it just so he could boast of uniting the entire original cast, or just so he could continue the Spock/McCoy feud. McCoy is a major character and could not be brought back for any flimsy reason. Yet it seemed he never really did anything except roam around the *Enterprise*. His medical scan of the Ilia-probe could easily have been performed by Dr. Chapel. And while McCoy is probably the best-qualified doctor to treat Spock, neither he nor Kirk could have predicted Spock's coming on board. True, according to the novel Spock's mind was touched by Kirk's when Kirk was called by Starfleet, but it is still a fact that Kirk was 100 percent surprised to see Spock when the turbolift doors opened. So why did Kirk get McCoy drafted?

Until your article, Joyce, I never realized how simple, yet vital, the reason was. Kirk gave us the entire reason in four words when he kept repeating to Bones, "I need you, badly." He didn't say this ship needs you, or we need you. Kirk specifically said, "*I* need you."

Kirk was miserable as an admiral. He was a desperate man when he literally stole command of the *Enterprise* from Decker. And Kirk had his doubts. Were his intentions really in the best interest of everyone, or just himself? He didn't know. Spock wasn't there. Only one other man could help him overcome his doubts and become the captain he used to be. That man—Dr. Leonard McCoy—was one of Kirk's closest friends.

And McCoy saw this. He knew that Dr. Chapel could perform the medical duties just as well as he. But here was his friend saying, "I need you." McCoy knew that Kirk would end up hating his promotion to admiral. He knew that one day Kirk would try anything to get the *Enterprise* back. And when he was drafted back into service, when the newly appointed captain of the *Enterprise* greeted him with an outstretched hand saying, "I need you, badly,"

McCoy knew that time had come. McCoy knew his friend, knew what made him tick. He saw how desperate Kirk was and how much Kirk needed him. McCoy could not and would not desert his friend. So he took Kirk's hand and Kirk knew that his friend would help him find the answers he needed.

And this is the primary reason McCoy was brought back. McCoy gave us an insight into how the years had affected Kirk. This one scene presented to us Kirk's doubts, guilts, drives, and the power of friendship without having to go into any long-winded speeches that would not have been even half as convincing. Star Trek is about people, and this is Star Trek.

If, eventually, new actors are cast as Kirk, Spock, McCoy, etc., these characters would no longer be the ones we've all grown to know. Shatner, Nimoy, Kelley, etc. have all brought their characters to life by injecting part of their own personalities into their roles. No other actor, no matter how great, could give Kirk the subtle gestures and inflections we have grown accustomed to and become familiar with. And after more than a decade of continuously watching Star Trek, seeing someone else playing Kirk would be like going to a mirror and not seeing your own face. And the key word here is *playing* Kirk. Shatner and the others *are* Kirk and company; anyone else would be merely playing the parts. (Kind of like no one but Charlton Heston can portray Moses.)

Instead, I propose a new direction for Star Trek. First of all, I would like to see Star Trek become either a series of theatrical movies or made-for-TV movies, limited to three or four a year. Definitely not a weekly series. Good science fiction cannot be cranked out on a weekly basis like doctor shows and sit-coms.

Now it would be next to impossible for every actor and actress to be available for every Star Trek movie. In addition, sad to say, they are not getting any younger. Therefore, in the first two or three movies it would be necessary for our *Enterprise* crew to introduce us to a variety of new, interesting characters around which entire movies can be made. We can even meet the principal crew members of another starship rather than just the captain (as it was limited to in the series). We can then experience the voyages of the starship *Constitution*, or *Constellation*, or

Excalibur. And these new characters must not be carbon copies of Kirk, Spock, and the rest, but new, unique personalities we can grow to know and love just as we do the crew of the *Enterprise.* Presented wrongly, an idealistic captain, a half-human science officer, and a country doctor could have been disastrous, but they were brought to life by the fine talents of Shatner, Nimoy, and Kelley, and became characters we cared about. There's loads of fresh new talent out there in Hollywood that can do the same thing with fresh new characters who would expand the Star Trek universe, allowing us to see other ways man has progressed, new philosophies, and how other persons of the twenty-third century react to the wonders of the universe. Furthermore, a new set of stars would be a group for a younger generation to become involved with, learn about, and care about, just as we did with Kirk and Company fourteen years ago. Star Trek would indeed live on and on and on.

And if this doesn't open up a flood of storylines (and I pray that they don't just rehash old plots with new characters), there is probably at least one movie for each of the original stars to solo in, explaining what happened to each of them between the five-year mission and the first movie. What happened in those two and a half years? What led Kirk to accept the desk-bound admiralcy? What finally led Spock back to Vulcan? Did McCoy finally become "just a country doctor"? Why did Janice Rand transfer back to the *Enterprise* after all those years?

In summary I'd just like to say this: No one else but Bill Shatner and the other original stars can be Kirk and Company. And while Kirk and Company are a major part of Star Trek, Star Trek is *not* just Kirk and Company. Rather, Star Trek is about people and the hope that mankind will survive, and ultimately it is a message that we do have the potential for greatness in this universe.

Janet Stumbo
Prestonburg, Ky.

I am a twenty-six-year-old from-episode-one-way-back-when Star Trek fanatic. Having successfully concealed this insanity from all but the immediate family and a few kindred souls for all these barren years, imagine my joy at recently discovering your *Best of Trek* series. Also imagine my employer's embarrassment when he and his fellow judges returned from lunch to find me in the robing room with my nose stuck in *The Best of Trek* (# 1), and *BOT* # 2 and # 3, *The New Voyagers*, and *The Trekkie Quiz Book* spread on the conference table!

You see, I'm a staff attorney for the Kentucky Court of Appeals, and we were in the middle of an out-of-town court session when I wandered into a bookstore. Thank heavens for Master Charge!

Gathering from the anything but sympathetic looks my treasures received that I had no fellow fans among the judges and other attorneys, I quickly stowed the books in my briefcase. I had trouble concentrating on the rest of the day's cases.

Just a week later the May HBO guide came out and there it was—*Star Trek: The Motion Picture*. I just finished watching it the second time and am in a state of bliss. Just think, I can see it four more times before the month is out! An embarrassment of riches.

It's obvious from the many exclamation points that I am in a state of barely controlled excitement. The reason for this is that here in eastern Kentucky there are no reruns, at least not on a regular basis. Each week I buy a *TV Guide* as soon as it comes out and read every listing. Star Trek has appeared here and there about every other week. I even missed the year's Kentucky Derby on TV because of an episode. (A cardinal sin for a Kentuckian, you know.)

About the movie, I agree completely with Walter Irwin—it improves with each viewing. I was distracted with watching for the characters to appear and the changes in the ship first time out, not to mention luxuriating in the glory of seeing Spock. Ah yes, Spock . . . what can I say that Beverly Wood didn't say in her "I Love Spock" article?

Anyway, thank you for lighting my life. I look forward to receiving *Trek*.

MONTGOMERY SCOTT: A SHORT BIOGRAPHY

by Bill Krophauser

*One of the most popular characters on Star Trek is the
lovable engineering officer, Montgomery Scott. His legion
of fans numbers in the thousands, and is fourth only to
the followings of Kirk, Spock, and McCoy. Yet, of these
four, we know the least about Scotty. Bill Krophauser offers some thoughts on what Montgomery Scott's early
years and career in Starfleet may have been like.*

In the latter half of the twenty-second century, in the Scottish port town of North Berwick, Kathleen Margaret Scott
presented her husband, William Donald Scott, with a boy.
As his parents were unable to agree on a middle name, the
boy was christened simply Montgomery Scott.

At twenty-five, William Scott was the owner of North
Berwick's third-largest watercraft rental establishment,
which he had inherited from his father. The business made
the Scotts a comfortable living, but it was a constant reminder to William of his father and he was not happy in
his work.

Kathleen Scott died of lymphatic cancer when Montgomery was five, and William was devastated. He was now
without a refuge: His home reminded him of his dead
wife, his business reminded him of his dead father. Kathleen's mother, Anne McDougal, came to North Berwick to

care for little Montgomery, and as William began to spend more and more time away from home and business, she gradually assumed responsibility in both areas. As Montgomery grew older, he helped his grandmother, and the experience served to mature him quickly. He grew very close to his grandmother, and she was to have a great influence upon him.

There were two general types of personalities among the people working on the Scottish docks. One type was very emotional, given to quick temper and deep depression. The other type was calm and stoic, a rock in time of crisis or danger. Anne McDougal was a stoic type, and she quickly taught the emotional Montgomery the virtues of calmness under pressure. The transformation was not as complete as she hoped, but it did give Montgomery a healthier, better-rounded personality, and made him a good man to have in a crisis.

Partly from necessity and partly from true interest, Montgomery developed an early interest in machinery. At ten, he could easily repair any of the latest-model aquatic pleasure craft, and he was soon tinkering with land-based vehicles as well. William Scott finally managed to overcome his grief, and by the time Montgomery was fifteen, he had rededicated himself to the business. Now that he had more spare time, Montgomery earned extra money by fixing any malfunctioning land or sea vehicle offered to him in his after-school hours.

Montgomery's first love was Maureen Ryan, a classmate in secondary school. Although Montgomery felt he was in love with her, Grandmother Anne doubted he really was and said so. The rightness of her prediction was proved when Maureen was forced to accompany her parents on an emergency trip to Mars. Upon her return six months later, both she and Montgomery were astonished to discover that the passion they had declared to each other as "undying" had metamorphosed into a simple, but lasting, friendship. The lesson wasn't lost on Montgomery, and it was to be quite a while before he would again mistake passion for love.

In addition to his proficiency with mechanics, Montgomery had also shown considerable promise in physics. Feeling that his future lay in engineering, a career which combined both of these talents, Montgomery enrolled in

Durham University in Durham, England. Over the course
of his college career, his interests ranged from advanced
physics to Karen Jensen, from aeronautic engineering to
Elizabeth Layton, from astrophysics to Christine Rudd,
from astroengineering to Debra Jo Martini, and finally to
advanced warp dynamics. He moved from subject to subject, from love interest to love interest whenever either
failed to hold anything more for him. Feeling that Earth-
bound engineering disciplines would be limiting, both aca-
demically and in mechanical challenges, he applied to and
was accepted by Starfleet Academy.

Once at the Academy, he applied himself a little more
to his studies and a little less to the ladies and soon
impressed his instructors with his already phenomenal
ability. He, in turn, was impressed by the caliber of instructors, whose ranks included the famous Dr. Kahn
Revox of the Deneva Research Station; Dr. Granville
Weber, teaching what was to be his last class in galactic
techtonics; Commodore Rex Opperman, more famous for
his service on the *SS Tritium* than his advances in warp-
drive modification; and Vice Admiral Winston Cauffield,
the man who helped design the Marshall Class cruiser.
Such a combination of inspirations for a cadet served to
push Montgomery to impressive accomplishments, culmi-
nating in his senior project, the theory and implementation
of a compact impulse-drive engine that was the first step to
developing the Constitution Class shuttlecraft. It was an
amazing breakthrough, especially for a cadet, and it won
Montgomery the Starfleet Academy Engineering Excel-
lence Award.

Like all cadets, Montgomery participated in pranks, but
only once did he get into serious trouble. After a drinking
bout to celebrate passing a difficult exam, Montgomery
and two similarly inebriated companions substituted a program of their own devising into the navigation control
simulator. When navigation cadets took their test the next
morning, they discovered that instead of navigating
through heavily populated Klingon battle zones they were
navigating through scenic vacation spots on Rigel IV. As
the drunken culprits had forgotten to remove their computer access codes from the log, they were located easily
and given a severe reprimand.

During his last semester at the Academy, Montgomery became deeply involved with fellow student Corinne Blackburn. Seeing in her a fiery drive that reminded him of his grandmother and a loving spirit that reminded him of his mother, he wished to devote himself to her. Corrine, however, was a very independent woman. To her, Montgomery's devotion and protectiveness was an attempt to dominate her. Although Montgomery's attentions were not malicious (he had similarly thrown himself wholeheartedly into all of his relationships), Corinne finally told him she felt as if she were drowning in the relationship and broke it off.

Although Montgomery was very hurt, he realized that Corinne was correct. Neither of them would change. With the resiliency and strength instilled in him by his grandmother's teachings, Montgomery was able to complete his studies. Yet, he felt he had found—and lost—the perfect woman. Some thirty years would pass before he was once again to meet a woman who would even come close to meeting the standard Corinne had left in Montgomery's mind.

Completing his studies, Montgomery graduated from the Academy with the rank of ensign and was immediately drafted by an anxious Starfleet to work on their grand new project—the Constitution Class cruiser.

Thanks to recent breakthroughs in warp-drive mechanics, computer duotronics, molecular transportation, and the like, it was decided to build an entire new class of cruiser, one based on the designs of the erratic genius Dr. Franz Joseph IV. The cream of Starfleet engineers, physicists, shipbuilders, etc. were assigned to the project, including many from the Academy. Admiral Cauffield was chosen to head up the team, and remembering Montgomery's skills, he requested him.

Completion of logistics and blueprinting took three years, by which time Montgomery had risen to lieutenant JG, and had also become one of Cauffield's most trusted aides. Knowing that Franz Joseph tended to lose interest in a project once theory had become construction, Cauffield assigned Montgomery to Joseph's crew. When Joseph suddenly became intrigued with his vision of an even smaller version of the Constitution Class ship and dropped his responsibilities to work on the designs, Cauffield chose

Montgomery to head up the crew. It was almost unheard of for an officer of Montgomery's rank to hold such a position, and Cauffield took some heat from Starfleet Command. But he remained firm, and Montgomery was given the position, determined not to let the admiral down.

The next five years were filled with problems and triumphs. Aside from construction headaches and design deficiencies, Montgomery also had problems with his crew, some of whom didn't like taking orders from a junior officer. Montgomery could have gone to Admiral Cauffield, but instead he worked harder than any two of his men. After a year of hard work (and, rumor has it, a couple of fistfights), Montgomery's crew was a tight and loyal unit that worked hard, drank hard, and fought hard against other gangs who dared mock the "boy wonder." The ship they were working on, the *Enterprise*, was finished ahead of schedule, and Montgomery was rewarded by being promoted to full lieutenant.

As the *Enterprise* was the first Constitution Class "ship of the line" launched, a shakedown cruise was immediately ordered. Montgomery naturally planned to be chief engineer on this cruise, under Admiral Cauffield's command, but Starfleet decided that there was no time for a traditional shakedown. Robert April was given command and the ship was sent out on a full mission. The time and expense involved in the Constitution project had to reap immediate benefits, and the *Enterprise* would be tested in action.

Montgomery was assigned to oversee completion of the remaining Constitution ships. Disappointed over his failure to get into deep space, he consoled himself with the glowing reports coming in on the *Enterprise*'s performance from Captain April. With time on his hands, Montgomery turned his talents to two dreams of his: designing his *own* starship, and writing a textbook.

Montgomery was continually discouraged in his Academy days by the uselessly outdated texts assigned in many classes. He felt that not enough emphasis was placed on individual experimentation, so he slanted his first effort, *Advanced Astrophysics*, toward that aim. It was enthusiastically accepted by the Academy, and Montgomery was asked to write another. He wrote two more, in fact, during this time; *The Essence of Warp Drive Mechanics* (co-authored with Admiral Cauffield), and *General Starship Engineering: Constitution Class*, based on his own experiences building the ships and reports coming in from the *Enterprise* and several other newly launched starships.

The starship Montgomery designed was the *Starstalker*, a sleek, small ship with impressive firepower and capable of speeds exceeding Warp 10. It was designed as a quick-strike ship, an answer to the Klingons' deadly Devastator Class of ships which they used primarily for ambush purposes. Even though Starfleet was banking on the impressive Constitution ships and had only promised a prototype would be built, Montgomery spent the next five years developing his ship. When completed, it was less than one-eighth the size of the *Enterprise*, yet could move faster and carry more firepower, thanks to the compact new warp drive and weaponry Scott and his assistants developed. So impressed was Starfleet at the end product that they ordered two more of the vessels built and tested.

But *Starstalker* was ready. Scott, never having stood for command, could not captain her, but he was happy enough being assigned as engineering officer. The captaincy was given to James Kirk, a brash young officer with a growing reputation for skill and daring. It was his first command, and as much of a test of him as it was of the ship.

Montgomery was dubious about Kirk, but his fears soon proved groundless. Like Scott's close friend and mentor, Admiral Cauffield, Kirk asked for "a little bit more" from himself and his crew. Kirk always seemed cheerfully optimistic that Montgomery could do anything he asked of him, and Montgomery, not wishing to disappoint his captain, always could. The two men worked together well, mercilessly shaking down the *Starstalker*, and became close friends.

The ship passed all of the tests set for it by Starfleet and Kirk and Montgomery (theirs were, naturally, much more imaginative and demanding), but at the end of the mission, it was decided to shelve the Starstalker project. A period of relative peace with Federation enemies had caused the inevitable cutbacks in funds after the horrendously expensive Constitution program, and the starships were proving both effective deterrents and valuable research vessels. Kirk and Scotty didn't actually disagree with the decision, but they made very sure that the three Starstalker craft were stored at strategic points around Federation space and in a near-ready condition. While the craft didn't fit into Starfleet's current schemes of exploration and expansion, they would be very valuable in time of war.

Assigned to command the *Hua C'hing*, Kirk asked Montgomery to come along with him. Unwilling to return to the dry, unexciting life of a designer, "Scotty" (as Kirk had taken to calling him) readily agreed. Their missions on the *Hua C'hing* were all successful, leading to promotion and rewards for them both. In what little spare time he had, Scotty authored his fourth text, *Applied Astroengineering*.

When he heard that Christopher Pike was being promoted to fleet captain, Montgomery toyed with the thought of applying for a transfer to the *Enterprise* under her new captain. He decided against doing so, however, for his loyalty to Kirk had grown, and he also, deep in his dour Scot heart, suspected that fate didn't want him to serve on the ship he had helped to build and loved so well. So he was taken completely by surprise when Kirk informed him that they would soon be transferring to the *Enterprise*. Having heard Montgomery speak lovingly of the ship many times, Kirk knew that nothing would make him happier.

However, when the transfer of command was complete, and Montgomery first stepped into "his" engineering section, he was horrified. Despite the meticulous care given it by previous engineering officers, the battles, stress, and general wear and tear of years of continuous use had left the ship in a sorry state. Scotty's memories had been of a shining, newly launched *Enterprise*; this one looked as if she had been in a gang war.

Pausing only to go to his cabin for a stiff shot of Scotch, Montgomery immediately put his engineering crew and drydock personnel onto a round-the-clock, marathon repair and refitting session. Only five days had been alotted for the refitting session. Only five weeks had been alotted from the busy starship's schedule for crew transition, and by driving himself and his men to the point of exhaustion, Montgomery was able to complete several months' worth of work. Although he was not satisfied with the state of his "bairns" (and never would be), Montgomery was very pleased by Lieutenant Commander Spock's comment that in his eleven years aboard the ship, he had never seen it functioning so well.

Scotty, happily ensconced aboard his beloved *Enterprise*, with a captain and crew he admired and respected, was at last a totally happy man. He knew from experience of that special relationship between the creator and the creation—how no one else but the man who built the machinery could get that little extra out of it, and how he could "communicate" with it on a level inaccessible to anyone else. He and Kirk had shared it on the *Starstalker*; and Montgomery "Scotty" Scott was now taking immense pleasure in again sharing it with Kirk on the *Enterprise*.

In the intervening years, Montgomery has shared many adventures with the *Enterprise* crew. He has faced (once even experienced!) death, fought battles, lost companions, fretted in helpless frustration as his ship was taxed beyond belief. Scotty fell in love, lost the woman to the "god" Apollo, fell in love again with the gentle Mira Romaine. They entered into a mutually acceptable open-end marriage contract, and have shared whatever time they could together ever since. But Montgomery's first love is—and always will be—the USS *Enterprise*.

Now once again, he is serving with his old friend Jim Kirk, the only person whose feelings for the ship come anywhere near Montgomery's. They are both happy and content, for they are again at home.

STAR TREK: CONCEPT EROSION
(Or Reality vs. Fantasy)

by Steven Satterfield

The heart of Star Trek is the believability and seeming reality of the "Star Trek universe"; a future of peace and goodwill where beings from all parts of the galaxy work together with fabulous technology for the betterment of all. But for such a universe to remain believable, it must remain consistent. In the following article, Steven Satterfield examines some of the areas where Star Trek's inconsistencies affected the "reality" of the show.

The future of Star Trek (in planned movies and/or television series) will be a direct outgrowth from the past of Star Trek. The aspects of the series which made Star Trek such a success have been dissected by many people. The failures of the series, on the other hand, are less well documented. Any new Star Trek production must incorporate the original's strengths and steer clear of its failures. This article is an attempt to identify the basic flaws and failures in the original Star Trek and, in some cases, suggest means to rectify them.

Star Trek's success resulted from the "reality" of the universe and characters created by Gene Roddenberry. The future, as projected in Star Trek, is a time of wonder, optimism, opportunity, equality, and adventure. In short, a *great* time to be alive! Even within the framework of such concepts as faster-than-light ships, phasers, gravity-field generators, and matter transporters, the extrapolated "reality" remained believable, highly possible, and significant to the viewing audience. The actions taken and opinions expressed by the characters were not limited solely to entertainment: They were relevant to *our* time and society, the ultimate test of any "reality."

Although the "reality" of the Star Trek universe was never allowed to completely disintegrate beyond all recognition, it was severely compromised in a number of episodes. This continual erosion of the basic concepts upon which the series was built was the paramount failure of Star Trek. (Compromises in characterizations was a collary to the erosion of the basic premises of the series.)

If the basic concepts of a science fiction series cannot endure examination, no amount of characterization can instill the needed "reality," for science fiction is the one branch of literature (or any other medium) that must have a rigorous respect for the creation and maintenance of a credible "reality."

The original science fiction concepts of Star Trek, while not completely faithful extrapolations of present knowledge, were very plausible for the most part. As they evolved from the "words on paper" stage, these concepts became the framework for the "reality" of the series; and so being, there must be no deviations from or contradictions to them during the entire run of the series, or else the "reality" of the show would be threatened. If it is decided that a concept *must* be altered, the change should be carefully and specifically explained within the context of the series, and thereafter remain consistent. A revision of the "reality" cannot be presented in a minor, offhand manner. It must be clearly expressed so as to avoid confusing the viewing audience.

A good example is the increase in the maximum safe cruising speed of the *Enterprise*. The original concept stated that the ship could safely travel at Warp 6 for extended periods of time. Although the engines have the capacity to produce greater speeds, the ship's construction is such that it can only withstand the strain of these greater speeds without buckling for a short time. An upward revision of this conceptual safe cruising speed—say perhaps to

Warp 8—would have to be presented in an episode of the series in which it would be explained how the structure of the *Enterprise* is reinforced against the strain of the matter-antimatter engines at greater speeds or how the engines have been improved to produce greater speeds without causing increased stress on the ship. For the "reality" to be maintained, it is important that such a change be established as a concept revision, and not just a whim on the part of the writer of a particular episode.

This particular facet of Star Trek's "reality," it is sad to say, did not pass the test of consistency or believability. The upper limit of safe operating speed for the *Enterprise* was not strictly adhered to. If a writer wished to inject "drama" into an episode, he would sometimes resort to the old cliché of having a "runaway ship" (with, of course, a "last-second save"). Many writers seemed to feel that this bit of so-called drama was all that was expected, and gave little thought to the speed at which they had the ship "run away." In many episodes, the fantastic speeds the *Enterprise* is shown enduring would have almost instantly destroyed it according to the original concept.

An even more distressing error of this sort occurred in "By Any Other Name," in which the Kelvans significantly improve both the structure and the engines of the *Enterprise* in no time at all. How they were able to perform this almost magical engineering feat is never explained in the episode. The mystery surrounding the exact nature of the Kelvans may have been a good idea, but it should not have been extended to include a mysterious ability to disrupt an established concept of the series. After the Kelvans have improved the *Enterprise*, it becomes a super-starship, capable of traveling at Warp 13 for three hundred years. At such speeds, it would be invincible against Klingon warships, able to run circles around them. But at the conclusion of "By Any Other Name," the Kelvans have been dealt with and the *Enterprise* returns home—only for us to discover the very next week that the *Enterprise* is no longer a super-starship. The improvements have disappeared—and so has the credibility of the Kelvans, the episode, and a signifcant portion of Star Trek's "reality."

If the "improvement" performed by the Kelvans had not been arbitrarily plopped down into the script, the plot would have been changed very little. It was little more than an afterthought. It seemingly did not matter that this afterthought produced ripples which could effect the entire "reality" of Star Trek. (It is interesting to note that in an earlier episode, "The Changeling," the Nomad probe affected the ship's engines to increase power and it was plainly stated that such speeds would destroy the ship due to stress.)

Another of the original concepts which was allowed to develop beyond its given parameters was the transporter. Even though the transporter was not particularly believable in the way it operated, it did provide an efficient method of getting the cast to and from the surface of a planet. The transporter could be accepted in the limited role it would play as an expedient to plot development and a means of keeping down the cost of production.

Due to the inherent possibilities of a machine which could convert matter to energy and back to the original matter again at a new location, it was vital that this concept be protected and its limited scope retained. If a writer does not take the time to analyze the implications of changes in this original borderline concept, he will explore the possibilities of the transporter to the detriment of the series "reality."

In "The Enemy Within," a duplicate Kirk was formed by a transporter malfunction. This incredible feat of wizardry not only created a formidable problem for Captain Kirk, but it also presented the Star Trek universe with another spreading ripple in its "reality." It has now been established that the transporter is capable of creating a living being out of random energy. The logical conclusion from this is that death need not be permanent, as the transporter now has all the capabilities needed to be an "immortality machine." The creation of new bodies out of old should be a simple operation of transporter mechanics.

On the other hand, it is obvious from the reactions of the characters that death is very real and very permanent. In the animated episode "Counter-Clock Incident," the transporter is used to restore crewmembers to their correct ages by tapping the stored data concerning their entire molecular structure, a process which is stated as being impossible under normal circumstances.

This contradiction between what we would logically expect and what actually is was the result of the alteration of the original concept. The transporter became a kind of magic wand. It was used to solve plot problems by many writers who had written themselves into a corner. The fantasy element of the transporter was allowed to overwhelm the science element, and an amazingly complex machine was reduced to the commonplace.

Consider, if you will, the complexities of storing the entire human molecular structure so the beamed energy can be converted back to the exact human that was transported. Every detail must be recorded. Multiply this by the maximum number of people that can be transported at the same time and you can see that the function of the transporter is not simple. This would account for the use of only one transporter in normal, nonemergency situations. The storage capacity of even the highly advanced computers on board the *Enterprise* would not be sufficient to allow a greater number of people to transport simultaneously while still monitoring and maintaining all other ship functions. The equipment and power necessary to convert matter to energy, project the energy to a programmed location, and convert it back to matter would also be very complex and would also tend to limit the number of people that could be transported. (In emergency situations, the "other" transporters that we are told exist on the ship could function, as in an all-out evacuation, all other ship's functions could be shut down.) These limited factors of the transporter pointed out how unlikely it was for it ever to be the miracle-worker it was sometimes made out to be.

If the creation of the "evil" Kirk in "The Enemy Within" is considered an incredible fluke which cannot be duplicated and the events of "Counter-Clock Incident" are left as a one-time-only occurrence, the concept of the transporter may survive. If the original concept is adhered to from now on, the alterations will still exist, but they will not be repeated.

The concept of full equality of sexes, races, intelligent beings, etc. in the Federation was never used to its fullest potential. Even though it was the main concept that sustained the optimistic philosophy of Star Trek, it was not developed beyond the first glimmerings of its ultimate potential: The existence and equality of intelligent alien beings was not presented consistently. Although the *Enterprise* was integrated and people of many races held important and demanding positions, the entire diversity of Earth's peoples was only hinted at. Too often the crew was presented as being made up of all too large a percentage of one particular skin tone. The equal role of women was ignored for the most part.

The concept of equality should have been presented in a very straightforward manner; a fact of existence, with no preaching concerning the evils of hate and prejudice. The existence of female starship captains, black starship captains, Indian starship captains, alien starship captains, or any other possible type of starship captains should have raised no eyebrows or garnered no double-takes. Star Trek should have taken care to show no extraordinary attention being paid to any being of any rank or position outside of the normal respect due to someone who has attained high rank or position. In the rare instances in which this was done, the audience was more than willing to accept the fact of equality in the Federation—and perhaps a bit more willing to accept the fact in real life.

The introduction of new concepts can also pose a problem with the continuity of a series. Such new concepts must be considered very carefully to ensure they will fit into the established parameters of the stated universe. The unwise use of new concepts not only caused individual episodes to fail, but their use can also open a Pandora's Box of future problems. As with the erosion of original concepts, the introduction of new concepts which are not well thought-out may harm the "reality" or create dead ends which can stifle character or plot development.

The Prime Directive is a fine example of just such a concept. On the surface, it is a completely proper and realistic addition to the Star Trek "reality." It is an outgrowth of the concept of equality, stating that no culture is inherently better than another. The rights of young, developing cultures are to be respected and protected from outside interference. The Prime Directive, as introduced, was absolute and uncompromising in its restrictions upon the actions that could be taken by Federation personnel in many situations.

But when this limited effect came into conflict with possible story opportunities, the Prime Directive was hastily shoved aside and given only lip service. It became little more than a device for meaningless discussion and empty conflict. The audience was aware that Kirk would not sacrifice his ship or crew to prevent interference in the development of cultures. On the contrary, Kirk takes it upon himself to interfere in the development of some cultures.

The mishandling of the Prime Directive caused a rip in the fabric of the compassionate attitude that was supposedly the hallmark of the Federation. If the restrictions of the Prime Directive were as stringent as originally presented, then Kirk was often in violation of Federation laws, or if he was allowed to so act, then the Federation was guilty of the grossest hypocrisy. Although the Prime Directive was a logical and entirely appropriate concept, it should not have been introduced into Star Trek's "reality," for strict adherence to it would have prevented Kirk and crew from acting (or even reacting) upon the cultures and situations they met on various worlds. That they did so anyway, despite the existence of the Prime Directive, eroded the "reality" of the series even further.

The events of "Journey to Babel" may offer some insight into the apparent contradictions concerning the Prime Directive. The internal strife between Federation members portrayed in this episode showed that there was indeed disagreement over policy. So it could be stated in a future episode that the member planets of the Federation are divided over the Prime Directive issue. Vulcans would probably wish a direct interpretation of it, Earth may interpret it in a less restrictive manner, while some Federation members may even wish to see it abandoned entirely. Such an approach would not only clear up apparent inconsistencies (Kirk's actions could be seen in the light that the Prime Directive is not specific, but open to interpretation in individual planetary situations) but would open up new avenues of story potential as well, especially when we see that all members of the Federation are not homogeneous in their beliefs.

The erosion of original concepts and the introduction of new, untested concepts not only destroys the "reality" of the series, but also severely lessens the optimistic philosophy of the series. This process of deterioration became even more pronounced as concrete science fiction concepts were sometimes replaced by pure fantasy. How can one be optimistic about the future when a model of that future is partially based on fantasy and not on extrapolation of the possible?

"Wink of an Eye" is an example of a Star Trek episode based entirely on a fantasy concept. We are expected to believe that a mysterious volcanic pollutant instilled the humanoids of the planet Scalos with super-speed abilities. They move at such an accelerated pace that they cannot be seen by the human eye, and the only evidence of their presence is a small buzzing sound. These speed demons raced about the corridors of the *Enterprise* faster than a phaser beam, every curl in place, no sonic booms to announce their passing, no harm from air friction, able to stop on a dime.

If we grant the impossible and accept the existence of humanoids who can travel at such accelerated speeds, we would still have to deal with physical laws. It would be virtually impossible for the Scalosians to stop within the confines of the *Enterprise* corridors once they had started, not to mention turning narrow corners or working delicate controls. Such a weak attempt to present something "daringly different" while ignoring known physical laws only obliterates the "reality." The audience knows the characters are involved in a situation which is impossible now and will still be impossible in the twenty-third century.

The use of fantasy was most pervasive during Star Trek's third season. Most episodes depended upon easy and unoriginal ideas and concepts based upon dubious pseudoscientific malarky. Mind powers (psychokinesis, transmutation of physical form or matter, etc.) were attributed to any number of humans or humanoids with no hint of a practical explanation. When an explanation was grafted onto an episode, it usually created more problems than solved.

Such severe deterioration of the quality of ideas and concepts was the inevitable result of the lack of care by the people involved in production of Star Trek during the third season. These production people had little or no idea what science fiction is. If a concept was strange or mysterious or powerful, that was the only test it had to pass to be considered science fiction. The fact that it might break an entire page of known physical laws or that it did not fit into the "reality" of the Star Trek universe was of no concern. Such a hit-or-miss approach must not be allowed to infect the return of Star Trek.

A reliance on "hard" science fiction, where the concepts are based upon the extrapolation of known facts, does limit the scope of the series. It removes many tempting opportunities for writers to use fantasy as a basis for scripts and to use fantasy as a means to erode the "reality" of already established concepts. The "self-destruction syndrome" has plagued science fiction on television since the beginning of the medium. Star Trek managed to overcome many (but not all) of the destructive urges due to Gene Roddenberry's capable guidance for the first two seasons.

The exclusive use of "hard" science fiction will tend to keep the "reality" of a created universe intact. However, it is very hard to maintain this approach. It forces writers to be original and to restrict their flights of fantasy, and forces them to pay closer attention to the characters and to the possible consequences this future society has on them. The future society should be carefully explored. Although "hard" science fiction does not rule out the known wonders of the universe to provide conflict and drama, it does force the writers to remember that science fiction is about people in a future society and not about Alice in Wonderland.

If the new Star Trek is to be a success, the failures of the original series and the animated series must not be incorporated into the new movie. The original concepts which have proved successful should be used and improved if possible, and the confusion surrounding others should be dispelled. In some cases, though, it may be wiser just to accept a concept as a mistake, learn from it, and vow never to repeat it.

Even with the number of failures found in Star Trek, it still managed to retain the greater portion of its "reality." Star Trek improved over all the science fiction television series that came before and have come since. No series has come as close to living up to its full potential as has Star Trek. The new movie must build upon this past and approach even closer to the ultimate potential. Anything less can only be considered a failure.

APPROACHING EVIL

by Joyce Tullock

If there's any science fiction subject that has even come close to approaching the popularity of Star Trek, it is Star Wars. One of the main reasons the Star Wars saga is so popular is the thrill we get out of watching the battles between the good Luke Skywalker and the evil Darth Vader. Joyce Tullock examines this classic confrontation, and compares it to the battles of good versus evil in Star Trek. As you will see, there's quite a difference in the way each series approaches evil.

Evil. Oh, how we love it! In the curious dark corners of our minds, we crave it, seek it out, revel in it. But we are intelligent, rational human beings. We are not supposed to be drawn to evil. We are supposed to be repelled by it. So we pretend to ignore our knowledge that deep down it is the bitter part of "us" that makes us human, and call it by other names not considered to be part of humanity—*alien, psychotic, unreal, possessed,* and many more.

Some of us, however, know how we feel about evil. We detest it as something which should be destroyed; we celebrate it as a way to have vicarious pleasure. Two recent filmmakers are among those who know that we must be exposed to evil to better know ourselves (as well as having a lot of fun in the process). These men are George Lucas and Gene Roddenberry.

Look at the great good vs. evil debates contained in the dialogue and events of *Star Wars/The Empire Strikes Back* and *Star Trek: The Motion Picture.* In the Lucas films, we are confronted with wicked Darth Vader, the "dark father" in every man, the dangerously seductive result of succumbing to the dark side of the Force—which is, in our terms, our own tendency to allow ourselves to be ruled by our id, the subconscious desires which drive us on the most primitive levels. Like Luke Skywalker, we must reject the dark side or at least overpower it, hold it in check. It is an ongoing battle, one which cannot ever be won as long as we retain our humanity.

But what if we lose, or cast aside, our humanity? Then we are confronted with the evil seen in Roddenberry's *STTMP,* the mighty alien which is the epitome of the "soulless man." A cast-off child of the twentieth century coming back to haunt men, even as our own careless acts will come back to haunt us.

Yes, evil is serious stuff, but as Lucas and Roddenberry have proved, it can also be big money and big fun. Through their films, we can have our cake and eat it too. We have the fun of watching our heroes fight against evil, we have the fun of watching the evil performed as well. And we have something to think about. With all of the proclaimed "shortcomings" of their work, Lucas and Roddenberry have almost singlehandedly provided modern movie audiences with something other than sex, horror, disco, soapy psychology, and crooked but lovable "good ol' boys." *Star Wars/Empire* and *STTMP* present two diverse and well-thought-out viewpoints on the topic of evil—and are wholesome, entertaining movies as well.

Of course, Star Trek had a head start; all those episodes in which evil (a term which must here be broadly defined to include all things thought to be "wrong") is so often discovered to be a misnomer for simple misunderstanding or alien behavior. It is an optimistic view; pure unadulterated evil for the sake of evil is rarely seen on Star Trek, one of the many ways in which the series mirrored real life. (One episode even prophesies that eventually the Federation and the Klingons—who *are* evil for the sake of evil, and love every minute of it!—will reach greater understanding and peace.)

As the Star Trek series very, very seldom dealt in the absolutes of good and evil, so does *STTMP* tread that in-between path. In *STTMP*, Roddenberry used his "alien" V'Ger to rip through the barriers of time and tradition to let us view ourselves a few hundred years hence. In the process, he provides us with a fine discussion of "evil" on psychological and surrealistic levels.

V'Ger is man's own "brainchild" gone off on its own. Like most failed pilgrims, it comes home changed and matured, but still lacking the answer to its most vital questions. But unlike most pilgrims who go out seeking the Creator, V'Ger went out seeking "all that could be learned," and was returning to the "Creator" to ask "What else is there?" It is a question to which our heroes have no answer. Indeed, the answer is probably what sent *them* out on their pilgrimage in the first place.

V'Ger appears to be the most mysterious, wicked, and dispassionate killer of all time. Its threatening behavior toward everything coming into contact with it affords only one explanation: It is obviously a thing of pure evil, without conscience or soul. In the words of Captain Kirk, it is a "thing— a thing which destroys, and must be destroyed. Kirk, illustrating the human tendency to label something which is frightening or misunderstood, wants to stop this "thing" before it reaches Earth. He will treat with it if he can, destroy it if he must, die trying if he cannot do either. It is the normal human reaction to evil's threat.

But Dr. McCoy speaks the line which represents Roddenberry's approach to evil's threat:

"Why is any object that we don't understand always called a 'thing'?"

We require that our enemies be inhuman, whether it be cloven-hooved Satan, bearded Klingon, or even a cartoon-like "monster from the id" as seen in *Forbidden Planet*. To perceive the enemy as a "man" is to hesitate over pulling the trigger. It is the kind of necessary thinking that requires your enemy to be a "bucktoothed, slant-eyed monkey," a "goosestepping kraut," or a "thing." It is easier to hate—and kill—that which is seen as "less than human."

But McCoy's sardonic question requires that we toss

aside our labels and slogans and consider our enemy not as a "thing" or as an "intruder" but as an entity which may contain sentient beings or may itself be sentient. Once "humanized," the entity cannot be considered evil, per se. Like our own dark recesses, it must be examined and evaluated.

McCoy's question is the movie's question, and the crew discover soon enough that the answer to it lies within themselves. In confronting V'Ger, the handiwork of their ancestors, they discover that in many ways it is like man, a true son of the father; it is logical and displays the ego of determination. Still, it lacks the human sensitivity and emotion of what we must call the "soul." It is out to "capture God," all right, and leave it to the sardonic doctor to tease us with one of his biting double-takes when he quips, "Capture God? V'Ger's liable to be in for one hell of a disappointment!"

Again, well put, for if there is no absolute evil in Star Trek, can there be absolute good?

It is a question which Roddenberry and his crew wisely refused to answer and it places Star Trek very securely in the realm of science fiction known as the "literature of ideas."

But at times we all like to rest our burdened souls in the world of "right and wrong." It is comforting to think of good as Good, as though it were some mystical pearl hidden within us, needing only to be uncovered to shine forth the beauty of our true self. That requires evil as Evil. We need to be able to tell ourselves that the wrong we do is only a temporary "flare-up" of the bad part of our natures, that we have momentarily slipped into the "dark side of the Force." Evil as a *thing* which can *possess* us and *force* us to do *evil things* relieves us of responsibility for our actions. We're not to blame, after all, if "the devil made us do it." But the temptations of the devil and the workings of the id are nothing but our own "Darth Vader" gone wild, however temporarily. We quickly assure ourselves that we are more Luke than Darth, and are comforted by the *Star Wars* promise that Good will triumph and endure.

So as we watch *Star Wars* and *Empire* we are mildly troubled by one nagging thought: Why is Darth Vader the most compelling character on the screen?

Darth is a beautiful creature indeed. He shines with evil and mystery and tempts us to look beneath the mask and helmet to the certain ugliness within. We become mesmerized by the dark side of the Force. Like Luke at the cave, we want to know what's "in there." We *have* to know. And also like our young hero, we wrestle with those "true feelings" which warn us that the ugliness within might be our own. Darth is the black mirror of the self, and we know it. We are enchanted by it. Even worse, we almost admire it.

And so *Star Wars* provides us with another concept of evil. Darth Vader is almost Evil personified. And if evil is so concrete a quality in *Star Wars*, so too, we must assume, is good. Unlike evil, however, good does not seem to exist in *Star Wars* as an accomplishment, a goal. For Darth, evil has become a source of pride; he even wants Luke to follow in his footsteps. No one, on the other hand, takes such pleasure in his (or her) goodness, not even Obi-Wan or Yoda. This is not a failing in the characters, no, for even though some of them are working against evil for less than altruistic purposes, they all still battle Vader and his evil bravely. The absence of pure good forces us, the audience, to become more involved. We must put aside our fascination with Vader and his works and actively cheer for Good. It is the adult parallel to children frantically clapping their hands to keep Tinkerbell alive.

Luke's stay with Yoda (which Luke refers to as a kind of dream experience) and his journey into the cave (where the dark side is strongest) are as Freudian and surrealistic as the *Enterprise*'s journey into V'Ger. But we know we're seeing fantasy, not science fiction, when Luke asks what he will find "in there," and Yoda answers, "Only what you take with you."

It's as fine a line as was ever uttered by a *Star Wars* character, and it encapsulates the concept of evil in *Empire* just as McCoy's statement does in *Star Trek: The Motion Picture*.

So what'll it be? Good versus Evil, or the rejection of traditional thought and a redefinition of both terms? Are we black/white spirits who continually struggle with our dual natures? Are we confused God-children seeking out our own worth?

After all, it's obvious that Lucas is right; there *is* a

"right" and a "wrong." Not only do we know it instinctively, we've been tutored in the reality of devils and angels since childhood. We've seen Hitler's evil, Mother Teresa's goodness. We've watched millions perish needlessly—and individuals perish horribly—and stood by with hands in the air, helpless. We have tried to explain the murky swirl of wretchedness shadowing human history, and have agreed on only one word: *evil*. Yet even it is a word which means different things to different people . . . and in different situations. If we cannot even agree on which things *are* evil, then how can we decide what evil *is*?

The bottom line is that each of us must decide for himself. "Some people," we are told in childhood, "are morally weak. They give way to the influence of evil. They fall into darkness and let Satan rule their lives. Evil is easy, 'broad is the road . . .' " So the Luke in us begins its noble struggle. The "best" of us grow up proud and strong, children of light in a darkened world. Like Luke, we "stand for something; for the right." We are proud of our goodness. We are certain of it. Then one day—and it happens to us all—we take a bold, swinging strike at the black mask of wickedness, eager to uncover once and for all the source of the world's misery. About that time we start looking for a new, more complex definition of evil.

The face beneath the mask looks a little too familiar . . . how can we doom ourselves to perdition? Once the polished surface dissolves, a truth is revealed: Hitler isn't Hitler anymore; Darth isn't Darth. We gaze for a moment upon our own "angelic" visage and, wondering and shaken, we turn away.

This is the pivot point of the dialogue of evil which exists between Star Trek and *Star Wars/Empire*. It's where Roddenberry and Lucas give each other a friendly nod as they continue along their opposing pathways. For as our shock settles into painful confusion, someone calls from the mist, "Evil doesn't exist, you know! It's only a term we use to set moral boundaries!"

Mankind isn't all evil, Star Trek suggests, it's merely a confused child reaching for the stars. In his effort to define himself, man has laced himself with a pearly chain. Afraid of his own power, he oppresses himself with goodness. He draws a circle of goodness and forbids himself to travel into the evil beyond. But still the Satan in him longs to defy the limits of definition and security; it needs to go where it should not, "to strange new worlds." It longs to touch the source (id! Force?), to understand Beginning, to look directly into the Darkness beyond the rim. And man gradually listens to that voice from the mist. He begins to doubt his own evil and goes so far as to question traditional concepts of right and wrong. Finally—inevitably—something in him wants to "cheat."

Thus was born the bastard child V'Ger. To the best of its youthful abilities, twentieth-century mankind creates a "thing" in its own mental image and sends it off on a pilgrimage to "Learn all that is learnable and bring it back." It returns a wayward child, a prodigal son, to a parent who has long since forgotten its birth. A stranger in its own land, an "alien," V'Ger is viewed as a thing of evil. No wonder, for it is determined to destroy all of mankind. It has returned to its father's house and found it a den of thieves, contaminated by parasitic biological life forms (something it deems useless—the logical equivalent of "evil"). In *STTMP* evil is nothing more than the Great Misunderstanding. Two aliens, man and V'Ger, face one another with total, threatening distrust. McCoy's "wisecracks" ring painfully true. Man has confronted the "thing" in space and found it to be his own seed altered and grown beyond its father's wildest dreams. After centuries of outworld "experience," poor V'Ger comes looking for its conception of the Ultimate God, wanting to finally join with its "Creator," only to find that its god is that heretofore hideous creature, man. God is a parasite! One hell of a letdown, indeed!

As we face our own innermost thoughts, as Luke faces Darth, so the crew of the *Enterprise* face the horror of itself; that must finally understand, accept, and become one with man to transcend that horror? V'Ger, Star Trek's grandest villain, is also its grandest hero. With the cooperation of the movie's other hero, Will Decker, V'Ger gives itself over to complete revelation. Casting aside its most valued traditional beliefs, its own concepts of "evil," V'Ger relinquishes its cherished right to "define" in order to transform into a greater, more complete entity. Decker's sacrifice is great, but V'Ger's is greater, for it is possessed of infinitely more profound and revealing experiences. But it gains much, perhaps even more than Decker gains. The Decker/Ilia/V'Ger transformation is nothing less than a visualization of the act of understanding. A very dramatic and graphic way of showing love for one's enemy.

In the fantasy world of Lucas' *Star Wars* and *The Empire Strikes Back*, evil is a thing to be rejected or overcome. It is clear-cut, black and white (and yet conveniently veiled with the mysteries of the "self").

Roddenberry's Star Trek and *Star Trek: The Motion Picture* tease us with a less concrete view of right and wrong. Evil is most often approached as a "label" for that which we do not yet understand.

The dialogue continues: Are man's sorrows the result of his giving in to the dark side of his nature? Or do they result from his failure to truly understand himself and his own worth? Is evil something to overcome? Or is it something to study and unwind from its source like some mystical puzzle?

It's a fair debate. A longstanding and beautifully irresolvable one. And it's enough to warm the heart of any true science fiction/fantasy fans. Hats off to both sides! Mr. Lucas, "May the Force be with you" always! Mr. Roddenberry, may your "human adventure" continue!

LOVE IN STAR TREK

by Walter Irwin

As we were shown in many ways in Star Trek, love is a universal constant. The question of what love is is one for poets, philosophers, or pundits, but we can see many examples of love in all its myriad forms in almost every episode of the series. Trek *editor Walter Irwin examines these examples, and draws some surprising conclusions from them.*

Love in Star Trek, as in life, takes many forms. Throughout the course of the series' run, almost every type of love which one sentient being may feel for another was presented. The need and desire for love was presented as an everyday, natural part of the characters' lives; just as it is with our own. Sometimes, love was the focus of an episode, as in "Requiem for Methuselah"; other times the tug of conflicting loves was the focus, as in "City on the Edge of Forever." Other kinds of love than the romantic were also pivotal to many episodes, such as brotherly love ("The Empath"), love of freedom ("The Menagerie"), paternal love ("The Conscience of the King"), and even love for inanimate objects ("This Side of Paradise").

Star Trek is, of course, based on love. The underlying theme of the series is that man will one day overcome his own humanity and learn to live in peace and brotherly love not only with his own kind, but with myriad other sentient beings throughout the universe. The love of freedom is also a very important part of the Star Trek concept. Each person is allowed the right to be free and desires the same right for all others. It naturally follows that love of individuality is the one theme which ties both of these together. As embodied in the Vulcan tradition of IDIC (Infinite Diversity in Infinite Combinations), it is the difference between beings which must be revered—and loved. The Star Trek concept was an optimistic one; especially for the turbulent times in which it was first introduced. So to make the series a bit more palatable for viewing audiences of the 1960s, Gene Roddenberry wisely incorporated mankind's love of adventure, exploration, mystery, danger, and the lure of the unknown into the format.

In the very first episode aired, we saw how all of these came into play. "The Man Trap" was a creature which survived by eating salt; but on another level, we could see how it also needed love to survive. Professor Robert Crater desired only to protect the Salt Monster as the last surviving member of its species, a creature he (and some of the *Enterprise* crew as well) felt deserved the same rights and respect as humans. It was also probable that he had come to love the creature as a mate, for it had assumed the shape of his late wife Nancy as a means of self-protection, and had apparently been cohabiting with him for quite some time.

Although the monster killed without hesitation, at no time did it "transform" itself into an object of horror. To the contrary, in every case the Salt Monster became an object of desire: McCoy's nostalgic memory of Nancy, Darnell's shapely crewwoman, Uhura's "perfect man." Even when it transformed into McCoy, it took a face and form which was loved, trusted, and extremely nonthreatening to the *Enterprise* crew.

It would have been ridiculously easy for the monster to use its telepathic powers and dredge up any number of horrific memories to paralyze crewmembers. Such visions would probably have served the creature's purposes much more quickly and efficiently. But it chose instead to appear as an object of love, leaving us to make the logical conclusion that it desired and needed to *be* loved—even for a brief moment before killing—to survive.

Even in this first episode, Star Trek proved that it was to be no ordinary TV show. It may seem that having McCoy kill the monster in a highly dramatic confrontation was pat histrionics, but the conflicts involved went much deeper than that. McCoy (and to a lesser degree Kirk and Spock) had to balance their "loves" against one another: the right of the Salt Monster to survive versus the survival of the crew; McCoy's nostalgic and idealistic love of Nancy Crater versus his love for Jim Kirk; and everyone's love for an "ideal" versus harsh reality. There was no hedging. It would have been easy for McCoy to stun the creature, have everyone make speeches about "passenger pigeons," and beam the creature down to a paradise of everlasting salt. But instead Gene Roddenberry had his characters make choices. It was a fine sign of things to come.

"Charlie X" wanted nothing else in the world but to be loved. Raised by the emotionless and noncorporeal Thasians, Charlie was deprived of the parental love and guidance he needed to be a complete being. His problem was compounded by his onrushing adolescence and his desire for Janice Rand, feelings which Charlie could not understand or control.

Charlie wanted to give love as much as he wanted to receive it, but again he didn't know how. He idolized Kirk as the father he never had, and naturally felt agonizingly betrayed when Kirk was forced to discipline him. Further "betrayed" by Janice, Charlie struck out in anger and despair. Like so many of us, he tried his best to "hurt the ones he loved."

The purest love in this episode, however, was not displayed by the humans, but by the Thasians. They quickly moved to correct Charlie's actions and removed him from the ship in order to protect not only the crew, but Charlie himself. The welfare of the humans was their primary concern. Even in the action of granting the psionic powers to baby Charlie in the first place, they showed their respect for the right of a fellow sentient being to survive—an act which was totally unnecessary to their own well-being and survival, an act which could only have come out of love. It is interesting to note that these beings without bodies and without emotions show just as much concern, compassion, and love for Charlie X as do any of the *Enterprise* crewmembers. One can only hope that with the passing of time, they have been able to communicate this love to Charlie Evans.

Friendship is examined in "Where No Man Has Gone Before." Not only is Kirk faced with the realization that his best friend, Gary Mitchell, is mutating into an advanced being, but he also learns that Gary has not been the true and trusted friend Kirk always thought him to be. It is a stunning blow for Kirk. He loses his friend twice—once by death, once by betrayal. It is not specifically spelled out in the episode, but we may assume that a long-standing "love-hate" relationship existed between the two men. They were both highly competitive, intelligent, and ambitious, a combination which more often makes for rivalry than friendship. It is amazing that Jim and Gary ever became close friends; it is even more amazing that they remained so.

Even when Kirk must face the realization that Gary has evolved to a point where he is willing to destroy them all to achieve his goals, he is still reluctant to take Spock's advice and have Gary killed. His love for Gary, even though it has been deeply shaken, is still so strong that he cannot bring himself to destroy him. It is only when Kirk becomes certain that Gary has lost all semblance of humanity that his love for his ship and crew finally overrides his feelings for a friend. With the help of Elizabeth Dehner, Kirk reluctantly kills Gary. It is more than the death of a friend; it is perhaps the death of Kirk's innocence as well. Never again will he give of himself so freely.

However, in the midst of his troubles during this episode, a new friend appears at Jim Kirk's side. Spock, forced to examine his own emotions in the light of events, and ultimately forced to confess them to Kirk as explanation for his insistence that Mitchell be killed, realizes that friendship is a stronger bond than he had ever believed. In a decision the difficulty of which cannot be underestimated, Spock offers his own friendship to Kirk at a time when the captain needs it the most. It is a moving gesture, one appreciated greatly by Kirk, and one which marks the beginning of the mutual respect and love the two men will share in the future.

It is, however, Dr. Elizabeth Dehner who shows the greatest love in this episode; she gives up her life for her fellow humans. This is a terrible and noble sacrifice, one which must have been very difficult for her to make, for she too is affected by the force field and is evolving into a superior being, and has to fight off the godlike feelings growing within her. Unlike Gary, she is able to retain enough compassion to understand that contempt and disdain are not the mark of a god. Elizabeth not only dies to protect the *Enterprise* crew, she gives up the opportunity to be a god. The amount of love and compassion such an act took cannot be overestimated—and is hardly typical of "a walking freezer unit."

The innermost feelings and desires of crewmembers were brought to the surface by a strange virus in "The Naked Time"; and in three cases feelings of love were involved. Nurse Christine Chapel became very affectionate and "dreamy," going so far as to confess her attraction to Spock. It is quite an intriguing question to consider who she was thinking of when she gazed so pensively into the sickbay mirror: Spock, or her fiancé, Roger Korby. Spock himself was overcome by debilitating grief and regret over the fact that he had never been able to tell his mother that he loved her. (Some bitterness toward his father was also displayed, although not overplayed.) This was the first indication we were given in Star Trek that Spock could feel—really *feel*—love, as well as the already displayed respect and friendship. It also told us much about his upbringing, a subject which was not forgotten and would provide much grist for future programs' mills. We also saw, for a brief moment, a tender side of Spock when he gently told Christine that although he could not return her affection, he understood and appreciated it. One can guess that memories of a girl named Leila prompted his gentle handling of the scene.

The most important revelation, however, was Jim Kirk's response to the virus. For the first time, we saw that Kirk loves the *Enterprise* more than he ever would any woman; loves her passionately and to the exclusion of all else. But she is a harsh mistress as well. Kirk also feels trapped by the *Enterprise*, by his duties, by the need to be "the captain" all the time. It is one of the few views we have of the soft inner core of Jim Kirk. Such doubts are not part of the Kirk we know. This assertive, aggressive, ambitious man is not the type to think in terms of failure or doubt, and is certainly not the type to be overly caring about inanimate objects. His cabin, save for a few books, is even more austere than Spock's. So why such a great love for a starship?

Kirk is in love with being the *captain* of the *Enterprise.* It is the position and the power—and the responsibility— which excites, motivates, and consumes him. This, and only this, is what he lives for. The affection he feels for his ship is an outward expression of these feelings, and one which makes him seem less single-minded and more human. His obsessive need for command is also tempered by a great number of positive and likable qualities, qualities which we like to think can be found within ourselves. He is a complete and very complex person.

We see more of this in "The Enemy Within," wherein Kirk's "good" and "bad" qualities are so evenly split between the two beings that each may be viewed as both admirable and flawed. The evil side, of course, is the most obvious, for Kirk's desires and ambitions come to the surface without control and subterfuge usually placed on them by society's constraints. What the "evil" Kirk wants, he takes. But it is unlikely that he would act in a consciously evil manner, such as betraying the ship to the Klingons, or murdering without reason. He is not amoral as was Kirk-2 from the "mirror universe," merely our own Kirk without the love and compassion which makes him a complete being.

The "good" Kirk, on the other hand, is completely ineffectual in even day-to-day matters aboard ship without the ambitious and somewhat ruthless qualities absorbed into the double. He is weak, and in many ways, more of a danger to the ship than the "evil" Kirk. At least the "evil" Kirk could fight a battle, even though his tactics would most likely be reckless in the extreme and quite merciless.

The split, however, is much deeper than one would think. Kirk's feelings for Janice, which must have had an element of love, however slight, come to the surface as animalistic lust in his "evil" half. This is an indication of the basic difference between the two Kirks: The "good" Kirk, containing all of Jim Kirk's enormous capacities for love and compassion, offers that love. The "evil" Kirk, the creature of ambition and ruthlessness, *needs* love. It is this eternal joining of love offered and love needed which finally allows the two entities to be once again combined into a complete, fully functioning individual.

The events of these two episodes seem to have had a cathartic effect on Kirk. The doubts expressed by him while under the influence of the virus seem to have lessened, as has the ambition which had heretofore driven him in his career. Both would remain, of course, but each in its proper perspective. Kirk's love for the *Enterprise* grew even stronger, for freed from the obsessive need to command, Kirk could now appreciate her as the beautiful realization of his desires for freedom and exploration. The ship was transformed into a symbol of his love for space, not a focus for his obsession with it.

Lust, not love, was the primary motivation in "Mudd's Women." The Venus Drug, while obviously having the power to make women beautiful (as was graphically illustrated), must have also had the ability to make them desirable in the extreme. (This was not played up in the show, for the subject of working aphrodisiacs wasn't standard television fare in the late 1960s.) But it must have been so, for the highly trained, strictly disciplined men of the *Enterprise* crew simply went bonkers over these women—leering at their backsides (as did the camera), falling over each other, tongues literally hanging out. These are supposedly men who are surrounded daily by over a hundred intelligent, healthy, and beautiful women (many of whom are much better-looking than Mudd's trio), deep-space veterans who would have had the opportunity to sample the sexual fruits of dozens of planets. It is almost certain that the drug provided the women with something like Ilia's pheromones—either that, or the ladies on board the ship were engaging in *Lysistrata*-like behavior.

There was, naturally, the obligatory infatuation with the captain, but it seemed as if Eve's refusal to attempt to seduce Kirk stemmed more from general disgust with the whole scheme than from any strong feelings for Kirk. (For the first time, we hear the phrase that Kirk is "married to his ship," and from Harry Mudd of all people! Perhaps Harry strode the straight and narrow in his youth and had a love for a ship of his own.) Eve's feelings for Kirk, whatever form they took, slipped away pretty quickly and just as quickly attached themselves to Ben Childress.

Even though her attachment to him begins as a sisterly chiding, we can see that it will soon blossom into a gentle, mutually caring, and mutually respectful love between them. Lord only knows what went on between Ruth, Magda, and the other two miners! If the men of the *Enterprise* went loony over the women, what then must have been the response of the poor miners who had been living in undesired celibacy for many months? Come to think of it ... poor Ruth and Magda!

The concept of love was so all-pervasive in Star Trek that beings who were not generally considered to be "alive" were shown to feel it in one way or another. Apparently, we were being subtly told that love is a state of caring and involvement, which does not necessarily need to be physical in origin or intent. Even machines could feel it.

The first examples of this are seen in "What Are Little Girls Made Of?" The android Andrea, apparently constructed by Roger Korby, feels inklings of emotion awakened by the appearance of Kirk and the other humans. Kirk takes advantage of Andrea's newfound interest to gain information. Although he does not intend his action to harm the android, it eventually leads to her destruction when she transfers that affection to Korby, for whom she probably had unawakened love all along.

Korby's case is a bit different. Mostly likely he created Andrea to satisfy his need for female companionship, and perhaps his sexual needs as well. Again, because of the mores of television, this subject was nicely skirted (except for a lovely scene in which the appearance of Andrea gets a raised eyebrow from Chapel), and we have no information either way as to whether Korby's android body wanted or required sex. But the enticing face and figure of Andrea would suggest it did.

Korby, although his judgment seems to be impaired by the transfer into the android body, still appears to possess a full range of human emotions, giving doubt to Kirk's assertion that Korby can no longer feel. Korby displays anger, sadness, ambition, and, especially, love for Christine. Their embrace upon meeting is certainly not the sort of faked emotion one would expect from an unfeeling android. As we know that Kirk is neither a fool nor a liar, we can only assume that he is glossing over the realities of the situation to spare Christine's feelings.

By her faith that Korby would someday be found alive, Christine shows a fine and pure love, the kind that does not die just because circumstances say it should. We know that in a special place deep within her, she still loves and respects Roger Korby very, very much. And if nothing else, she has a good friend on the *Enterprise*. The touching scene where Uhura hugs Christine, sharing her happiness that Korby is alive, is the only time we see that these two are close. We'd have liked to see more of this friendship.

But what of Ruk? Although he is the last of his advanced android design, and he and his contemporaries were responsible for destroying the inhabitants of Exo III, he acts out of his own strange kind of love of logic and order. One suspects that the creators of Ruk went around killing each other just as Korby and the *Enterprise* crew do. He is more than willing to help Korby when things are peaceful, and it isn't until strong emotions begin swirling about him that he reverts to his former aggressive ways. The lesson of Ruk is overlooked by everyone involved, and it should not be.

The sweetly painful first love of adolescence is the heart of "Miri." The young woman of the title is beginning to enter puberty after a horrifyingly extended childhood, and who should appear just at the time she is beginning to feel the stirring of her sex but Jim Kirk, virile, sexy, totally *male* Jim Kirk. Like millions of viewers, Miri is immediately smitten.

Kirk is flattered, of course, and at first allows Miri to hang around mooning while the team works to find a cure for the viral infection. But when Miri sees him comforting Janice Rand—to our eyes a totally sexless scene, but to Miri, total disaster—she turns on him with all the force of a woman scorned. Poor Miri. She has two of the strongest adolescent burdens forced upon her at once, puppy love and jealousy. And she has to contend with her unfamiliar emotions without the benefit of adult example or advice. She has no mother to teach her or comfort her in her misery, and the only other woman around is her "rival."

To Kirk's credit, he does not take the tack of "If you really love me, you'd tell us" when trying to convince Miri to bring back the communicators. He instead appeals to her growing maturity and attempts to explain why the children turn into "Grups." He is successful in this, for Miri has the children return the tools when another child goes mad. Although Miri still admires Kirk, we can see that she's beginning to get over him—just as we all get over our first love.

Also in "Miri" is the first inkling of the love and devotion shared by the members of the *Enterprise* crew. When McCoy develops a serum for the disease, everyone insists on being the one to test it. McCoy, showing for the first time his lovable combination of compassionate man and curmudgeon, naturally uses himself as the guinea pig.

In "Dagger of the Mind," Kirk and Dr. Helen Noel are the victims of an artificially induced love thanks to Dr. Tristan Adams and his "neural neutralizer." Although Kirk feels passion for Helen (and has memories of a Christmas party that led to a night of love), he rather easily overcomes his feelings and goes about destroying Dr. Adams' operation. Again, his love for his ship and crew have proved stronger than the imprinted feelings for a woman. We suspect that however deep the "love" for Helen was implanted in Kirk's brain, to him that love was not so different from the many other infatuations he has had over the years. Now if the good doctor had used Spock as his guinea pig, it might have been a different story. . . .

In "The Corbomite Maneuver," we see Kirk show great compassion when he returns to aid the small First Federation ship, thereby proving the humans' worth to Balok. Balok (and presumably his race) is a bit more pragmatic, preferring to offer "brotherly love" to those who prove deserving of it—and to destroy those who fail the test. One can only hope that the association with the UFP has helped Balok's people to be a bit more open-minded. Perhaps not, for we haven't seen or heard from them since. Maybe they feel the United Federation of Planets, while an acceptable presence in the galaxy and no threat to them, is a little too liberal for their tastes.

"The Menagerie" is a feast for those looking for instances of love in Star Trek. We have the various sexually enticing forms of Vina that are offered to Pike; the unspoken feelings of both Number One and Yeoman Colt for Pike; Pike's own desires for peace, rest, and love; Kirk's feelings when he thinks that Spock has betrayed him; and, of course, the very great love that Spock shows for Christopher Pike by his dangerous and oh-so-wonderful actions. Each of these is deserving of discussion in detail.

Vina was the sole survivor of the crash of the SS *Columbia* on Talos IV, and although rescued by the Talosians, she was horribly disfigured. Living alone for many years with only the company of the intellectual and inward-directed Talosians, Vina must have suffered immense loneliness. The arrival of the Earthmen and the subsequent capture of Pike must have been like a dream come true for Vina. She was willing (at least in the beginning) to go to any lengths to keep Pike with her, even to the extent of allowing herself to "become" such a total sex object as a Green Orion Slave Girl. Vina only wanted Pike to love her and stay with her, but she soon found herself falling in love with him. In a reaction which must have completely astounded and dismayed her, that love took the form of helping Pike to escape.

Easier said than done, however. Vina spoke of the mental tortures which the Talosians could inflict on a human, and we could tell from the shudder that went through her that she was speaking from bitter experience. (Pike's brief taste of "hell" was frightening enough!) The Talosians, in their never-ending search for new experiences to mentally relive, must have found Vina's memories and subconscious fantasies a treasure trove. We can imagine only a mere fraction of the experiences they must have forced her to endure—experiences both pleasurable and painful. And like Pike, she would have found the mental images distressing because she would always *know* that they were not real, no matter how graphic or tactile they seemed. How would any of us like to spend eighteen years reliving our lives—and our fantasies and our nightmares—over and over and over again?

It has been suggested that Vina did not (thanks to the Talosians) see Pike as *Pike*, but rather as her "ideal dream man." Three things argue against this: First, Pike saw her as herself, admittedly a perfect, extremely beautiful image, but he stated that she was unknown to him, even as a fantasy image. The fact that she was a constant in each of the illusions was his first clue to their unreality. Second, because of the aforementioned enforced "reliving" of her life and fantasies, it is unlikely that Vina would be overly excited by her "ideal man," any image of which would have long since been pulled from her mind and placed into the illusions by the Talosians. Last, the need of the Talosians to draw Pike into their scheme required that he respond to Vina as a real woman, and having her see him the same way would heighten the intensity of the illusions. It was this that backfired against them.

Vina also displayed one other kind of love: self-love. Not unhealthy narcissism, but a self-respect and dignity that allowed her to reject the dream-existence of the Talosians to remain with Pike and the others and face death by phaser overload. It would have been very easy for her to slip back into the existence she had lived for so long, and it took a great deal of courage for her to choose not to. By so doing, Vina reclaimed her humanity and individual rights. Even though the Talosians gave the illusion of her beauty back to her (and the illusion that Pike was staying, in the original script), we can assume that they no longer "used" her for illusion-casting and that she was treated as much more of an equal.

When they discovered that their plan to have Pike respond to Vina was failing, the Talosians pulled Number One and Yeoman Colt from the ship. Figuring quite wrongly that all a human needed to be happy was a compatible mate, they cited health, youth, and intelligence as their criteria for choosing this new "breeding stock." But they carefully looked into the women's minds as well. In Yeoman Colt's mind, they found a natural and strong infatuation for the captain, one which could easily grow into love under the proper circumstances. They also mentioned her "strong female drives," which could mean a number of things, but probably referred to her desires for a home and children, as this is what the Talosians were hoping for a couple to develop. But we may suspect what they found in the mind of Number One was one heck of a lot more enticing for their parasitic urges (and one heck of a lot more interesting for us to speculate on): She had often had fantasies concerning Pike.

Christopher Pike's mind was on other things at the time, but you can bet he gave that little revelation quite a bit of thought when he returned to the *Enterprise*. Number One was as about as emotionless as a human could be, as well

as coldly efficient to an almost robotic degree. It is highly
unlikely that Pike ever had any fantasies concerning *her,*
and it must have come as quite a surprise to him to discover that the reverse was true. Both were professionals,
however, and we may assume that the incident was never
mentioned again. Forgetting about it, however, was another matter, and it would be interesting to somehow see
the reactions of the two when future command duties
forced them together.

It must be noted in Number One's favor that when the
Talosian made his pronouncement, she did not react with
embarrassment (as did Yeoman Colt), but instead showed
the same determination and defiance as did Pike.

Christopher Pike is one of the most complex individuals
ever to appear on Star Trek. We learned more about him
(and had more questions raised about him) in one hour
than we ever did about many other characters who appeared far more often. Unlike Kirk, Pike did not seem to
have an overwhelming need for command. He saw it more
as a duty he had to take on simply because he was one of
that "special breed." It was a job that needed doing, and
he could do it better than anyone else. He yearned for
relaxation, peace, comfort, and an end to tensions, decisions, and responsibility. In many ways, this makes him a
better man than Jim Kirk; but in just as many ways, he is
not a better starship commander than Kirk. We have seen
how often Kirk is plagued by doubts. How much worse it
must have been for Pike, a man who was not "born to be
a starship commander," but had it "thrust upon him." Although he was an extremely successful commander (the
respect he gained from Spock speaks for that), he probably was not a daring or imaginative one. He was not totally happy commanding the *Enterprise*, but as Dr. Boyce
pointed out, he probably would have been unhappier doing anything else.

Unlike Kirk, Pike yearned for love. He would have liked
nothing better than to share a life of quiet contemplation
with a woman he loved. It is highly indicative that the
most convincing fantasy presented him by the Talosians
was just such a pedestrian, peaceful situation, drawn from
his uppermost desires. When protecting Vina from the Ri-
gellian warrior, he was performing his "duty"; when in the
midst of the hedonistic slavers, he was out of place and

disgusted with them and himself. It was only in the simple picnic setting that Pike looked at ease, however briefly.

Spock, although he did not appear to be close to Pike at the time of the Talosian incident, grew much closer to him in later years. His telepathic powers, always more sensitive to those he cared for, would have involuntarily "picked up" Pike's desires for love and the simple life. That knowledge probably played a major part in his decision to help the crippled Pike return to Talos. The Talosians could give Pike not only "freedom" from his injuries, but a perfect illusion of the peaceful life he so fondly desired and never found. Kirk, the fighter, would have received Spock's help in another form; perhaps by transference into an android body like those on Exo III, so that Kirk could once again roam the stars and command his beloved *Enterprise*. The illusions of Talos would not have pleased a crippled Kirk as they did Pike; they would have only served to magnify his distress at not really being in space.

Having responded to Spock's hesitantly proffered friendship, only shortly before these events, Kirk is quite devastated by the Vulcan's seeming mutiny. It is one of Kirk's worst dreams come true—to again have his friendship betrayed, as had been done by Gary Mitchell (and apparently several others). The vindictiveness Kirk shows briefly would have been caused by this hurt, although his natural sense of fairness and his affection for Spock soon return him to normal. When Kirk finally learns the truth, he is relieved not only because Spock will not have to face charges of mutiny, but because he is at last able to cast aside all doubts about the Vulcan's loyalty. His gentle chiding to Spock about "this distressing tendency toward emotionalism" is more than joshing; it is an affirmation that Spock is once again his trusted friend.

Spock is also Christopher Pike's trusted friend. There is no doubt of the great love Spock holds for Chris Pike; he shows it in the most graphic way possible. Spock risks his life, his friendship with Kirk, his career, and most important to a Vulcan, the chance of disgrace to help Pike. Had Spock been apprehended at the Starbase, he would most certainly not have offered to explain his actions, even under threat of court-martial and death. Such is not his way; Spock neither makes excuses nor speaks of his emotionally motivated actions. But his help to Pike is an emotional action, an action of completely selfless love, for Spock has absolutely nothing personally to gain, and very, very much to lose.

But, as always, his actions, no matter how emotionally motivated, are logically planned in infinite detail. How like Spock to do something absolutely quixotic, absolutely emotional, absolutely out of love, and then to compute not only each step of the process, but its eventual chance of success as well.

The only regrets we viewers must have over Spock's actions in "The Menagerie" is that we are never allowed to see any instances of the great friendship he and Pike shared. We must assume that it was Pike who was responsible for bringing Spock out of his totally Vulcan shell and introducing him—however reluctantly and grudgingly—to the value of experiencing and controlling his emotions rather than suppressing them. It is not too farfetched to feel that Spock is quoting some long-ago advice given to him by Chris Pike when he speaks so movingly of "this simple feeling" after his encounter with V'Ger in *Star Trek: The Motion Picture.*

Also in "The Menagerie," the concept of Star Trek is strongly restated in the realization of the Talosians that humanity so loves freedom that men and women would rather die than lose it. The yearning to be free, and to grant others freedom, is vital to the characters in Star Trek; one of the reasons why man first reached into deep space. Like the pioneers of old, they needed more "elbow room."

The Talosians also exhibit, if not love, at least compassion in their unwillingness to force the humans to remain on Talos IV, and in their action of granting Vina her illusion of beauty and of having Pike. More, they show that they truly care for the humans as a race, fearing that the secret of mental projection will spread beyond their world and destroy others as it had their own. Their help to Spock in returning Pike to Talos IV is an indication that they have become a more loving and understanding race.

In "The Conscience of the King," Lenore Karidian displays a great love for her father, Anton Karidian, also known as Kodos the Executioner. Her love is so great, in fact, that she slips over the edge of madness and resorts to murder to protect him. Her insanity becomes complete when she is the cause of his death. There was an unhealthy undercurrent of incest in Lenore's feelings and actions, subtly displayed by having her first seen playing Lady Macbeth to her father's Macbeth. Again, it was only a suggestion, for nothing could be overtly shown or stated on television.

Love culminates in marriage—almost—in "Balance of Terror" as Kirk is about to officiate at the wedding of Robert Tomlinson and Angela Martine. It is the only instance we were shown of crewmembers marrying or being married, although it would not be uncommon on the long voyages of a ship like the *Enterprise*. Perhaps while not forbidding the practice, Starfleet did not encourage it. The realism of Star Trek's world would have benefited by having a few married couples aboard the ship, and it would also have been an indication that things have changed greatly since our time. Angela's grief after Robert's death is realistically underplayed with the kind of dignity, even resignation, one would expect from a seasoned, professional Starfleet officer.

Then again, maybe she wasn't all that broken up. If Star Trek adventures happened in the sequence in which they were aired, Angela got over Robert's death pretty quickly, for in the following episode, "Shore Leave," Angela was happily flirting with Lieutenant Esteban Rodriguez and fantasizing about Don Juan. She also had a mysterious name change to Martine-Teller. If she was still grieving over Tomlinson, one would expect her to be more reserved, or for "Don Juan" to at least resemble poor old Robert, or for her to have changed her name to Martine-Tomlinson in his memory. Apparently Ms. Martine is a lady who quickly puts the past behind her and gets on with life. Kind of like a certain captain we all know.

Also in "Balance," we saw that the Romulans could share deep, loving friendships; the commander and the centurion are longtime friends. Their relationship is akin to that of Kirk and McCoy. We also see that the Romulans, as embodied by the commander, are occasionally men of great honor and character, assets which are often prerequisites for the ability to love.

We see Dr. McCoy work his Southern charm on a lady for the first time in "Shore Leave." The charmingly shy and genteel affair shared by Bones and Tonia Barrows is refreshing to watch, for it showed us a side of Star Trek (as well as the doctor) we hadn't seen before. Until this episode, love affairs in the series were the hinge upon which the plot swung, and therefore were played to the hilt with all the *Sturm and Drang* of bad theater. McCoy's spooning of his lady, on the other hand, was simply an enjoyable subplot to the show. (True, Tonia's "wish" for a White Knight led to McCoy's "death," but that could have been just as easily accomplished in any number of ways. At least it tied in with the plot better than the relationship of Martine and Tomlinson, which was included only to give us a look at some ship's personnel interacting, and to tug at our heartstrings when Tomlinson died.) It was fun to watch Bones work his winsome wiles on a totally willing young woman, and it's a shame we didn't get to see McCoy "romanticizin' " more often.

One of Kirk's old flames also pops up in the course of the episode, and their first meeting evokes a rare air of tenderness and nostalgia in Kirk. Ruth must have been very special indeed to Jim, for he pauses in his breathless chase of Finnegan to contemplate the flower that reminds him of her. What little we see of Ruth indicates that she was a gentle, quiet, and loving woman, one who was about Kirk's current age, and therefore most likely the "older woman" who gently and graciously introduced a young Jim Kirk to love in all its most sensitive and enjoyable forms. It is a part of Kirk's past we seldom get a glimpse of, and all the more pleasant for the sweetness of it.

Trelane, "The Squire of Gothos," flirts outrageously with Uhura and Yeoman Ross, but his behavior is based on his observations of eighteenth-century Earth, and like a child playing cowboy, he's imitating the actions of his heroes. He makes no serious overtures toward them, and one suspects that if they'd made overtures toward him, Trelane would have fled in frightened confusion. Had Kirk, or one of the women, figured this out quickly, the crew would have most likely been given speedy leave to go ahead. Trelane, like most boys, probably wouldn't like that "mushy stuff." His desire for love is that of a child, to be made much of and flattered for his cleverness, admired, and feared. In that respect, Trelane was much like Charlie Evans. But unlike Charlie, Trelane has only been playing, and like all children who get too rambunctious with their toys, his loving but stern parents make him go to his room.

In "Courtmartial," Kirk not only suffers a bittersweet reunion with an old girlfriend, Areel Shaw (who is serving as his prosecutor), but he again meets with betrayal from an old friend. Finney's framing of Kirk is compounded by the bitterness of Jamie Finney, who blames Kirk for her father's death and professes hatred for him. Jamie's forgiveness when Finney is revealed to be alive doesn't help Kirk much. He has permanently lost another friend. Although they had not been close for years, Kirk would have overlooked Finney's resentment and still considered him a friend. Helping assuage the pain a bit was his relief at being cleared and a nostalgic kiss from Areel—with perhaps a promise of renewed closeness in the future.

The power of love to lead a person down the wrong path is examined in "Space Seed." Lieutenant Marla McGivers falls helplessly for Kahn's mesmerizing charisma and *macho* disdain. So captivated is Marla by this living example of everything she has always considered to be the "best" in a man that she almost worships him. In one repellant scene, Kahn grips her wrist painfully and forces her to her knees to prove her loyalty to him. After suffering such degradation, it is only a small step to betraying the *Enterprise* into his hands. Although Marla turns on Kahn when he intends to let Kirk die, she is still madly in love with him and is willing to suffer Starfleet's punishment if he can be spared. Kahn, impressed by her loyalty (and probably even more by the bravery she showed in defying him), "forgives" her and asks if she will accompany him in his enforced exile. She agrees, realizing that in his own chauvinistic way, Kahn loves her too.

(If, as rumored, the upcoming *Star Trek II* movie shows the civilization built by Kahn and his followers, perhaps we may see the changes wrought by Marla's influence, maybe a kind of turnabout "Taming of the Shrew.")

In "This Side of Paradise," we meet the Woman from Spock's Past (somehow we always *knew* there was one), and thanks to the intervention of the inhibition-loosening spores, we have the added treat of seeing Spock fall in love with her.

Not much is revealed about Leila Kalomi, save that she fell in love with Spock during his sojourn on Earth and

tried her best to break down his Vulcan reserve. As Spock
must have found the teeming millions of illogical humans
on Earth trial enough for any Vulcan to bear, the appearance of a beautiful young woman who professed love for
him would have just about driven him crazy, especially if
he found himself beginning to reciprocate the feelings.
Spock gently, but forcefully, told Leila that he was incapable of loving her, and he may have believed it at the time,
but as we saw when he was under the influence of the
spores, he was wrong.

It was not that Mr. Spock was incapable of loving
Leila; it was that he was incapable of showing that love,
or even of admitting it to himself. (Remember the surprise
in his voice when he told her, "I *can* love you!" He was
surprised—Leila wasn't.) Thanks to his strict Vulcan upbringing and his own natural shyness and reticence, Spock
was disturbed by strong emotion . . . especially if those
emotions were his own. To enter into a love affair, no
matter how desirable the object of his affections might be,
would be unthinkable for Spock. Unable to even consider
the prospect, he put Leila out of his life completely. Shattered by his dismissal, Leila joined the mission to colonize
Omnicron Ceti III, probably hoping to find a new life and
new romance. But as she is still unattached when the *Enterprise* crew arrives, she obviously could not forget Spock.

Spock, his emotions now completely unfettered, leaps
into a joyous love affair with Leila. He laughs, appreciates
beauty and pleasure on an emotional level rather than an
intellectual one, and is most happy to be sharing it all with
Leila. If it were not for the fact that the spores' influence
destroyed all ambition and drive, such a situation would
be perfect for Spock.

It is interesting to speculate whether or not Spock would
have remained in love with Leila if he had been forced to
remain on Omnicron Ceti III. The first rush of emotional
release, coupled with the proximity of a beautiful woman
who already loved him, would certainly cause Spock to be
smitten with her, especially since he had been strongly attracted to her on Earth. But it was truly first love that
Spock was experiencing, and such love seldom lasts. It
could have been that once his infatuation with Leila began
to cool off, Spock would have acted like any normal human male and begun to play the field. It was not stated in

the show, but one would suspect that a by-product of the spores' influence would have been the acceptance of free love within the colony group and its recent additions from the *Enterprise*. We shall never know.

It is enough for us to know that deep within Mr. Spock, no matter how carefully controlled and craftily hidden, there exists the capacity for joyful, sharing, and fulfilling love. Sadly for Spock (and for Leila), it was all too brief. But we can take comfort in the fact that for once in his life, Spock was happy. Perhaps the memory of that happiness will someday help him to break through the barriers of his training and tradition without the help of artificial influences and he will again share such a love.

"The Devil in the Dark" is the Horta, and the Horta is a mother. Like any loving mother, she acts in a most definite—and violent—manner to protect the lives of her young. It is again brotherly love which allows Kirk, Spock, and McCoy to save the Horta and her children from destruction and grant them the respect and rights they deserve as sentient beings.

The Organians in "Errand of Mercy" also practice brotherly love; but like Balok's First Federation, it is on their own terms. It is the second time (and will not be the last) that Kirk and his crew are presented with such an attitude from an advanced race, and one would think that the Federation and Starfleet would begin to consider the rightness or wrongness of such a policy. But again, beyond an occasional reference to the Organian Peace Treaty, nothing more is said of it.

James T. Kirk is the man who considered sacrificing a universe for the woman he loved.

That is the plot of "The City on the Edge of Forever" in a nutshell, but what a nutshell it is! It is our first glimpse of the kind of woman that Kirk would consider "perfect"—Edith Keeler. Edith is warm, loving, compassionate, and something of a visionary. She is also very lovely, but we can consider that to be beside the point. Kirk doesn't go out looking for a beautiful woman to spend a night with; he falls in love with Edith gradually, as he is forced to remain near her awaiting McCoy's arrival and is able to see her day-to-day activities. Seeing that she lives what she preaches, Kirk loves her for what is inside of her, not because she happens to be extremely lovely. (It is interesting to note that in his original teleplay for "City" Harlan Ellison stipulated that Edith Keeler not be beautiful, but possess a lively, fresh vibrancy that makes her lovely to behold.) It is testimony to the spirit of Edith that Kirk, involved as he is in trying to right his world, cannot help falling in love with her.

And fall he does. It is very plain that Kirk has *never before* felt this way about any woman. For the first time, he is willing to abandon his ship, his career, even his closest friends to remain with Edith. He almost abandons the future.

But Kirk's love for Edith is not the strongest love he displays in "City." The love that he has for unborn millions is greater. It is that love—not duty, not responsibility, not logic—that *love* that forces him to make the most difficult movement of his life and prevent Dr. McCoy from saving Edith's life. It takes a great love for a man to lay down his own life; how much greater then must a love be for a man to lay down the life of the only woman he has ever truly loved and at the same time sentence himself to an eternity of loneliness? That is the love story of "City" and it is a sad and beautiful one.

It is interesting to note that Spock could have erased the memory of Edith from Kirk's mind as he was later to erase the memory of Reena Kapec. Why didn't he? Because by removing Jim's memories of Edith, he would have also removed the memory of Kirk's sacrifice. Spock would have logically, and rightly, concluded that the pain of Edith's death would be lessened for Jim every time he considered the wonders and beauty of the twenty-third century. The existence of billions, the opening of the universe, the untold *good* that could be done—all of these and more would stand forever as a tribute to Edith in Kirk's mind. Removing the painful memories would have been a compassionate, loving act on Spock's part. Leaving them was an even greater one.

Kirk's love for his brother "Sam" and his sister-in-law was quite evident in "Operation Annihilate," but because of the urgency of the situation, he had little time or opportunity to express his grief. Coming so soon after his loss of Edith, this must have shattered Kirk, but he bravely managed to oversee the destruction of the cell-creatures. His control almost breaks when he thinks that Spock has been permanently blinded, and he takes out much of his anger and grief on McCoy, but he still goes on. The fact that his nephew survived (and that Spock's blindness was temporary) would have helped Kirk recover a little quicker, but so much emotional battering in so short a time would most certainly have left some very deep mental scars. Luckily for Kirk, some leave time was coming up, and he would have a chance to rest and recover.

He needed it. No sooner had the *Enterprise* set out on the second year of its mission when apparent tragedy again struck. Mr. Spock began to suffer the throes of *pon farr*, the inbred urge of a Vulcan male to return to his home planet and take a mate, or die. There was little love involved between Mr. Spock and his intended bride, T'Pring, but quite a bit of love was shown by Jim Kirk, who risked his career so that Spock would not perish. For a man like Kirk, this was much more of a personal sacrifice than risking his life—Kirk had risked his life for Spock and others of his crew many times, and would not hesitate to do so again—this time Kirk was risking the loss of his ship and his position, another matter entirely. Without them, Jim Kirk might as well be dead. Yet, because Spock's life was in danger, and because he was Kirk's *friend*, Kirk unhesitatingly and willfully disobeyed a direct order from Starfleet and diverted the *Enterprise* to Vulcan.

And once there, he allowed himself to be drawn into a battle to the death against that same friend. True, Kirk thought he was protecting Spock by acting as T'Pring's champion, but he still placed himself in quite a bit of danger. The lust-maddened Spock could have easily killed or severely injured Kirk. And once Kirk discovered that he couldn't just spar around long enough to make it look good and then take a quick dive, he could have taken the safe way out and used his more rational thinking to quickly dispatch Spock. Instead, he chose to fight a defensive battle, hoping that somehow Spock would come to his senses. Had Dr. McCoy been a little more slow-witted or Kirk a little less nimble, we know that Kirk would have allowed Spock to kill him. Even knowing the agonies Spock would go through once he returned to normal and discovered he had killed him, Kirk couldn't have killed Spock. Death at the hands of his best friend wouldn't be the sort of death Jim would prefer, but as he said to

McCoy, "I didn't bring Spock all the way to Vulcan to kill him."

McCoy showed love for both of his friends by managing to come up with the knockout plan under unbelievable pressure, then showed it again by emphasizing his anger to the point of seeming hatred when accusing Spock of murdering Kirk. We know that the doctor was only letting off some steam, but it also served the purpose of protecting Spock's honor and position. His was also the most profound joy at seeing Spock's emotional scene when the Vulcan learned that Kirk was alive, yet he chose to mask it in his usual cynical manner. It was his way of repaying Spock for the compliment of being invited to attend the ceremony (and the tacit acknowledgment it carried). Spock understood. His riposte was logical, calm, and quite warm and affectionate—*and* an open invitation for McCoy to have the last word. It was his way of saying, "Thanks, Bones!"

But what of the Vulcans, those coldly logical beings who disdain emotions such as love? Well, if ever a couple was in love, it was T'Pring and Stonn. He was willing to risk his life in battle to win her. She was willing to risk the shameful state of "chattel" to the victor to escape marrying Spock. Each of them had equal courage, and it is very difficult to determined whose love was the greater. Seemingly, it was Stonn, for we can't help but see T'Pring as a cold and calculating bitch, incapable of loving anyone or anything save power or position. Yet she chose Kirk to be her champion, not Stonn. Her reasons for doing so were so perfectly logical that even Spock congratulated her upon them, yet we can't help feeling that her primary motivation was to protect Stonn. Whatever the circumstances that threw them together and led them into the illicit affair, the love that grew out of it must have been a very deep and passionate one, for to keep it, they had to fly in the face of Vulcan tradition and law. While there's no arguing the fact that T'Pring was crazy, maybe we can amend it to "crazy in love," and hope that Spock's prediction did not come to pass, and that Stonn found the *having* of T'Pring just as satisfying as the wanting.

Apollo wanted not only to be loved, but to be worshiped. His race, having landed on Earth at the time of the ancient Greeks, were considered gods and worshiped as such. The feeling was, of course, narcotic, and Apollo demanded the same devotion from the *Enterprise* crew. In return, Apollo promised "love" to the humans, but it was not truly love he offered, but instead the kind of condescending protectiveness one would give to a likable but not particularly important or intelligent pet. Man had changed much since the time of Apollo's sojourn on Earth, and Apollo was quite surprised at the adamant refusal of Kirk and his crew to bow to his superiority. When he finally realized that he could not longer have the worship he needed, he cast himself onto "the winds of time" and vanished. But it was the lack of love—blind, obedient, adoring love, the only kind Apollo could understand or accept— that destroyed him.

Although the attention and affection he showed her was never more than physical, Carolyn Palmas fell deeply in love with Apollo. Whether it was because of his charm and mighty mien, or because of some dim, half-remembered memory supplied by her Grecian ancestors, it was a strong love. Like Marla McGivers, she became so enthralled with an enemy that she temporarily forgot her allegiance to Starfleet and abetted him in actions against the crew. But also like Marla, Carolyn soon realized that helping Apollo to victory would serve to destroy everything she had devoted her life to, so she aided Kirk in defeating Apollo. Such loyalty, even in the face of overwhelming love, shows how deeply each of these women loved their fellows and the principles of the Federation. It is to be hoped that the same love resides within each of the crewmembers on the *Enterprise*. Carolyn had to make a choice between love and loyalty, and loyalty won. We can only hope that the tag to the original script (and in James Blish's adaptation) was true—that Carolyn bore the child of Apollo, and thereby had a living, loving memory of him throughout her life.

Carolyn loved Apollo—but Scotty loved Carolyn. For once, the master engineer placed his beloved *Enterprise* second to a woman. We were never told exactly what it was about Carolyn that attracted Scotty so. Yes, she was an extremely beautiful woman, and seemed vivacious, sexy, and intelligent, but so are many women on the *En-*

terprise and we do not see Scotty constantly falling in love with them. Carolyn didn't even work in engineering, where a common interest and propinquity could have led to growing affection on Scotty's part. She also did not seem to care for Scotty overmuch. She was friendly and polite, but not at all loving in her actions toward him. We must assume that Scotty was—for whatever reasons—simply infatuated with Carolyn. Had the events on Pollux IV not happened, he probably would have tired of her indifference after a while, and forgotten about her completely when the next intriguing technical problem came along.

Her choice of Apollo over him, and her actions on Pollux IV, probably left him with more bitterness than he would have otherwise felt, but Scotty is that dour sort who looks at life cynically anyway, and he would have chalked it up as another in what is probably a long series of romantic disappointments. He probably drained a bottle of scotch, played a few mournful songs on his pipes, and immersed himself in his technical manuals. We can assume by the time the *Enterprise* made for its next port of call, Scotty was just about his old self again.

There is a distinct lack of love in the "mirror universe." The principles upon which the United Federation of Planets is founded would probably be a source of great amusement to the ruthless minions of the Imperial Starship *Enterprise*. But there was a smattering of love seen in "Mirror, Mirror." Most of it was simple lust: Sulu-2 wanted Uhura; Kirk-2 wanted a beautiful Captain's Woman. Yet the Captain's Woman, Marlena Moreau, did respond to Kirk's tenderness and probably would have fallen quite deeply in love with him given the chance. Surely, the (so she thought) uncharacteristic treatment he afforded her was enough to soften her cynical attitudes. Spock-2 also displayed the beginnings of a love of freedom, not only for himself, but for all the peoples enslaved by the Empire. We can assume that he and Marlena would work from within to destroy the Empire—and their first objective would have been the conversion of Kirk-2, Spock-2 using his Vulcan logic, Marlena using her feminine wiles. (And in the matter of our own Kirk and the USS *Enterprise*'s version of Marlena Moreau—well, knowing Jim Kirk, we can guess that he had his *own* Captain's Woman, albeit temporarily.)

Love of principles was taken to the extreme by the Halkans of both universes. They were quite willing to die as a race for what they believed in. This is quite often the case with members of Starfleet as well, but men such as Kirk, Spock, and McCoy also recognize the value of compromise and the need to often make tough decisions about the relative rightness or wrongness of a situation. It is much easier to simply say no than it is to evaluate both sides of a question and choose one of them. For all their admirable qualities, the Halkans were obviously a stagnant and fearful race. They did not love peace, they worshiped it. And as Kirk realized in the case of Apollo, that which is worshiped is often a harsh and stultifying master.

Sex is more the question than love in "The Apple." The childlike inhabitants of Gamma Trianguli VI are complacent, simple, and extremely happy. They do not love, they simply peacefully coexist. It is not until the humans arrive and display affection to one another that the "people" begin to relate to each other as sexual beings. The tenderness with which they treat each other gives a seeming idyllic loveliness to their tentative advances, but there is no question that when their glands and instincts begin to work in full force, peace will be ended and jealousy, lust, and killing will begin. In freeing them from Vaal, the crew of the *Enterprise* condemned the "people" to thousands of years of strife and bloodshed, something the godlike computer was obviously designed to end in the first place. If a team of experts was not dispatched to Gamma Trianguli VI very quickly, Kirk and his men may very well have been guilty of genocide.

In "The Doomsday Machine," we saw how Commodore Matt Decker, a man very much like Jim Kirk, was completely shattered by the destruction of his ship and the deaths of his entire crew. It is an indication of how distraught Kirk would be in similar circumstances, but let us hope he would not go off the deep end, thanks to the friendship he shares with Spock and McCoy. Decker appeared to be a particularly friendless and insular man (much as his son, Will Decker, appears to be in *Star Trek: The Motion Picture*). Perhaps this is the curse of starship captains to lose close friends and loves in their quest to be the best. We know that Chris Pike became fast friends with Spock, as did Kirk. Such friends are apparently rare, and Kirk is probably one of the luckiest captains in Starfleet, for he has *two* of them. Their very presence increases his chance for survival.

Love, as Mr. Spock would be the first to point out, is an emotion, and when human emotions are suddenly thrust upon a being who has never experienced them, chaos can result. In "Catspaw," we see how the overwhelming sensations of Sylvia's newfound emotions drive her to acts which cause her mission to fail. She lusts for Kirk, tempting him with a variety of sensuous female personas, and like poor little Miri, becomes furious when Kirk spurns her advances. Her companion, Korob, seems to be somewhat less affected by taking on a human form; although he does show all-too-human uncertainty and fear. His help to the *Enterprise* crew does prove that his race can—if only under the influence of human form—fell compassion, and that bodes well for any future contact between the two races.

"Metamorphosis" is strictly a love story, *and* one of the few instances we saw in Star Trek of love between a human and a nonhuman. It is to be noted, however, that the Companion was a creature of force, without a physical body, and therefore nonthreatening in the sense of interbreeding. It is also female, a subtle indication of the double standard which has always pervaded television. When Zefram Cochrane learns that the creature is female, he is very upset, terming it "disgusting." It's difficult to rationalize his feelings, seeing as how he was completely satisfied to have a symbiotic relationship with the Companion while he believed it to be sexless. He's willing to have an "affair" with a sexless alien, but not a female one. Curious.

But the situation is quickly remedied when the Companion enters the dying body of Nancy Hereford, and becomes, for all intents and purposes, a human female. Now Cochrane is not disgusted; indeed, he seems more than anxious to have the relationship progress onward to the physical. He seems to ignore, or be ignorant of, the fact that it is the mental processes—the soul, if you will—that is the major distingushing difference between all living beings. Cochrane is a chauvinist of the worst kind: He refuses to love a "female" Companion; he courts an equally alien "human" just because she now appears to be of the "right" race.

It is the Companion who is the truly sensitive and loving one in this relationship. She has cared for Cochrane for many years, met his every need (and probably demand) without question or complaint, and once in the vulnerable human form, would probably be willing to go with him back to Earth and an untimely death if he demanded. If nothing else, she has given up relative immortality for him. And all of this without any overt return of her affection by Cochrane through all those years—even after he professes disgust at her femininity. She is a beautiful example of love incarnate, and much, much too good for Cochrane. We can only hope that she is able to soften his attitudes as they live together—or failing that, the Nancy Hereford half of her personality becomes dominant, and that she is is presently in the process of unmercifully nagging him to death.

In "Journey to Babel," we meet one of the most loving individuals ever presented in Star Trek: Spock's mother, Amanda. She is totally human, warm and smiling, obviously happy in her life with Sarek, yet just as obviously a sensitive and intelligent individual in her own right. She may defer to Sarek in public as a good Vulcan wife should, be we can be sure that she has her say in private. We got to see a little bit of it in "Journey," and that was outside the confines of their own home, in a milieu where Amanda would have constrained her feelings and comments even more than she usually did.

We shall probably never know the true story of how Sarek and Amanda came to fall in love and marry. Sarek will only say that it seemed like the logical thing to do at the time. Surely it was. Even an "emotionless" Vulcan would not be insensitive enough to let a treasure such as Amanda escape. Their love is shown poignantly in the small glances and gestures they share. It is a quiet love but a strong one; who would expect trumpets, bells, and fireworks from a Vulcan? This is mostly due to Amanda, we suspect. She would have patiently overlooked Sarek's reluctance to give of himself, while at the same time accepting and subtly encouraging such small indications as we saw in "Journey." That Sarek deeply loves her there is no doubt.

Amanda loves her son just as much as she loves her husband. Perhaps she treasures him even more. Spock must have inadvertently given his mother much pain during his childhood. She would have suffered with him through every rebuff, every insult, every setback. And it would have pained her as well to see him embracing and accepting the Vulcan way of life, with all of its constraints of behavior and denial of emotion. Emotion Amanda *knew* her husband felt; how much more then would the half-human Spock feel it?

Amanda treats Spock as an adult Vulcan male of accomplishment and position should be treated. Beyond a simple but extremely warm greeting, she does not fawn over her son, even though it has obviously been some time since she has seen him. Naturally, her first reaction is to find out whether or not he still insists on continuing the grudge situation with his father; it is the thing uppermost on her mind and has been for many years. As happy as Amanda's life with Sarek has been, her happiness has been marred by the breach between Spock and Sarek, and she wishes more than anything for it to be healed. But both of her men are stubborn, and loving them both as she does, she will not and cannot take sides.

Sarek and Spock love each other, but because of their pride, they refuse to acknowledge it. We know that Spock devoted his first two decades to the Vulcan life-style, but had to leave for Starfleet to gain any kind of measure of individuality. Sarek, expecting Spock to follow in his footsteps like a good Vulcan son, refused to give his blessing to Spock's plans. Neither would acknowledge that the other had a point; and being Vulcans, neither would acknowledge that hurt feelings were the primary motivation for the split on both sides.

But Sarek is extremely proud of Spock, nonetheless. It can be seen in the way he gives a slight nod of approval when Spock speaks as a Starfleet officer. And when he feels that Amanda has belittled Spock in front of his peers, he lets her know in no uncertain terms that she is wrong. Thanks to the circumstances surrounding the voyage to Babel, Spock and his father are reunited. But one suspects

that Sarek is more impressed by Spock's refusal to help
him when in command of the ship than he is by the fact
that Spock's blood helped him to survive the operation.
Spock acted correctly, without undue emotion, and, above
all, *logically* in Sarek's opinion, and that, more than anything, proved to Sarek that his son was correct and successful in his choice of career. Now it was possible for
Sarek to display the respect and honor due a fellow Vulcan—and the small, almost indistinguishable indications of
affection to a son.

Amanda, filled with relief that her husband and son
both survived the crisis and that the break between them
was finally healed, was aghast that they did not show more
emotion. It was a warm moment, with all of the three enjoying a good "laugh," once again a complete and very
loving family.

It is love for her unborn child in "Friday's Child" that
causes Eleen to disobey the tribal command that she take
her own life because she is carrying the child who would
be the next chieftain. Dr. McCoy is instrumental in guid-
ing Eleen to this decision, his own love for humanity
showing her the wrongness of destroying an unborn innocent to satisfy custom.

The onset of extreme and debilitating age in "The
Deadly Years" presents us with one of the strangest "love
affairs" seen on Star Trek. Dr. Janet Wallace was attracted
to Kirk, but seems to be even more so when he begins to
age. Perhaps she only had a preference for older men, but
it could also be that she saw Kirk as a father figure, an
eventuality which would give her attraction to Kirk's
"elderly" self an unhealthy tinge. Kirk seems to be put off
by Janet's attentions, and although he has more important
concerns on his mind, he cannot decide if she is attending
him out of pity or affection. The impending loss of his vi-
rility would also have bothered Kirk quite a bit. It is interesting to note that Kirk is somewhat standoffish to Janet at
the conclusion of the episode.

Kirk's affection for his former, late commander, Captain Garrovick, is the cause of his "Obsession." Feeling
that as a junior officer his failure to blast the "cloud creature" quickly enough resulted in Garrovick's death, Kirk
was consumed with both guilt and an overriding desire to

destroy the creature. The presence of Garrovick's son, now an ensign on the *Enterprise*, only serves to heighten Kirk's obsession, for he feels that young Garrovick blames him for his father's death. Although we are not told so, we can assume that young Garrovick has an uncanny resemblance to his father, which would have disturbed Kirk all the more. And although Kirk claims to be especially interested in and helpful to Ensign Garrovick, we don't see any indications of it in the episode. In truth, Kirk probably was even more standoffish to the ensign than he would have been to anyone else. With Kirk's history of losing those close to him, forming a close association with another Garrovick who could meet death at any time would not be something Jim would be eager to do. Garrovick disappears from the *Enterprise* soon after this episode, and we can suspect that he was as glad to get away from Kirk and the constant reminders of his father as Kirk was glad to get rid of him.

Kirk fears that Scotty has become a "Jack the Ripper" in "Wolf in the Fold" because of an injury to the engineer caused by a woman. We might also suspect that Kirk had some thoughts about Carolyn Palmas' affair with Apollo and the pain it caused Scotty, adding to his resentment of women. This was the only episode of Star Trek in which out-and-out murder was the problem faced by the crew; and sure enough, it *was* Jack the Ripper doing the kill-ing—at least an immortal creature with the ability to possess bodies and feed off the fear instilled in the victim at the time of the murder. Much more interesting, but of course downplayed, is the hedonistic culture of Argelius II. A society based on pleasure and its gratification was pretty strong medicine for television in the sixties (and probably would be now, in this age of "let's talk about it, but never do anything" titillation shows). It's pretty tasty medicine for Kirk and McCoy, however, as they gleefully look for-ward to sampling the pleasures of Argelius II; McCoy even displays an expert's anticipation we would not have expected from him. The character of Morla of Cantaba Street is also fun to watch, for his is the unthinkable crime of jealousy and (gasp!) preferring a monogamous relation-ship with the dancer Kara.

Tribbles are the only love you can buy in the Star Trek

universe (unless you can be satisfied with the varieties on Argelius II), but they are a royal pain in the turbolift if they get out of hand. It is nice to think that they are currently spreading love and affection throughout the Klingon Empire.

In "The Gamesters of Triskelion," Klok not only introduces Shahna to physical love (however far it went off-camera), but to his own love of freedom and the unknown. It is this which helps to save his life when Shahna refuses to kill him, even at the risk of her own life, for she now knows that killing for the pleasure of the Providers is wrong, as is living in enforced slavery. Her action is taken as an individual; she is not trying to force the Providers' hand, she is merely taking a personal stand, saying, "No more killing." It is a poignant echo of Kirk's avowal of what makes a person civilized: "We will not kill . . . today." She has become a thriving, growing person, and we feel that the various races on Triskelion will grow with her. For once, Kirk's use of a woman to achieve his own ends has a beneficial effect beyond that of ending his current crisis.

It's also amusing to look back at Chekov's distress at the overtures of the thrall Tamoon. But the question remains—was her deep voice and mannish demeanor what distressed him? Or was it the fact that he might be on the verge of losing his virginity?

Love is used wrongly in "A Private Little War" by Nona, the Witch Woman. She attempts to coerce her husband Tyree to war on the village people, threatening to withhold her sexual favors if he does not comply. Later, she saves Kirk's life, but the potion used is one which reputedly causes the recipient to fall helplessly in love with the one administering it. Kirk seems to be strongly attracted to her, but manages to overcome the witchery without too much effort. It would have perhaps worked better on someone with a little less practice at disengaging himself from love affairs. All Kirk had to do was operate on his well-honed instincts. Nona, of course, meets a bad end, killed by the very village people to whom she was attempting to betray Tyree.

It's interesting to note that in Star Trek, the punishment for misuse of love is swift and sure. Those who twist and corrupt love for their own nefarious purposes usually die, or at least end up suffering the fate they most fear. Because love is such an important and integral part of the series' premise, it apparently must be graphically illustrated that utilizing love as a tool of evil leads to destruction and ruin.

Sargon and Thalassa in "Return to Tomorrow" shared a very great love indeed. It endured throughout not only thousands of years, but also the alienation of having their consciousnesses trapped in globes of force. It is a very touching moment when they are reunited in the physical bodies of Dr. Anne Mulhall and Captain Kirk. One suspects that their love is all that has kept them alive while the others of their race have died. (Henoch, of course, stayed alive because of his hatred and ambition, but it is somewhat confusing as to how he managed to conceal this from Sargon, for they were both telepaths.) Perhaps Sargon realized all along that they would never again be able to exist with humans, and so allowed the plans for android bodies to be built—and the opportunity for Henoch's treachery—to go on, knowing that it was the only way he could convince Thalassa to give up her dreams of once again living in a physical body. In any case, he displayed a great love for humanity—"his children"—by sacrificing his and Thalassa's chance to live in android bodies because he feared their presence would ultimately prove harmful to the humans.

In "By Any Other Name," the Kelvans (like Sylvia) are undone by the onrush of sensation and accompanying emotional response caused by their newly acquired human forms. Love, or at least one of the signs of burgeoning love, jealousy, is felt by Rojan when he realizes that Kirk has been making advances toward Kelinda. While Kelinda handles her newfound emotions more successfully than Sylvia did, she is still quite willing to have Kirk teach her more about them. Kirk convinces Rojan that his own jealousy and anger, Kelinda's confusion, and the emotional responses of the other Kelvans are just the beginning of a full range of emotional sensations that will shortly cause them to become human in feeling as well as form, and virtual aliens to their own people by the time they reach Kelva. The Kelvans agree to abandon their quest, and allow Kirk to return them to the planet where they were discovered, where, we can assume, they remain to this day, happily experiencing and enjoying life as loving, laughing, fighting, emotional humans.

In "The Omega Glory," we have perhaps the strongest statement in Star Trek of man's desire for and love of freedom. The Yangs have spent many years, and countless lives, fighting to reconquer their homeland from the Kohms. The enormous respect and veneration with which they treat the "sacred documents" is indicative of the feelings which Gene Roddenberry holds for the Constitution and our other testimonials to democracy. Like so many of us today, the Yangs really didn't understand the words, but they knew very well what the documents stood for: freedom.

In "Assignment: Earth," we meet (for the only time, sadly) Gary Seven, an Earthman raised by mysterious alien beings and returned to Earth to assist in its survival and development. In the course of his efforts to prevent a disastrous rocket launch, Seven is both aided and encumbered by his secretary, Roberta Lincoln. Roberta is somewhat scatterbrained, but lovely and lovable. Seven is quite singleminded about his mission, and although his intelligence and skills are such that Spock would envy them, he has a full range of human emotions, including a wry and well-developed sense of humor. We see a growing affection between the two; and although it is unlikely that Seven would desire to be drawn into an affair with Roberta, they are two healthy young humans, and between such, anything can happen. Complicating such an event, however, is Seven's other assistant, Isis. Isis, a beautiful black cat, sometimes appears as a sultry, dark-haired beauty of a woman. She also seems quite possessive about Gary and disinclined to let Roberta get too close to him. We would have liked to have their relationship—*whatever* it was— explained (as would Roberta!), but as this "pilot" show wasn't picked up by the networks, our imaginations will have to supply the details of this rather strange, but very interesting, triangle. It's hardly the classic one!

Editor's Note: In a future article, we will examine the various forms of love in Star Trek's third season, the ani-

mated series, and Star Trek: The Motion Picture; *as well as in some selected Star Trek fiction, fan fiction, and comic books. The relationships of the various crewmembers will also be examined.*

SHADOWS

by Rowena Warner

He wanders the ship's corridors at night,
Quite, somber, a shadow among shadows.
His footsteps are soft, carrying him in
    directions his brain does not comprehend.

     For his thoughts are lost
Drifting in the dark canyons of his mind.

It is easier during the day.
That cringe of fear is suppressed,
As anxious eyes watch his captain tread
    the line of danger once again.

That disagreement with the doctor to mask
    his friendship.
      But he knows.
      They both know.

At night, though, it is different.
The lights are dimmed, there is a shadow
    beyond every door.
A shadow of today, yesterday.

     Why is it harder at night?
Why do the emotions seem to overflow,

threatening to suffocate him with their
intensity.
        CONTROL.
The brow furrows.

Ah, to sleep.
Perchance, to dream.

NO!

The slim figure moves silently, his shadow
    blending with those surrounding him.
The tangible, the elusive, yesterday and today.

About the Editors

Although largely unknown to readers not involved in Star Trek fandom before the publication of *The Best of Trek* (*#1*), WALTER IRWIN and G. B. LOVE have been actively editing and publishing magazines for many years. Before they teamed up to create TREK® in 1975, Irwin worked in newspapers, advertising, and free-lance writing, while Love published *The Rocket's Blast—Comiccollector* from 1960 to 1974, as well as hundreds of other magazines, books, and collectables. Both together and separately, they are currently planning several new books and magazines, as well as continuing to publish TREK.